IMPERFECT TRUTH

Visit us at www.boldstrokesbooks.com

By the Author

Edge of Awareness

The Courage to Try

Imperfect Truth

IMPERFECT TRUTH

by

C.A. Popovich

2016

IMPERFECT TRUTH

ISBN 13: 978-1-62639-787-3

This Trade Paperback Original Is Published By
Bold Strokes Books, Inc.
P.O. Box 249
Valley Falls, NY 12185

First Edition: October 2016

CREDITS
EDITORS: Victoria Villasenor and Cindy Cresap
PRODUCTION DESIGN: Susan Ramundo
COVER DESIGN By Sheri (graphicartist2020@hotmail.com)

Acknowledgments

Thank you Len Barot, Sandy Lowe, and all the other hardworking folks at Bold Strokes Books for all you do to help me fulfill my dream of writing. I also want to thank Victoria Villasenor and Cindy Cresap, editors extraordinaire, for helping me make this work so much better.

To Sandi, who answers my equine questions and offers her support and research help, I'm grateful for all the ways you're in my life.

And thank you, Lois, for your expertise and suggestions regarding the world of social work.

Finally, thank you to all the readers of lesbian romance. Your support means everything.

Dedication

To Abby and MacIntosh

Chapter One

A lex Reed closed her laptop and sighed. She knew she'd be taking a chance by going to the lesbian Meetup, but her trips to work and home hadn't drawn the attention of any suspicious characters, so maybe she'd be all right. She couldn't drop her guard, but would attending one social event be so dangerous? She was supposed to begin a new life, after all, and sitting alone in an empty apartment wasn't a life.

Two years ago, her life had been turned upside down when her father's court testimony had led to the incarceration of a drug dealing gang leader, and he'd made a number of other drug dealers decidedly uncomfortable, but failed to put them away. The credible threats to his life and his family had sent them into the federal witness protection program, or WITSEC. She knew she couldn't ignore their instructions, or she would be on her own. Which meant she'd probably be dead. She wondered when the paranoia would end.

She finally felt safe enough in this "neutral site," after a year and a half, to sleep through the night without a baseball bat under the covers. Now it leaned within reach against her nightstand. If she'd been given a choice as to where she and her sister would have been relocated, she wouldn't have chosen a state where the average yearly temperature was lower than the coldest day in winter in her home state of Florida. They'd spent six months in a safe house getting used to and writing their new names before being permanently located in the northern state of Michigan.

She allowed herself a brief, prohibited thought of her previous life, where she would be floating in her backyard pool enjoying the humidity of July in Naples, Florida. She was supposed to purge all those memories and make this her new existence. The staff psychologists had told her she'd settle in eventually. Her shorter, highlighted, spiky haircut and new name, Alexandra E. Reed, were becoming more comfortable, but lately she had been having a hard time suppressing the futile dream of finding someone special with whom to share this new life. Maybe she could find a friend to relax with and practice her fabricated identity, before she tried for something more intimate.

Alex picked up her phone, scrolled to her contact labeled Uncle Joe, and exhaled in relief when she received clearance to attend the Meetup hiking event. She could have waited until the weekly check-in with her WITSEC inspector, but she didn't want to wait three days for permission to begin meeting new lesbians and potential friends.

She grabbed her dog's leash. "Come on, Abby. I've got to get to work. We've got just enough time for a walk around the park." She smiled at her black Lab mix bouncing in anticipation. She and Abby followed their favorite path as the warm July sun started to chase away the morning chill. As much as she hated the winter snow, she loved the greenery of the state in the summer. Alex breathed deeply. It wasn't the familiar, humid heavy air of *before*, but she would get used to it. She had no choice.

A few joggers passed, and Alex wondered if any of them had aliases. She knew full well she and her sister weren't the only ones living in the world as imposters. *Can you really ever know anyone is who they say they are?* She shoved away the pointless pondering and mentally reviewed the coaching she'd received from WITSEC on how to deflect questions and change the topic when people asked about her past. "At least I don't have to change your name, Abby." She chuckled as Abby tilted her head and wagged her tail.

Alex organized the contents of her backpack when she returned home, tossed in a bag of Fig Newtons, and made herself a sandwich for lunch before heading out into a world that still felt slightly alien.

❖

"Good morning, Betty." Alex greeted the hotel manager as she stowed her backpack in her locker and changed into her work uniform. A blue blazer with the hotel logo on the lapel, a white blouse, blue slacks, and a perpetual smile was now her daily work attire. She had been strongly advised not to make use of her master's degree in social work in her new life, so at forty-two, she'd tossed away six years of college and found the job of desk clerk at a local hotel convention center. It paid enough to end the government stipend, and she got to meet some interesting people, but she struggled to let go of the concern for her former clients.

Alex would never know what the woman she had dated for three months thought when she hadn't showed up for a date and never called. Never would call. She had a new life and new memories to make now, no matter how hard it was or how much she hated that it had to be that way.

Her father had chosen to stay alone in the small house in Plymouth, Michigan, where they'd originally been relocated. She worried that her father would fall back in with the drug group he had helped to break up, but she had to trust the marshals to keep him safe.

She and her sister had said good-bye to their dad, and their inspector had moved them into a safe house for a month before settling them into an apartment building a few miles away from their dad's place, even though they weren't supposed to see him all that often. Now, they each had their own place, where they had quietly begun to heal from having their lives ripped apart.

Alex's paranoia still ran deep, so she would follow the rules. If not for herself, for her baby sister. She pushed away all thoughts of the past and concentrated on greeting a group of visitors from Canada.

Alex knocked three rapid thumps on her sister's apartment door, counted five seconds, and knocked twice. She counted out another thirty seconds before pulling out her cell phone. The door opened before she had to call.

"Hey, sis. Come on in."

"Good morning, Jen. Ready for the farmer's market?" Alex set her purse on a table by the door next to Jen's ever-present overnight bag. *When will the fear diminish?* She had decided months ago to ignore Jen's mistrust. If being ready to move again at a moment's notice helped her transition, so be it. At least she seemed comfortable with her new name, Jennifer B. Reed. Alex still had trouble thinking of her that way, but she'd get used to it. *One day.*

"Sounds good. All I've been doing lately is working, so I'm ready for our weekly outing. I took on a couple of extra clients at Dr. Parker's. Her dental practice is growing, and I'm getting better at my job," Jen said.

Alex drew her into a hug and kissed her cheek. "I'm proud of you." She stepped back but kept her hands on her upper arms, grounding herself in familiarity. The touch cracked her defenses and flooded her with banned memories. She'd spent hours helping Jen, five years her junior, with her homework, and encouraging her to consider more schooling until she'd finally agreed to take a couple of classes at the community college. She'd never finished, but enrolled in the dental hygienist program, locally, a year ago.

"Thanks. I can't believe it took what happened to me...to us, to finally find a job I love. Did I tell you I got a raise? Ruth, Dr. Parker, can't hire me full time yet, but she told me she'd like to as soon as I finish my degree. For now, I get first choice of how many patients I want to see. The other hygienist, Sue, is super nice, and I don't mind sharing the work. I think we could be friends." Jen turned tear-filled eyes to Alex. "That would be okay, wouldn't it?"

"Of course, honey. You'll settle down and make lots of friends." Alex brushed the backs of her fingers lightly down Jen's cheek and smiled. "We're starting a new life with new friends. It'll take time, but I think we should try to look forward to it. I'm going to a Meetup at the state park next week."

"Yeah? Cool. We'll be okay."

Jen's response, a statement rather than a question, encouraged Alex. She needed to remain positive for Jen's sake as well as her own. She didn't disclose to Jen her own deep loneliness and longing for someone special in her life. She knew she would never be able to disclose her true past, but changing her name didn't change who she was inside, the person she hoped to someday share with someone.

Alex watched Jen go through her ritual of checking the locks on the two windows and reviewing the room before they left. She'd told her she liked to memorize where everything was so she'd know right away if someone broke in and disturbed anything. She locked the deadbolt on the way out and double-checked it before they began the two-block walk to the outdoor market.

"Let's get some zucchini, and I'll make us some zucchini bread," Alex said. She grabbed Jen's hand as they crossed the street like she'd done so often when they were growing up.

"Yum. I'll chop the walnuts."

Alex smiled at the sparkle in her eyes. She vowed to do whatever it took to make sure it stayed there.

CHAPTER TWO

"Bought I just met these women, Kristen. I'd feel like I'd be crashing their wedding." Debra Johnson stood in the shade of a huge oak tree sipping an iced tea. She scanned the expanse of land surrounding the throngs of people gathered for the Independence Day celebration. The property bordered the Saint Clair River, and she caught glimpses of sunshine sparkling off the water through the evergreens lining its banks. The turn of the century, well-maintained farmhouse sat atop a rise on the property, and she could see part of a newer outbuilding located behind it at the end of a gravel driveway. She'd been told the building was a kennel for the owner's Irish wolfhounds, and she planned to check it out before leaving.

"Dana and Maria invited you. Same-sex weddings will be taking place all over Michigan now, after the Supreme Court's decision. They want to share their day with as many lesbians as they can. You're my friend and they want you there," Kristen said.

"I get it, I do, but I won't know anyone there except you guys, and I'll have to find a date." Debby pushed her hair over her left ear and shook her head.

"Maybe it's time, my friend." Kristen squeezed Debby's shoulder before continuing. "Not everyone is like your ex. There're many trustworthy lesbians out there, and a lesbian wedding will be fun. It's an historic time in our country, and our state."

"That's true, and I'm happy for them, but I don't know. I'll think about it." Debby took a sip of tea and stared out over the crowd.

"Bring Kelly if you want. She likes to dance."

"Maybe I will, or I'll see if Mary from the club wants to go. She likes all kinds of dancing. They do that stupid chicken dance at weddings, you know." Debby grinned and poked Kristen in the shoulder.

"Lesbian wedding. No chicken dancing." Kristen clucked and did a little chicken dance step. "I'm going to get another hot dog. Can I bring you one?"

"No, thanks. I'll get something in a minute. You know how bad those are for you, don't you?"

"Yeah, yeah. I saw some boring veggies on one of the grills. You should be safe with them. Come sit with us later. We'll be at the picnic table down by the water." Kristen walked toward the smoking grills next to the house.

Debby took a deep breath and slowly expelled it before sitting on the grass to lean against the giant tree. She'd been friends with Kristen Eckert since high school and appreciated her attempt to include her in the events of her life. Since Kristen had met her partner and local veterinarian, Dr. Jaylin Meyers, she hadn't seen much of her except at the local barrel racing events. Now she wanted to drag her to a wedding where she wouldn't know anyone. *It's probably no different than going to the club alone.* She stood, intending to follow Kristen to the food, when someone gripped her forearm.

"Sorry. I didn't mean to startle you. Debby, right?"

Debby recognized Dana Langdon, one of the soon-to-be newlyweds. "Yeah. Good to meet you in person." She shook Dana's hand as she spoke.

"I'm glad you made it today. Kristen's told us so much about you that I feel like I know you. I wanted to extend an official invitation to our wedding. I hope you're available."

"Thanks, Dana. I'm excited for you and Maria. September fifth, right?"

"Yep. It's the anniversary of our 'sort of' first date. We went to a wiener dog race." Dana grinned, and her eyes sparkled. "Bring a date if you'd like. We're hoping to have a huge turnout. Pastor Wright has agreed to marry us in his little church, and Maria would be ecstatic to have standing room only. We'll be mailing out invitations next week."

Debby's stab of envy surprised her, and she hesitated. Going to the dance club and hooking up with a woman for the night was very different from extending an invitation for a date to a wedding. She clung to the security of her list tucked safely away in her desk drawer. "I'll plan on it."

"Good. I'm going to go find my honey and get some food. Enjoy the party."

Debby watched Dana stop to say hello to a few people on her way toward the house. She could do this. If she had to, she'd invite Kelly. She was a good friend and safe. Content with her decision, she went to fill a plate and find her friends.

"Over here." Kristen waved as she called to Debby. "We saved you a seat."

"Thanks." Debby settled on the end of the bench at the picnic table with her plate of grilled zucchini, corn, and a burger.

Kristen swallowed her bite of hot dog before speaking. "I missed you last weekend at the stump race."

"I've been covering for the vacationing pharmacist at the store in Waterford for two weeks, so I haven't had time for much of anything except getting home, feeding Shadow, and crashing. I hate working in retail pharmacy more and more every day." Debby stabbed a chunk of zucchini and popped it into her mouth.

"Have you talked to the nursing home yet?" Kristen asked.

"Yeah. I've got an interview in two weeks. I can't wait."

"Good luck. I know Kelly's been happy working there for years. Let me know how it goes."

"I will. Thanks." Debby finished her food and stood to stretch her back. "I'm heading home. You guys enjoy the rest of the party, and I'll talk to you next week."

❖

Debby tossed her daypack on the chair next to her front door and hung her keys on the hook mounted on the wall. She had used the hour-long drive across town to reflect on her social life, or lack of one. By the time she had pulled into her driveway, she had convinced herself that attending her new friends' wedding would be fun. She hadn't been dancing at the club for several weeks, and she missed the connection of holding a woman in her arms. Surely she could find someone interested in joining her for a lesbian wedding without thinking it was some kind of weird commitment thing.

"Okay, okay, you fat cat." She picked up her mewling seal point Himalayan and hugged him until he squirmed and pushed himself out of her arms. She put down some kibble and checked his water bowl. "I'm going to make myself a cup of tea if that's all right with you." Debby chuckled at her cat purring his approval as he ate.

Debby went out to toss some hay into Shadow's hay feeder and set up his stall for the night before returning inside to settle into her favorite chair with her laptop and cup of green tea. She had heard her pharmacy tech talking about a bike ride she had attended with a group of people she had met on something called a Meetup. She Googled it and began her search.

Half an hour later, she had narrowed down her search to two lesbian groups in her area that were interested in social events. The first event was a hike through a nearby state park. *This could work.* Maybe this was a good place to find a woman who would respect her boundaries and be willing to accompany her as a platonic companion. She knew her friend Kelly would be risk-free, but the other women in her life were either, coworkers, one-night stands, or wanted more than she was willing to give. *I need someone new, but safe.*

"This sounds promising doesn't it, Buddy?" Buddy had nestled in her lap as she was browsing, and she absorbed the serenity of his purring as she stroked his soft fur.

She printed out the meeting information and pulled her list from the desk drawer. Her list was her protection from anyone daring to venture close to her shattered heart. It consisted of the mandatory requirements in a lover. Top of the list were openness and honesty. She wasn't going to repeat the pain she'd suffered with her deceitful lover of six years. She reviewed the important requisites and reverently placed it away, certain she wouldn't need to refer to it, but always reassured by its presence.

❖

"Thanks for covering for me tomorrow, Jake. I appreciate it." Debby glanced at her fellow pharmacist as she pasted a label on a prescription bottle she'd filled.

"No problem. Patsy's working a twelve-hour shift, so I'd just be home watching the baseball game and eating pizza and ice cream. My wife and my waistline thank you." Jake grinned and began counting pills onto a pill counter.

"That sounds pretty good to me. You sure you wouldn't want the down time?"

"Nah. I'd rather have the time off when Pat and I can do something together. We've been talking about a trip to the zoo since May. It seems like whenever we plan a date day, our daughter calls about our granddaughter's soccer game or baseball tournament." Jake stopped what he was working on and turned to face Debby. "So, what's up tomorrow? You've been awfully tightlipped about it. Is everything okay?"

Debby avoided Jake's gaze as she considered how much she wanted to share with him. She'd worked with him for three years and considered him a friend, but she didn't want to put him in a position to lie to their boss if asked where she was. She needed to meet with the administration of the nursing home before letting him know she might be leaving.

"Yeah. Everything's fine. I'm just burned out, you know? I need a day to do nothing."

"I get it. It's pretty hectic around here, especially in the summer when we have to cover for people on vacation. I'll be right back. I've got to go to the back to finish filling this script." Jake squeezed past her and disappeared through a door at the back of the room.

She was used to working alone, so Jake's departure didn't bother her. She filled prescriptions and tried her best to avoid answering the phone. A daily occurrence lately was someone with twenty questions about his or her prescription, and this day was no exception. The large woman standing at the "consultation" area shifted from foot to foot and drummed her fingers on the counter.

"Hello. Can I help you with something?" Debby had quit bothering to introduce herself to customers. *Pharmacist* and her name were clearly imprinted on her lab coat. They didn't care who she was, anyway.

"I want to know why I can't eat grapefruit anymore." The woman, wide-eyed and red-faced, leaned against the counter, pushing toward her. Debby retreated a step.

"What medication are you on, ma'am?"

"It's for cholesterol. My doctor didn't say a word about this. The pamphlet that came with this stuff says to avoid grapefruit. How am I supposed to lose the weight he wants me to without eating grapefruit? What's the problem?"

Debby took a settling breath before replying. "There's a compound in grapefruit that interacts with some of the cholesterol lowering drugs called statins. Which medicine are you taking?"

"How am I supposed to know? You're the pharmacist."

"Okay. What's your last name?" Debby moved to the computer.

"Zantis," the woman said.

"First name, Ginger?"

"Yes."

"Date of birth?"

"Why do you people always ask me that?"

"It's for security purposes, Ms. Zantis."

"You know, I don't care. I'm going to continue my grapefruit and egg diet. I don't have time for this nonsense." She turned and hurried out the door.

Debby logged off the computer and headed to the employee restroom where she splashed water on her face and stretched to relieve the tension in her back. Her job interview the next day couldn't come soon enough.

"Hey there. What're you doing here?" Kelly Newton, the day shift nursing supervisor, and Debby's long-time friend, stood in the hallway outside the nurses' station.

"Hi, Kelly. I'm here for an interview for a position in the pharmacy. I've got an eight a.m. appointment," Debby said.

"Cool. I'm glad you decided to try Serenity Care. I love it here. Are you here to see Janis?"

"Yes. That's who I spoke to on the phone," Debby said.

"Come on, I'll show you to her office." Kelly handed the patient's chart she was holding to one of the nurses at the desk and led Debby through a set of doors at the end of the hall. "You'll like Jan. She pretty much singlehandedly runs the place and does an excellent job of balancing the patient's care with the financial realities of a nursing home. Here's her office. Good luck, and stop and see me on the way out."

"Thanks, Kelly. I will."

Debby took a seat opposite the empty chair at a beautiful mahogany desk. A svelte woman with salt-and-pepper short hair and an engaging smile entered the room within a few minutes.

"Good morning. I'm Janis Smith. You must be Debra."

Debby took Janis's outstretched hand in a firm grip. "Yes. I'm Debra Johnson. It's good to meet you in person, Ms. Smith."

Debby glanced at the clock above the desk and noted Janis's punctuality. Her gaze was direct and her body language laid-back. Everything she hoped for in a boss.

"Please call me Jan. So, you're a pharmacist looking to get out of Walgreens."

Jan's grin and easy nature were soothing. "Yes to both," Debby said. "And please call me Debby."

Debby explained her situation, and they talked for an hour before Jan checked her watch and smiled.

"I've got a meeting in ten minutes. Let me show you the pharmacy. It's on the way." Jan stood and leaned on her desk. "We have a board certified geriatric consultant pharmacist on staff, and I think you'd be an excellent addition to our group. When can you start?" She offered her hand again in acknowledgment.

"Thank you. I look forward to joining your staff. I'll report for duty in two weeks, when I've worked out my notice."

Debby couldn't contain her grin as she made her way back to Kelly's station, but Kelly was nowhere to be seen, so she left a message with the nurse on duty and left. She sat in her car for a few minutes reviewing all she and Jan had talked about. She planned to apply for the geriatric pharmaceutical exam in the fall and show Jan she was willing to do whatever it took to be the best she could be in her new position. The pharmacy looked well stocked and extremely organized. She couldn't wait to get started and meet the rest of the staff. She thought of Jake and his friendship for the past few years and realized that was the only thing she'd miss. She blew out a breath and rested her head against the headrest for a minute to enjoy the feeling of anticipation.

CHAPTER THREE

Debby pulled into the park ten minutes before the Meetup event was scheduled to begin. She parked and headed to the pavilion, where she saw a group of women standing near the picnic tables. She sighed in relief when she didn't recognize anyone. At least she wouldn't have to deal with the awkwardness of running into an ex-one-night-stand. One woman stood out from the crowd. She stood off to the side, looking shy. She seemed to be taking in the whole group, looking around almost warily. Her short, highlighted hair shone in the afternoon sunshine, and her tan legs below her khaki shorts looked toned, as if she walked on a regular basis. Her long-sleeved T-shirt pleasantly hugged her breasts but seemed a bit much for the warm summer day.

Debby approached the woman and stuck out her hand in greeting. "Hi. My name's Debra Johnson. Most people call me Debby."

She lost her train of thought for a moment as the woman turned her wary gaze on her. Her eyes were gray, with tiny gold flecks that seemed to emit light rather than reflect it.

"Nice to meet you, Debby. I'm Alexandra Reed. Please call me Alex." Alex enveloped her hand in a warm, soft, and solid grip.

A tingle raced up her arm and heat rose to her face. Alex was an inch or so shorter than her but with a presence that declared she could take care of herself. She wondered about Alex's first impression of her, and that thought disturbed her. She reverted to the safety of item three on her list. *It doesn't matter what others think.*

"This looks like fun. There's quite a few women here," Debby said.

"Is this your first Meetup?" Alex asked.

"Yeah. I hadn't even heard of them until a coworker mentioned she'd found a group to bike ride with. I Googled it and found this bunch. I prefer the idea of walking the paths of the state park as opposed to peddling for miles. How about you?"

"I've heard of Meetups, but this is the first one I've tried, and I prefer walking to riding a bike, too."

Their conversation was interrupted by a tall blonde signaling for attention.

"Hello, everyone. I'm glad to see such a good turnout. My name's Nat, and I initiated this Meetup. Some of you may know about this park, but if you're new here I'll let you know that the hiking trails are not long, but well-marked, and I love walking them. I hope you all enjoy yourselves. Like I said, my name's Nat and this is my partner, Joy." Nat took the hand of her much shorter partner and kissed her palm. "We'd love to get to know all of you today and on future Meetups. We're taking the longest trail that starts there." Nat pointed in the direction of a small picnic area to their right. "We plan to stop at the first turnout, which is about a mile away. We look forward to chatting with you."

The group of women followed Nat and Joy to the paved path and broke up into small groups. A woman named Leslie introduced herself and fell into step with Debby and Alex. She stopped every few feet to point out a mushroom and prattle on about its type and poisonous properties. Debby feigned interest and listened politely until her patience ran out.

"Do you care about fungi?" Debby whispered to Alex while Leslie cooed over a particularly large capped mushroom.

"Not a bit," Alex whispered. "I don't even like to eat them."

Debby laughed. "Well, at this rate we won't reach the one-mile mark until tomorrow, but I suppose I ought to consider it a learning experience."

"Right. You never know when you'll be asked about a mushroom." Alex looked serious until a slight grin gave her away.

Debby refrained from reaching to hold her hand, surprised at how natural it would feel. She and Alex fell into an easy gait and walked in comfortable silence, content to let Leslie give lessons on the spore-bearing fruiting body of a fungus.

She liked Alex's sense of humor, and she seemed nice, but she needed to find out if Alex was single before making a decision on the invitation to the wedding. No way was she getting in the middle of a couple. The incredibly important number two on her list: *a single lesbian.* She didn't know why she kept associating Alex with her list. The wedding was her concern, not a real date, which meant the list didn't apply.

"Do you live around here?" Debby asked. Leslie had wandered off the path to look at some moldy thing she found particularly exciting.

"Not far. In fact, I walk my dog here. It's usually not too crowded, and I like that the trails are paved. Do you live nearby?"

"I live just outside of Novi, so it's pretty close. Just you and your dog, then?"

"Yep."

Alex's response probably ruled out a lover at home waiting for her. "I see the group is congregating. Let's grab a seat at the tables."

She followed Alex to the pavilion. She would plan to attend the next event with this group, spend a little more time with Alex, and make a decision to ask her to the wedding after that. There was no hurry, and even if she was only looking for a friend, she was determined to be careful with her heart.

Alex silently chided herself for nearly telling Debby about her previous walking group. She needed to work harder at thinking of her prior self in third person, but she found herself distracted by the way Debby's beautiful brown eyes twinkled when she smiled, and the small laugh lines around her eyes indicated they were probably the same age. She was tan and her body toned, as if she worked out. Alex vowed to work harder to lose the ten pounds she had put on over the past year. Debby was a little taller than she was, and Alex noticed how comfortably they could have held hands as they walked. She pushed away the unexpected attraction and concentrated on how to deflect any questions about her past.

The group had arrived at the meeting point Nat had chosen and settled onto a few picnic tables located under a pavilion. Debby sat across from her, and Leslie took the spot on her left.

"So, did you two come to the Meetup together?" Leslie asked.

"No," Alex answered quickly, and Debby shifted, looking uncomfortable.

"No. We just met today," Debby said.

"Oh. Sorry." Leslie waved her hand in the air as if dismissing her own idea. "I just love it here, don't you? I'm going to sign up for all their hikes. Hey, would you guys like to help me start our own Meetup? We can go hunting mushrooms throughout the woods of Michigan." Leslie beamed, spread out her arms, and looked back and forth at them.

"I'm going to pass on the mushroom hunting," Debby said.

"Me, too, I'm afraid. I don't know anything about them," Alex said.

"I'll be happy to teach you." Leslie hugged the pile of accumulated mushrooms she had deposited on the table.

Alex looked at Debby across the table and smothered a giggle. She looked like she was struggling not to laugh, too.

"You post the Meetup, Leslie. I'm sure there're plenty of other people interested," Alex said.

Leslie looked slightly disgruntled as she scooped up her mushrooms and deposited them into a plastic bag she'd pulled from her daypack, before leaving to join another group of women.

They sat enjoying the bird sounds and the light chatter of the group for a few minutes before Debby spoke.

"I'd like to join this group on another hike. It was fun walking with you. I hope you can make it, too."

"I'd love to plan on it. In fact, I'll bring my dog, Abby. She'd enjoy the walk, and she's great with people. I suppose I should ask if anyone minds first, huh?" Alex looked for Nat but couldn't see her anywhere.

"I see Joy at the far table. I'll walk over with you."

Alex confirmed that she could bring her dog on the next outing and began the walk to the parking lot with Debby.

"This walk is certainly more peaceful without the drone of lessons on mushrooms." Debby chuckled and kicked a fallen branch off the path in front of them.

"Yes, it is, but Leslie was nice. I liked her enthusiasm, even if I didn't share it."

"She was nice. We'll probably see her again trying to convince someone to join her mushroom hunting group."

They strolled the rest of the way in companionable silence, and Alex stifled the yearning to drop her guard. She mentally reviewed her lessons on keeping the focus off of herself.

"Do you have any pets?" Alex asked.

"I do. I rescued a cat a couple of months ago, and I have a horse that I ride in barrel racing competitions."

"Cool. I love horses. I used to…never mind." Alex fumbled for her keys in her waist pack and hoped Debby didn't ask questions. "I'll see you at the next walk." She rushed to her car, the ever-present feeling of panic surging through her. She gave Debby a weak wave as she drove away, trying to ignore the slightly puzzled expression on her face. *Running. Always running.*

Alex pulled into her carport, turned off the engine, and closed her eyes as she tipped her head back. *Why is this still so hard?* All she wanted to do was meet new people and make a few friends. She loved Jen dearly, but she was tired of having no one but her with whom to go out to dinner or a movie. No coaching from the federal marshals had prepared her for the constant stress of having to avoid revealing her past.

Inside her apartment, she opened her laptop and Googled Debra Johnson. She thought about the minimal information available on Alexandra Reed. She avoided all social media and used an alias for her email account. The U.S. Marshals had done their best to erase her former self from the Internet, but she had Joe to worry about that. She couldn't find a Facebook page or LinkedIn account for Debby, but she found a bio with a picture on the Michigan Pharmacists Association website. Debby looked great in a white lab coat. She allowed herself a brief fantasy of revealing her true self to her and living free. Free to enjoy the sparkle in her eyes and free of the constant vigilance to contain the banned memories. She shut down her computer and took Abby outside before heading to Jennifer's.

Alex began the knocking signal, and Jen answered within a minute. "Hey, sis."

"You're early. Didn't the Meetup go well?" Jen asked.

"It was fun but not a long hike. More like the walk I do with Abby, but I might have made a new friend with a horse." Alex hung Abby's leash on a hook next to the door and hugged Jen.

"A horse? You love horses." Jen stepped back out of the hug to look her in the eye. "You didn't tell her about Mr. Ed did you?"

"No. But almost. I let myself get too comfortable and nearly made a mistake." Alex shook her head and blew out a breath. "Want to order a pizza and watch *Criminal Minds* tonight?"

"Sure. You okay?"

"Yeah. I'm okay. Just a little frustrated. I can't believe it's still so difficult."

Alex plopped onto the couch and picked up the TV remote. Jen sat next to her and wrapped her arms around her. Alex didn't move away.

"Yeah. Extremely difficult. The good news, though, is that each day we're here living our new lives, and becoming our new selves, we're safer. We settle and blend in, so it'll get easier."

Jen smiled, and Alex wondered about her newfound confidence. She sat up and stared at her. "When did you get so comfortable?" She looked closer at the room and realized the overnight bag was gone.

"Yep. I put it away. I'm tired of living in fear, and…I've met someone."

Alex knew it was bound to happen eventually. Jennifer was a nice looking woman, and she had been dating a guy in Florida. Alex stood and shook her head in an attempt to dislodge the memory she was supposed to expunge. It made sense that someone would ask Jen out sooner or later. "You met someone, huh? When did this happen? You haven't said a word about him."

"I met Phil at work. He's a cop, and I feel safe with him. We've only had three dates, but I like him a lot."

"Joe will want to meet him." Alex knew their WITSEC inspector wouldn't object to Jen's dating, but they were required to let him know about anyone new in their lives.

"I already called him. He'll be here next weekend because Phil's coming over for dinner on Saturday. You'll be here, too, won't you?"

Alex smiled and nodded. "Of course I will. I can't wait to meet this new man of yours. Did you call Dad?"

"I did. No surprise that he declined the invitation."

"I talked to him last week, and he seemed okay. We may have to go visit him if we want to see him." Alex shook her head.

"Yeah. I wish he'd get over his guilt. I keep telling him we love and support him, but I don't think he'll ever forgive himself for tearing our lives apart." Jennifer sighed and stood to get her phone. "Hey, bring that horsewoman with you."

The thought had crossed her mind to invite Debby. She was good company and they could probably be friends, but she worried she'd slip again. She was unsure of how to involve a new friend in her life's untruths, but the only way to find out was to try.

"I don't have her number. I don't even know where she lives."

"She was at the park with you. She can't possibly live too far away, right?"

"Maybe, but I don't have any way of contacting her." Alex stood and went to the kitchen to fix a cup of hot chocolate.

"Okay. I won't bring it up again."

Alex heard the concern in Jen's voice and returned to the living room. "I'm sorry, Jen. I'm just not sure I trust myself completely yet. I almost slipped today."

"No problem. You gonna make a cup for me, too?" Jen pointed to the steaming cup Alex set on the end table and grinned.

"Well, that was fun, Buddy. I'm going to do it again." Debby tossed her car keys on her kitchen counter, stretched her back for a few minutes, and grabbed a beer from her refrigerator. Her cat purred and sprang onto her lap when she settled into her swivel rocker. She tipped her head back and enjoyed the tranquility of having a purring cat in her lap. Her thoughts drifted to Alex and their outing. She couldn't remember ever feeling so comfortable with a woman she didn't intend to sleep with. Maybe that's why it was comfortable. Having no expectations for a change felt refreshing, liberating. She pushed away the sliver of fear by reminding herself of her list. She had never used it to guard against friendship before, but those lines seemed blurred with Alex. Her mind kept calling her a potential friend, but her heart wondered if there could be more. *This is ridiculous. I just met her.*

She logged on to her computer and double-checked the meeting time for the next Meetup before turning her thoughts again to Alex and the hike that had turned out to be merely a stroll through the park. It didn't matter. She got plenty of exercise riding her horse. Alex had expressed excitement at the fact that she had a horse. Then it was as if she had stopped herself from admitting something. Debby wondered if Alex just misspoke or if she was trying to hide something. *Will I ever trust anyone? Is anyone actually trustworthy?*

She typed Alexandra Reed into her search engine and scrolled through various results. She didn't find anyone that sounded like the woman she'd met. She found no Facebook or LinkedIn account, or anyone living in Northville.

Debby sipped her beer and rested her hand on Buddy's warm back. "At least I know I can trust you. We're going to order Chinese food and watch *Criminal Minds* tonight." She set down her beer and called to order her dinner. Her life wasn't perfect, but it was safe. And that's how she liked it.

CHAPTER FOUR

Debby filled the last prescription of her last day working at Walgreens and placed it into a customer bin. She took one last look at the line of impatient customers ignoring the sign behind which they were to stand to protect others' privacy. They juggled items in their arms as they tried to balance their purchases. A harried looking woman yanked on the arm of a toddler attempting to grab anything within reach from the shelves. A bearded man leaned on a cane and stared blankly at the pharmacy tech, who was explaining about his pain medication prescription. A pair of teenaged girls, standing in the hair product aisle, giggled as they stuffed items into their backpacks. The last task on her last day would be to call security. She wouldn't miss this chaos. She phoned the front office to report the girl's shoplifting and said good-bye to her coworkers. She promised Jake she'd stop by and say hello once in a while, and left without looking back.

She opened her car door and was about to slide into the driver's seat when a familiar figure crossed the parking lot. She waved just as Alex stepped onto the sidewalk in front of the building entrance and looked her way.

"Hi, Debby."

"Hey. How're you doing?" Debby watched her stride toward her. She wore tailored pants with a matching blazer. As she got closer, she read Hyatt Place stitched on the lapel. She looked professional without hiding the fact that she was a sexy woman.

"Great. I needed to pick up a prescription on my way home. Do you shop here?"

Debby drew her eyes away from Alex's breasts filling out the front of her blouse as she unbuttoned her blazer. "I used to work here. Today was my last day."

"I hope that's a good thing. That it was your choice, I mean."

"Oh, yeah. I'm a pharmacist who's totally fed up with working at a retail pharmacy. I'm looking forward to a new position in a private nursing home."

"Ah. I'm glad you're going to do what you want."

"Thanks. I see you work at the Hyatt. Do you like it?" Debby leaned on her car door as she spoke, trying to quell the tiny butterflies she felt at seeing Alex again.

"I do. I've only been there a year, but I find it interesting. We have guests from all over the world since it's connected to the showcase and convention center."

"That's the one off the expressway, isn't it?"

"Yep."

"I've never stayed at the hotel, but I go to the horse expo every year." Debby smiled, and the blush creeping up Alex's cheeks surprised her.

"I love that show. The equestrian expo is in November. Maybe you'd like to go? I get complimentary tickets since I work at the hotel." Alex hesitated and continued. "I don't mean we have to go together if you don't want to." She looked nervous.

"I'd love to go together. It'll be fun." Debby didn't tell Alex she already had the event highlighted on her calendar. She was looking for someone besides Kristen with whom to attend the event, so she appreciated her invitation.

"Cool." Alex shifted and looked like she wanted to say more. "I...uh...my sister is having a little dinner party next Saturday. Do you think you'd like to come? I know it's last-minute, but she doesn't have many friends and loves to cook. There'll probably be enough food for ten people and it's just dinner." Alex's voice trailed off and she took a breath.

"I need to be clear about this, Alex. I'm not interested in dating anyone, so if that's what you had in mind—"

"No!" She blushed and smiled slightly. "I'm not looking for a date either. I just need a friend. Someone to do things with, like the horse show. We seemed to get along well at the Meetup hike, so I thought it would be nice to have you for company. That's all."

Debby smiled as Alex wiped her palms on her pants. Alex was cute when she was nervous, but she didn't want to make her any more uncomfortable, so she pulled out her phone. "Let's exchange numbers and emails, and you can let me know where I need to be and when I need to be there. Lots of food sounds good."

Alex visibly relaxed, and Debby's fears evaporated in the heat of her smile. This was what she wanted. A non-sexual relationship with a woman she liked, with whom she could share life's various events. Still, she began her mental recitation of the items on her list.

Alex eyed the flashing lights of the police car parked on the side of the building. She entered the drugstore but was stopped midway to the prescription counter by one of the officers.

"It'll only be a moment, ma'am," the tall cop said as he kept one eye on his partner, who was leading a female in handcuffs past them. Memories she was supposed to purge surfaced as she watched the girl who couldn't have been older than fourteen being led away in shackles. That young girl, probably shoplifting, could have been her younger sister at that age if she hadn't been there to guide her away from trouble. Her heart ached for the girl.

The policeman waved her on and followed the captive out, and Alex proceeded to the pharmacy counter. She waited in line and wished she would've used this drug store before. She would've enjoyed seeing Debby's beautiful smile and sparkling eyes. She paid for her purchase and left the store.

Alex sat in her car for five minutes, examining her feelings. She was glad Debby's intentions about dating matched her own. She still worried about slipping up, but if they only saw each other occasionally at public events, it would be easier for her to keep her story straight. It might have been a mistake to invite Debby to Jen's dinner party, but when she saw her in the parking lot, all her reservations had disappeared. She was definitely attracted to Debby, but she would never act on it. They were friends who enjoyed each other's company and liked to do things together. That would be all, and that needed to be enough. *It's a start. It's one more friend than I've had, anyway.*

She looked at Debby's number in her phone and realized it was the first time since relocating that she had someone other than Jen and Joe to text. *Now to figure out what to say.*

"Hey, Buddy. We're celebrating the end of working for a drugstore tonight." Debby filled her cat's bowl with his favorite canned food and watched as he settled in to eat. His quiet purring did little to calm her uneasiness with her decision to spend time with Alex. Her original plan to ask her to attend the wedding had somehow morphed into plans for two other events. She wanted someone to do things with, but she hadn't planned to feel so comfortable and attracted to the one she chose to hang out with. Items five and six on her list mandated a high level of comfort and attraction in a lover, but Alex could only be a friend, and although she was comfortable with her on a surface level, who knew what they'd be like if things got serious? They'd agreed to no dating, and she would hold up her part of the bargain. She would probably find an essential flaw in Alex anyway if they spent enough time together. She pulled a bottle of water out of her refrigerator and headed to her barn to feed Shadow.

"Feeling neglected, boy?" Debby tossed a flake of hay in the corner of her horse's stall and filled his grain bucket for the night. "We'll ride with Kristen and Zigzag this weekend." As soon as she spoke, she realized the barrel racing event was Saturday. The day she'd agreed to go to Alex's for dinner. She pulled out her phone and sent a text.

Alex, what time is dinner next Saturday?

She put her phone away and began brushing Shadow as he munched on his hay. She had only finished brushing one side when her phone pinged.

Hey, Debby. Good to hear from you. We're planning dinner for seven o'clock. Problem?

Debby thought for a moment before replying. Seeing Alex at dinner, in her own environment, could help her decide for sure if she wanted to ask her to the wedding.

No problem. I was hoping to ride in a barrel racing event on Saturday and wanted to make sure I'd have enough time. Should be okay.

Alex's reply was immediate.

Barrel racing? Is it a private event or can anyone attend?

Debby hesitated. Should she invite Alex to the fairgrounds? It was one of the last few scheduled competitions for the summer, and it was open to spectators. *Friends invite friends to that sort of thing, right?*

Anyone can come and watch. Debby took a breath before continuing her text. *I'd love a cheering section, if you're interested. Be at the Novi fairgrounds at 1 p.m. Ring number four.*

Alex's positive reply came five minutes later, and Debby pushed aside her excitement at the prospect of seeing her. *It's just good to have a friend, that's all. Nothing more.*

❖

"I'm glad you invited her," Jen said.

"I didn't intend to, but I saw her in the parking lot of Walgreens and decided I wanted to. Thanks for including her."

"Does she like fish? I was thinking of baking some fresh salmon with steamed asparagus tips."

"God! I've no idea. But if she has some food allergies or hated something, wouldn't it be up to her to tell me?" Alex paced the kitchen, regretting her snap decision to invite Debby to dinner.

"Yeah. I think you're right. I'll bake a couple of Cornish hens, too, with wild rice and acorn squash. If she doesn't like any of that she can have a bologna sandwich." Jen grinned and Alex relaxed.

"Thanks. I'll bring my yogurt and Cool Whip pie."

"Ooh, make the peach one." Jen's eyes lit up and she clapped.

"Peach it is. And if Debby doesn't like it, she can eat leftover Girl Scout cookies." Alex and Jen laughed, but Alex wondered if she should be worried. Debby was the first friend she had allowed into her life since her relocation, and she wanted to make it work.

"Thanks for picking up my prescription, by the way. The frequency of my migraines has subsided considerably since I found this doctor and the medication."

"I'm glad they're working for you. I'll bet the tension of the past few years hasn't helped any."

"Probably not. But I've been doing yoga and meditation with Sue at lunch every day, and that seems to be a huge help, too. You should give it a try."

"Do you have a DVD or something?" Alex asked.

"I do. Come on, I'll show you."

Alex followed her into the living room where she laid out two thin mats on the floor, and within five minutes, Alex was struggling to keep up with the flexible woman on the DVD. She was nearly folding her body in half, and Jennifer was keeping up as if she had done it her whole life.

"This is hard." Alex blew out a breath and plopped to the floor out of the silly position the instructor was demonstrating. "When do we get to the meditation part?"

Jen fast-forwarded to the end of the disc. "This is called yoga nidra. It's a guided meditation, so just lie on your back and rest."

Alex reclined on the floor, and for the next ten minutes allowed the soothing voice of the narrator to carry her into a world of peace and tranquility. She felt her body become heavy and melt into the floor as she allowed her awareness to float outside of the room and back again. She let go of any residual stress of her day, relaxed totally, and fell in love with yoga nidra.

CHAPTER FIVE

Debby pulled into the fairgrounds with her horse trailer an hour before the start of the event, intending to walk Shadow in the ring a few times. It had been several weeks since they'd competed, and she hadn't had much time for training. She waved to Kristen, who was waiting for her with her horse.

"Hi, Deb. I'm glad you could make it. It should be a good match. Kelly'll be here with Pogo, and Tom's riding his new palomino, Ginger." Kristen led Zigzag to the waiting area of the barn and waited for Debby to unload Shadow.

"I'm a little rusty, but I think Shadow's looking forward to this. He loves to compete."

"Let's do a practice run before anyone else gets here," Kristen said.

"Sounds good."

"I think you two will do fine," Kristen said after their practice turn, as they walked the ring to cool down. "You looked great out there."

"Thanks. I've missed it, for sure." Debby dismounted and bent to stretch her back.

"When do you start your new job?"

"Monday. I took an extra couple of days off before starting. I needed the break. It'll be wonderful to have most weekends off now." Debby scanned the area around the ring, searching for Alex.

"Expecting someone?" Kristen asked. She closed Zigzag in a stall and stood next to Debby.

"Yeah. I met a woman on that Meetup I went to last weekend, and she wanted to watch us ride today." Debby pulled out her phone and checked for text messages.

"So, you met someone." Kristen grinned and sat on one of the benches lined up against the barn. "Don't think you're going to get away without telling me all about that, my friend." She patted the seat next to her.

Debby put her phone away and sat next to Kristen. She shook her head at Kristen's expectant expression.

"She's just a friend. We got along well on the hike and that's the whole story."

"That's great, Deb. I'm glad you found a new friend. I can't wait to meet her."

Several of the other riders had arrived and were preparing their horses for the match.

"I guess we should get ready soon," Debby said. "I'm going to look for Alex."

Her phone pinged just as she pulled it out of her pocket.

I'm at the fairgrounds, heading for the bleachers at ring four now. A

Debby replied, taken unawares by the tingle of anticipation at seeing the text.

I'll meet you at the concession area after the race. D

She tucked her phone away and joined the other contestants, confused by her delight at having Alex there to watch her.

Alex sat on the end of the first bench of the stands directly across from the area where Debby would be riding. She watched the horses and riders prepare for the contest and allowed the disallowed memories to flow. Mr. Ed was too old for barrel racing and pole bending, but she had won quite a few first place ribbons riding him in Western Pleasure events. Other uninvited memories surfaced, and she shut them down to watch Debby maneuver her big dappled gray through the course.

She cheered for Debby as the match pitted her against a solid looking pinto ridden by an incredibly attractive blonde. The pinto had narrowly edged out an impressive looking Appaloosa, and she doubted Debby could beat them. Her prediction was accurate as she watched Debby race out the end of the course a full length behind the faster pinto. She considered how she would let Debby know how much she knew about horses without disclosing the past she wasn't supposed to have. She could make something up. She was getting better at it every day, but for some reason it felt more difficult with Debby. She wanted to know her and be known by her. All of her. She pushed aside the dangerous thoughts and took a deep breath to ground herself in reality.

"Hey, Alex. I'm glad you could make it." Debby waved at her from a round table positioned next to a large white trailer with "fresh squeezed lemonade" painted on the side, along with a picture of a lemon.

"Hi." Alex relaxed into one of the white plastic chairs across the table from Debby. "It was fun watching you ride. Thanks for telling me about this."

"We have these events nearly every weekend throughout the summer. There'll be a couple more before Labor Day."

"Well, I'm going to plan on attending them. I loved it. Who's the blonde with the pinto? She's fast."

"That's Kelly and Pogo. It's either them or Kristen and Zigzag who win most of the barrel racing."

"Is that the Appaloosa?"

"Yep. Kristen and I've been friends since high school, and I met Kelly at one of these events a few years ago. They'll probably come by here in a few minutes. Would you like a lemonade?"

"Yeah. Thanks." Alex pulled her wallet out of her waist pack.

"It's on me," Debby said. "You can buy next time."

Alex tilted her head and caught Debby's eye. She held her gaze for a moment before speaking. "I'd love a next time."

"Hey, Deb. Great riding today."

The nice looking woman who had ridden the Appaloosa strode toward them holding the hand of a woman with beautiful hazel eyes. They made a striking couple, and Alex squelched the surprise envy. The hazel-eyed woman smiled at her as they approached, and Alex relaxed. She radiated serenity, and her non-judgmental, direct gaze reflected acceptance, as if having secrets was irrelevant. She smiled back.

"Thanks," Debby said.

Debby's dark eyes sparkled when she smiled. Hazel Eyes was beautiful, but looking at Debby made her tingle. She squelched that feeling, too.

Alex offered her hand to Kristen in greeting. "I'm Alex. You had a great ride today, too, and your horse is gorgeous." She hesitated to say more and scrambled for an explanation as to how she knew about horses in case she asked.

"Thanks, Alex. It's good to meet you. I'm Kristen, and this is my partner, Jaylin." Kristen lifted their joined hands and kissed Jaylin's knuckles.

"Nice to meet you, Alex," Jaylin said. "You're a friend of Debby's?"

"Sorry. I should have introduced Alex. We met at a Meetup a week ago, and I invited her to watch us ride today." Debby had moved closer as she spoke, and Alex felt herself flush at her nearness.

"We're always happy to have someone here rooting for us. We'd join you for something to drink, but Jaylin has a surgery patient she needs to check on this afternoon. Hopefully, we'll see you next week," Kristen said. She and Jaylin waved as they turned and left.

"Is Jaylin a doctor?" Alex sat back in her chair and watched Kristen and Jaylin stroll away. She smiled as they bumped playfully against each other as they walked.

"She's a veterinarian at that equine practice in Novi."

"She's an equine vet?"

"No. Sorry. She's the small animal vet in the adjacent building. Feel like a light lunch at Tony's? Hot dogs and burgers are the only options here, and my cholesterol level needs no assistance."

"Sounds good except I promised Jennifer I'd help her this afternoon. Can I have a rain check?" Alex remembered the concern over Debby's food preference. She wouldn't need the bologna sandwich.

"Sure. Jennifer must be your sister. I'm looking forward to meeting her."

"I think you two will get along well. I guess I'll head home now. Thanks again for telling me about this event."

"I'll walk you to your car." Debby tossed their empty cups into the garbage bin and rested her hand on Alex's lower back as they walked to the exit.

Alex felt the heat of her touch through to her belly and shivered at the cold when she moved away to get into her car.

❖

Debby hung her keys on the hook by the door and pulled a cold bottle of water out of her refrigerator before settling into her favorite chair. Buddy's loud mewling reminded her to check his food bowl.

"All right, you. I've already fed the big guy, so it's your turn."

She stood and winced at the shooting pain in her back. She slowly bent forward until the tight muscles relaxed. Arthritis from years of riding and too many tumbles off her horse reminded her of her forty-four-year-old body. *Time for a trip to the chiropractor.* She loved riding her horse and had no intention of quitting, but maybe it was time to slow down a little.

Buddy purred and rubbed against her leg. She picked him up and cuddled him as she carried him into the kitchen.

"I've got to get changed, Buddy. I'm going to a dinner party." She set him on the floor next to his bowl and filled it with kibble before stroking his back and heading to the bathroom.

Debby allowed the hot water to cascade down her back and thoughts of Alex to drift through her mind. She'd looked good today at the fairgrounds. Her highlighted hair shone in the summer sun, and she'd smiled more often than when they had first met. Kristen and Jaylin seemed to like her. Number seven on her list. *Must be accepted by her friends.* She wondered again why she was even using her list for Alex. They were *not* dating.

She squeezed scented body wash onto her hands and cupped her breasts. She massaged slowly as her nipples stiffened and tickled her palms. She slid one hand down to her belly circling her fingertips lightly just below her belly button. But as she moved them lower, her body's reaction to her own touch reminded her that it had been a long time since she'd hooked up with a woman at the bar. It was soft gray eyes she saw, however, that coaxed her over the edge as she shuddered, engulfed by her orgasm.

Debby stepped out of the shower and dried off quickly, dismissing her intense arousal as a normal reaction to the fact that Alex was a beautiful woman. It didn't mean anything.

She decided on a pair of black slacks and white Western shirt with turquoise embroidery. She polished her boots and mentally reviewed the directions Alex had sent her. She glanced at her watch as she grabbed her keys. She'd have just enough time to pick up flowers for Alex's sister. *Never show up empty-handed or under dressed.* She smiled at the old family wisdom and at the feeling of excitement.

❖

"Is there anything else I can do to help? I got here early so you wouldn't be overwhelmed." Alex sat at the kitchen table with a cup of tea watching Jen flit from the stove to the counter and back again. "You look a little manic there, sis."

"I'm fine."

"Okay." Alex retrieved plates and silverware and set the table while Jen continued her preparations. She was about to ask when Phillip, Jen's new guy, was due to arrive when the buzzer sounded. "I'll get it."

"Hey, Joe. Come on in. Jennifer's in the kitchen cooking and being nervous." Alex smiled and hugged the tall deputy marshal who had been with them throughout the transition. He was the one she had yelled at in frustration when they had been moved to their third safe house. He was who they called when they needed to talk to someone who knew the truth. She could easily think of him as Uncle Joe.

"Hi, kiddo. So little sis is nervous, huh? I'll go talk to her."

"Good. I'll make you a cup of hot chocolate." Alex followed Joe into the kitchen where Jennifer looked much calmer.

"It's good to see you." Jen turned off the burner and turned to hug Joe.

"It's good to see you, too. You look great." He stepped back holding her at arm's length. "I'm looking forward to meeting Phillip." He turned toward Alex and continued. "And I understand you have someone you've invited today, too?"

Alex shifted in her seat. "Yes. A new friend. I met her at that Meetup I attended."

"Well, I'm looking forward to meeting them both. I'm glad you two are moving on and settling in. Remember, I'm here for anything you need." Joe looked back and forth between them.

"We know that, and we appreciate it," Alex said.

"Yeah. We probably don't let you know often enough how much we appreciate how you've helped us make our transition tolerable." Jen spoke as she turned to the stove to stir homemade carrot soup that smelled wonderful.

Alex left Joe with his cup of hot chocolate to answer the door. She took a step back as a tall, dark-haired man smiled down at her from the doorway.

"I'm Phillip Donohue. You must be Alexandra."

Phillip wasn't only tall and dark, but also handsome. *For a man.* He didn't look like a cop. His hair was a tad shaggy and hung to his collar, not the buzz cut that most officers wore, and he had a mustache. His chocolate eyes scanned the room and rested on Joe standing in the kitchen doorway. She noticed an infinitesimal nod before he focused back on Alex.

"That would be me. Please call me Alex." She ushered him into the room and called to Jen in the kitchen. "And this is our uncle, Joe Murphy."

"Good to meet you, Phillip," Joe said.

"You, too. Call me Phil, please."

The men shook hands, and Alex got a sense of their posturing.

Jen entered the living room just as the buzzer sounded again, but she ignored it to focus on Phil, so Alex opened the door for Debby. "Hi. Any trouble finding the place?"

"None. You give good directions." Debby grinned and held out a small bouquet of flowers. "For the cook."

"Thanks. Come in and meet her." Alex handed the spray of mixed blooms to Jen. "Jen, this is my friend Debby."

"Thanks for the invitation," Debby said. She smiled, and Alex realized how much she was beginning to look forward to that sparkle in her eyes.

"I'm glad you could make it. Dinner's almost ready. I'll show you where the drinks are so you can help yourself." Jennifer led the way into the kitchen and arranged the flowers in a vase.

"And I'm going to fill water glasses," Alex said.

"Can I help with anything?" Debby followed Alex to the small dining area off the living room.

"You can sit." Jennifer carried in a pot of soup and began filling bowls.

"This is great." Debby spoke between spoonfuls of soup. "Everything's fantastic, Jen. This salmon is perfectly prepared. Where did you learn to cook like this?"

"I took a cooking class years ago."

"At the local college? I hear they have a great culinary program."

"Ah. No. It was somewhere else." Jennifer looked down at her plate and took a big bite of her salmon.

"So, do you do much cooking?" Alex faced Debby as she asked.

"Not much. I do the basics. Baked chicken, salad, and steamed vegetables. I'm too busy with my job and my horse to have time for anything fancy. Which reminds me. You seem to know so much about horses, that I wanted to know if you've ever owned one." Debby set her fork down and took a drink of water.

"No. I just like horses." *True. Mr. Ed was leased.*

"Do you live in Northville?" Joe asked from across the table.

"No. I have a house in Novi. I've lived there for most of my adult life. Where're you from, Joe?"

"I don't live too far from here." Joe ladled soup into his bowl.

Alex interrupted the ensuing awkward silence by retrieving her pie from the kitchen. "Anyone ready for desert?" She hoped Debby wouldn't ask any more questions.

Alex could feel Jen's anxiety, and her own apprehension was flaring. She looked at Phil and said, "So, tell us about your job. You must have some crazy stories."

To her relief, it worked. Phil started talking about various things he'd dealt with during his years on the force, and it filled the rest of the time perfectly. As long as Alex remembered to ask questions to keep him talking, and Joe did a lot of that as well, it kept away the questions that were too hard, too personal, to answer.

Chapter Six

I don't know about you, but I need a walk after that huge meal," Alex said. "Is it all right if I stop to get Abby? She's been inside since before noon."

"Of course. I'd love to meet her."

"Here we are." Alex unlocked and pushed open the door, hoping Debby didn't notice the folded gum wrapper fall to the floor. She wasn't ready to come up with an excuse for making sure no one had broken in.

"It must be nice to be so close to Jen." Debby knelt to pet the bouncing dog as they entered the apartment.

"It is. The rent's inexpensive here, so I told Jen about it when she was looking for a place." *Almost true.*

Debby walked through the living area, and Alex straightened the pile of yoga magazines on the coffee table as she passed. "I have a house outside of town that has a similar layout. I like walking into the living room and having the kitchen off to the side." Alex followed her through the kitchen with Abby close by her side. "I have a back entrance to my kitchen, though. This is nice. Cozy." Debby turned toward her, smiled, and their gazes locked for a heartbeat.

Alex swallowed and pushed down the swift rush of arousal. "Thanks. I sometimes think I'd like a bit more room, but this works for now. Shall we walk?"

"Let's."

Alex locked the door behind them and discreetly stuck a new piece of paper between the door and frame while Debby walked away from her.

"So, is your uncle from your mother or your father's side of the family?" Debby stopped to stretch her back after they'd walked for a couple of blocks.

"Actually, neither." *The truth.* "He and his wife have been friends of the family since I was a baby. We've always called him uncle." *Almost the truth.*

"Well, he's nice. And your sister's great. Has she been dating Phil long?"

"Not really. I believe they've only had a few dates, but they seem well suited for each other." Alex took a deep breath, hugged herself, and tried to relax in the cool of the summer evening.

"You cold? Here." Debby reached around her waist and pulled her next to her so their hips were touching. "Better?"

Alex stiffened at the unexpected contact but didn't pull away. The connection felt good, right.

"I'm okay. Thanks." She stepped out of the one-armed hug, gently took Debby's hand, and squeezed. "I'm not much for temperatures below eighty degrees." She released her hand and at once felt the loss.

"I kinda guessed that you were a warm weather person at the Meetup. You were the only one wearing a long-sleeved shirt. Have you lived in Michigan your whole life?" Debby had moved so a foot separated them as they walked.

My whole life as Alexandra Reed. "Mostly."

"Here in Northville?"

"Yes. I lived farther south in the state before here." *In two other safe houses.* "How 'bout you? You said you had a house, so have you lived in Michigan your whole life?"

"I was born in Lansing, Michigan, and my family moved to Novi when I was twelve. I've lived there ever since."

"Any siblings?"

"I've a brother, an Iraq war vet, who still lives in Lansing, and a sister in Arizona. That's it." Debby stopped walking to bend and stretch her back.

"Back issues?" Alex asked.

"One too many spills from atop my horse, I'm afraid. Nothing too serious, just arthritis that I aggravated by riding today."

"Ah. I know what arthritis is. Have you ever tried yoga?"

"Yeah. I hate it."

Alex laughed. "Me too. But Jen showed me some body stretches that've helped me. I could show you, if you're interested." Alex imagined the two of them lying on the floor stretching and moving together to the soothing voice of the instructor on the DVD. She liked the vision.

"Maybe I'll try it. I don't like taking anything for pain and lately I've had to." She bent side to side as she spoke.

"Cool. We'll make plans for next week. You ready to head back?" Alex tugged on Abby's leash and began walking back without waiting for an answer. She considered the information she'd divulged and mentally reviewed the various methods of memory retention she'd practiced. She needed to be able to keep her story straight, especially if they were going to spend more time together. All the coaching during her transition hadn't prepared her for the anxiety of possibly tripping over her story, or how in the world to deal with a simple dinner party, but she was beginning to believe that getting to know Debby was worth it.

Debby tried to figure out what bothered her about Alex. She had appeared relaxed and unguarded at dinner, but uneasy at times while they had walked, as if hesitant to divulge too much information. Jennifer had seemed reluctant to discuss herself, too. And what was that piece of paper in the door about? Some kind of strange OCD thing? Debby shook off the desire to reach beyond Alex's defenses and know her better. She needed to ask her to attend the wedding with her, say good-bye after that so they didn't get too close, and then concentrate on her new job. They could be surface friends and occasionally run into each other, but that was all. Alex could keep her privacy, and she would go back to the club and her no strings hookups.

Alex rapped on the door three times and hesitated as if counting before opening the door. Jennifer and Phil sat on the couch facing the door, and Abby rushed to jump on the couch and snuggle next to them when Alex unhooked her leash.

"I'm glad you two made it back. Phil got called into work and has to leave soon, but he wanted to say good-bye." Jennifer hugged Abby close as she spoke.

Phil stood and placed his hand on Jennifer's back when she rose. "We'll probably see each other again," he said. He smiled as Jennifer leaned into him.

"I'll be heading home now, too," Debby said. "Thank you for a lovely dinner. It was great to meet you all." She waved at Joe, who waved back from where he was leaning with his back to the wall.

"Glad to meet you, Debby. I hope we'll see you again," Joe said.

"I'm gonna go, too. I've got a large group coming in tomorrow for a private wedding reception, so I'll be on my feet all day. I'll walk you out, Debby." Alex hugged Jen and waved good-bye to Phil and Joe as she called to Abby.

"Thanks for the invitation today. Your sister is a phenomenal cook," Debby said as they headed downstairs.

"You're welcome. I'm glad you made it to help consume the feast, but I'm sure she'll be bringing me leftovers for days." Alex placed her hand on her belly and smiled.

"Before I leave, I have something I want to ask you." Debby leaned against the wall and pulled out her car keys. "I've been invited to a lesbian wedding next month, and I'd rather not go alone, so I wondered if you'd like to come with me. Just as a friend. Like we agreed. It's on Saturday, the fifth of September."

"That's Labor Day weekend. I'm scheduled to work on Monday rather than the weekend, so yeah. I'd love to go with you, as a friend."

Alex smiled, and Debby's gut fluttered. "Great. I'll let you know what time when it gets closer. Have a good evening."

"You, too. Take care." Alex turned to leave and pulled Abby's leash.

Debby pushed away from the wall and followed the sway of Alex's hips as she led Abby toward the stairs. She needed to get a grip on her reactions to Alex or she'd regret having asked her to the wedding.

Debby reviewed the evening as she drove the few miles home. She had surprised herself when she found herself relaxed and enjoying the easy flow of conversation. Alex and her sister obviously cared about each other, and she had noted several times when they had exchanged glances and moved at the same time as if reading each other's minds. She envied their connection. Her own sister lived in Arizona, but with her husband working overtime and two kids in school, the time and financial restraints meant they only saw each other maybe once a year. Her brother lived and worked less than thirty miles away in Lansing, Michigan, but was struggling with post-traumatic stress, so she didn't hear from him often.

Phil and Jennifer seemed to be closer than she would have expected for a new relationship. They seemed as comfortable with each other as a long-term couple, and her jealousy took her by surprise. It seemed she had shaken off that feeling several times in the short time since Alex had entered her life, and she vowed to squelch it by consulting her list as soon as she got home.

Alex double-checked the guest list for one of the biggest wedding events the convention center had hosted all year. Sundays in July were big days for wedding events, and they usually took up the whole facility. She pasted on her smile and prepared to greet the guests streaming into the room. Her stomach clenched when she read the groom's name. Maybe Martinez was a common name, like Smith or Jones. She checked in several guests as she searched the group for the wedding party but saw no one who stood out. She'd never seen a wedding so formal. All the guests were in tuxedos and evening gowns.

"I'll be right back, Betty," she whispered to her boss while scanning the crowd again, then grabbed her cell phone and headed to the employee parking area.

"Martinez." She pronounced the name clearly over the phone to Joe.

"Does he have a first name?"

"Miguel. Miguel Martinez. God, Joe, is he related to that offshoot of the La Familia cartel I read about? Is he one of the bad guys that knew my father?"

"Take it easy. The whole Martinez family, and the Knights Templar cartel, is under surveillance. They're a newer group, and your dad was never involved with them. Remember when I told you we would protect you at all costs? I meant it, kiddo. You relax, and I'll look into this Miguel for you. He might not even be part of that cartel. It's a pretty common Hispanic name, so try not to worry about it. I'll get back to you soon, okay?"

"Thanks, Joe. I'll wait to hear from you."

Alex disconnected the call and took a settling breath before heading back to work. She wouldn't panic. She had a new identity and there was no chance she would be recognized by this Martinez, even if he was part of the cartel. Her father was involved with the drug gang, not her. She settled behind the front desk and let the other employees take care of the wedding guests.

She was able to avoid working with the wedding party for most of the day, but an hour before she was due to leave, her boss asked her to work overtime to take over for one of her coworkers who had to leave early. She took a deep breath and agreed to stay. She thought of Debby's calm strength, and the constriction in her chest eased. The relief was short-lived as she realized she couldn't even mention her fears to her. She sighed and phoned Jen to ask her to take Abby out. She saw no need to tell Jennifer anything until she heard back from Joe. No sense in both of them being on edge. She put her phone away and went to check on the wedding's food preparation.

Alex spent the last hour of her shift confirming reservation information in the hotel's computer. She noted which room Miguel and his new bride were staying in, surprised that it wasn't one of the suites. It seemed they'd reserved those for their guests. Maybe he wasn't an evil drug lord after all. They were due to check out the next day, and she hoped that would be the last time she ever saw them.

Chapter Seven

"Hey, good morning, Deb." Kelly leaned across the counter at the nurses' station located by the employee entrance. "You're starting today, huh?"

"Yep. First day, and I couldn't be more excited. I don't know exactly what to expect yet, but maybe we can get together for lunch."

"Sure. You go check in with Jan, and I'll come by the pharmacy later."

Debby followed the hallway to the center of the building past Janis's office and had nearly made it to the pharmacy entrance when she started at a scream coming from one of the rooms. She quickly turned to investigate as two nurses scurried past her.

"It's okay, Mrs. Wilson. You're safe now." The nurses' practiced movements and calming demeanor must have been what Mrs. Wilson needed because her shrieking stopped. "Just relax and we'll bring you your medication."

Debby retreated down the hall to the pharmacy. If medication was needed, she wanted to be ready to learn what was being dispensed. She was surprised to find the pharmacy door unlocked but the room dark. She flipped on the light switch and called into the empty room. "Hello? Anyone here?" She was surprised and a little dismayed that the room full of drugs was left unlocked and unattended. She was about to leave in search of Janis when one of the nurses she had seen with Mrs. Wilson entered the room.

"Good morning. I'm Rita, one of the day shift nurses. You must be the new pharmacist Janis told us about. I'm hoping you can help me with one of the patients this morning."

Debby smiled at the nurse standing in the doorway looking completely relaxed. "Yes. I'm Debra Johnson. I think I need to settle in first and get my bearings, Rita. This is my first day, and I'm not familiar with the procedure here."

"Just look her up in the system, for goodness sake. You do know how to use a computer don't you? It's Cora Wilson. She takes two milligrams of Xanax, three times a day. It's over there." Rita pointed to a locked cabinet behind Debby.

"That sounds like a high dose. I'll confirm it in the system and get back to you. Okay?" Debby bristled but stifled an impatient retort. She hoped this incident was an anomaly and not the norm.

"Just open the cabinet and give me the pills. I'll let her doctor know about it." Rita stood unmoving, with her hands on her hips.

"I'm sorry, Rita, but like I said, this is my first day, and I don't even know where the keys are to the cabinets."

"They're right there. Hanging on that hook." Rita pointed to a wall where several keys hung for anyone to reach.

"Is this where they're kept all the time? It seems unsafe to leave them where anyone can get to them."

Rita shrugged and Debby wondered what she'd gotten herself into just as Janis entered the room.

"Good morning. I see you've already met Rita." Janis turned to address the nurse. "I'll explain our system to Debby while you fill out the requisition form."

Rita looked irritated, but turned and left the room.

"Sorry about that. Rita can be a bit pushy when it comes to her patients. Come on. I'll show you the ropes. Penny, our other pharmacist, called in sick today, so you'll be on your own."

"Thanks. Can we start with why the keys to the drug cabinet aren't put away in a drawer?"

"We've been short staffed for a few months, and regulations have slipped. You find a good spot for them, and I'll make sure everyone is aware of the change."

Debby didn't mind working alone when she knew where to find things. She just needed to learn the facility's process and figure out what was up with Rita. *This may be more than I bargained for.* Odd that she now had two new people in her life she couldn't quite figure out. Thoughts of Alex reminded her she was going to mention the next barrel racing event to her. She liked the thought of Alex watching her ride. She stretched her back and remembered she was going to learn some yoga moves. She made a mental note to call her at lunchtime.

❖

"So how's your first day going?" Kelly and Debby sat across from each other in the employee break room eating their lunches.

"So far, so good. I wasn't sure what I was getting into first thing this morning, though."

"What happened?"

"A nurse named Rita came into the pharmacy demanding some Xanax for one of the residents, but I'd only just walked in the door and had no idea what the procedure was. Fortunately, Janis rescued me and explained how the system works."

Kelly's laugh surprised Debby.

"Rita can be a handful. I'm sorry you had to experience her exuberance on your first day. She takes her responsibilities extremely seriously. It was probably Mrs. Wilson who needed the Xanax. Her doctor keeps her heavily dosed or she gets extremely agitated. We've had to sedate her several times over the past few months so she wouldn't hurt herself or anyone else."

"Huh. Well, I looked up her record, and the dose Rita requested was indeed what was prescribed, although I thought it was pretty high." Debby finished her sandwich and sat back with a cup of tea.

"So, how's your love life these days? It's been a while since you talked about the club," Kelly asked.

Debby balked at the turn in the conversation but decided to be honest. "I've sort of lost interest, you know." She took a swallow of tea and contemplated telling her about Alex, but Alex was only a friend. *Why do I need to keep reminding myself of that?* "I miss dancing, but the one night hookups have sort of lost their appeal. It almost seems like more work than it's worth."

"Whoa. I never thought I'd hear you say that. I know I've been a little off my game since I lost Kristen to Jaylin. I was hoping maybe we could hit the Rainbow Zone together this weekend. You up for that?"

Debby considered the invitation. A night out was probably just what she needed to let off some steam and keep her focus off Alex. She recalled she was going to call her to invite her to the fairgrounds and remind her of the yoga. Maybe she'd wait until next week, give it some time to feel less…interesting.

"Yeah. Let's plan on a Saturday night adventure."

❖

Debby settled into her seat and took a sip of her beer as she watched Kelly dancing with a young brunette in a leather skirt and knit top that barely covered her breasts. Kelly caressed her bare midriff, and Debby turned to watch the other dancers.

A couple moved past her line of sight, and she caught her breath as one of the women stepped away then twirled back into the arms she'd left. She could have been Alex, with her short spiky hair and shapely body. She shook off the desire to be the one holding that body and searched for her own dance partner. An attractive blonde caught her eye, and she watched as the woman waved and went to join a group in the back of the room. For some unknown reason, she felt no inclination to follow her. She sat back and waited for Kelly.

"Are you going to just sit there like a bump on a log all night?" Kelly asked. She plopped into her chair and took a long pull on her cold beer.

"What do you mean? I'm just relaxing." Debby shifted in her seat, willing Kelly to ignore her. Her idea of an adventure had been wishful thinking. The only woman she'd wanted to dance with was one that reminded her of Alex. This wasn't good. Alex was only supposed to be a friend, not someone against whom she needed her list for protection.

"You haven't danced once tonight, and there are some hot women here."

"I think I'm just tired. I'm so sick of retail pharmacy that it's important to me to do a good job for Janis. I worked hard today and I think I'm just wiped out." Debby knew Kelly wouldn't buy her excuse.

"I've seen you work a fifty-hour week and still stay out all night dancing. You sure there isn't something else going on?" Kelly leaned back in her chair and twirled her beer bottle with one hand, looking prepared to wait for as long as it took for Debby's reply. "Does it have anything to do with that nice looking woman I saw you with at the fairgrounds last week?"

"That was Alex. She's just a new friend I met at a Meetup last month." Debby stood abruptly. "I'm going for another beer. Can I get you anything?"

"No. I'm good. Hey—" Kelly rested her hand on Debby's arm to stop her. "We can leave if you're not having a good time."

Debby dropped back into her chair. "I'm sorry. I don't want to squash your fun."

"You're not squashing anything. I'm ready to get out of here, too. I don't know, maybe I'm getting old, but this doesn't seem as satisfying as it used to. Let's go get an omelet at Pete's."

"Sounds good. We've turned into real party animals, haven't we?" Debby stood and stretched her back.

"Those bulging disks bothering you again?"

"Just a little. God, now I feel old. Let's get the heck out of here."

Debby fed Shadow and set up his stall for the night when she got home and then dropped into her swivel rocker to read the letter from the Michigan Pharmacists Association. She held up her arms so Buddy could jump into her lap while she read it aloud. "Due to conflicts in scheduling, the venue for this year's event will be changed to the new convention center in Novi."

She set the document aside, unsettled by the tickle of pleasure at the thought of seeing Alex again so soon. The second Meetup was planned for the same weekend as the MPA conference, so she had told Alex she wouldn't be there. She thought she heard relief in her voice when Alex told her she would have to work that weekend and couldn't join the group either, but it could have been wishful thinking. She realized that Alex rendered item three on her list irrelevant. She cared what Alex thought of her.

Buddy jumped off her lap and rubbed against her leg. She leaned to stroke his back as he arched into her hand.

"Who's got who trained here?"

Buddy leapt back into her lap and rubbed his cheek on her arm before curling up and ignoring her. She stroked his fur and closed her eyes, his purring lulling her to sleep.

Debby awakened to a stiff neck and numb leg. She groaned as she gently nudged Buddy off her lap and stood to stretch. "My days of sleeping in this chair are over, Bud." She strode to her bedroom thinking of Alex's offer of learning yoga stretches. She would call her in the morning to make arrangements to give it a try. *It couldn't hurt.*

She fell asleep to thoughts of Alex's backside in yoga pants.

CHAPTER EIGHT

"Thanks for helping with this, Jen." Alex paced the length of Jen's living room, anticipating Debby's arrival.

"No problem. You know I love doing yoga, so I'm happy to include Debby." Jennifer doubled over to touch her palms to the floor.

"Show off." Alex grinned.

Alex jumped when the buzzer indicated Debby had arrived and stopped short when she opened the door. Debby wore a white T-shirt that fit snuggly over her breasts, a pair of loose fitting knit pants that hugged her shapely ass, and a pair of new looking white sneakers.

"Am I early?" Debby looked puzzled.

"No. Sorry. Come in." Alex stepped aside, happy to have found her voice. She took a settling breath before continuing. "Jennifer's already flaunting her flexibility, and I'm standing around watching."

"Okay. I wasn't sure what to wear so…well…here I am." Debby raised her arms to the side. "And I brought water." She handed Alex a plastic bag containing several bottles of water.

"You look just fine. The key is to be comfortable while you do the ridiculous poses. I'll put these in the kitchen, and we can join Jennifer in the living room."

Alex worked to concentrate on the movements of the instructor on the TV screen and ignore Debby lying less than a foot from her. Several times, as they did a cross-stretching move, her hand brushed Debby's, sending warmth up her arm. She seemed to have no trouble keeping up and was even enjoying the workout.

Alex let out a sigh of relief when they reached the yoga nidra portion of the DVD.

"Hmm. I like this part." Debby slowly raised, then lowered, her arms as she spoke. "I feel like a limp noodle."

"You sound like Alex. The first time she tried this, her favorite part was the meditation." Jennifer sat up in a lotus position and breathed deeply.

Alex didn't want to move. She remained on her back, but when she turned toward Debby, their gazes locked, and she changed her mind. She wanted to roll over on top of her and kiss her silly. She felt herself blush and pushed herself into a sitting position.

Debby stood slowly, flexing her neck and rolling her shoulders. "Thanks, Jennifer. I think I feel better. I can see what you like about the last part, Alex. I've never experienced guided meditation before."

Alex struggled to get control of her runaway libido. "Yeah. I'll admit it. I'm only in it for the lying around part. I'll get us some water." She stood, grateful for the distraction.

Debby and Jennifer were seated on the couch when she returned with three bottles of water. They all sat quietly drinking the water until Jennifer's phone interrupted the serenity. She left to take the call in the kitchen, and Debby stood and stretched her back.

"I do feel better. I never would've thought I'd consider doing yoga again after the last time I tried it."

"Sounds like a story there. Care to share it?" Alex sat back and took a drink of water.

A loud siren blared outside, forcing them to wait for a moment before continuing the conversation.

Debby sat at the opposite end of the couch facing Alex. "It was quite a few years ago, when I was young and stupid. I was practicing barrel racing and fell off Shadow twice. Nothing hurt too much, so I hopped back on him." She took a drink of water and tilted her head, considering. "It was a silly thing to do. I pushed myself to impress my lover at the time. I managed to dismount but hobbled for days afterward. She was big into yoga and convinced me it would help my back, so I decided to give it a try to avoid a trip to the doctor. I went with her to a class taught by a guy who'd trained with a Swami in India. Well, after the class, I felt no better, and to make matters worse, before leaving, I discovered my lover in a back room beneath the instructor." Debby took a deep breath in an attempt to expel the memory. She had healed physically, but shut down emotionally, with her list to protect her. "And that's the story of why I'm not big on yoga."

Alex had moved closer to her at some point during her story, and she set her water bottle on the coffee table and pulled her into a hug. "I'm so sorry you had to go through that. You deserve better." She sat back, and Debby felt a chill envelop her.

"Hey, you two. Sorry I was so long. That was Phil on the phone. He's managed to get tonight off work, so we're going to a show." Jennifer sat in a chair opposite the couch and took a drink of water.

"We'll leave you to get ready," Alex said and stood.

"Thanks for the lesson, Jennifer. I'm thinking there may be something to this yoga stuff." Debby smiled and stood to collect the empty water bottles.

"I'm convinced yoga helps me deal with the stress of life. You can leave those bottles. I'll recycle them."

"Okay. Thanks again." She reached to shake hands, but Jen opened her arms wide for a hug.

"See you next week. Have a good time tonight." Alex hugged Jen before heading to the door.

She followed Alex out into the hallway, feeling hesitant. She couldn't remember the last time she'd told anyone about the day her six-year relationship ended. There'd been plenty of pain and anguish after, but it was that day it had truly ended. What was it about Alex that inspired so much trust?

"How about lunch at my place?" Alex asked. "Tuna fish sandwiches?"

Debby's uncertainty vanished under Alex's smile. "Sounds good. That yoga builds up an appetite, if nothing else."

They walked the short distance to Alex's apartment in comfortable silence.

Abby bounced into the air as they entered the room before grabbing one of Alex's shoes as she removed it. She raced around the couch and crouched into a play stance, waiting.

"Abby wants to play 'shoe.'" Alex pointed to the floor in front of Abby, and the dog immediately dropped the shoe and came to sit next to her. "Good girl. We'll play later."

Debby watched the interaction between Alex and her dog. Alex was gentle yet firm and obviously cared a great deal about Abby. She thought of her own connection to Shadow and to her now healthy stray cat who had wandered into her life skinny, matted, and full of fleas. For reasons she didn't want to consider, she checked off another item on her list. *Must love animals.*

❖

"Now that we have 'Miss Center of Attention' taken care of, does tuna fish on whole wheat sound okay?" Forbidden memories surfaced as she remembered her "go-to" meal for herself and Jen when they had been left to fend for themselves while her father was gone searching for her schizophrenic mother. Peanut butter was the backup if they were out of tuna, usually just eaten out of the jar with a couple of spoons. Those days were gone. She had a new life with a full pantry and a well-stocked refrigerator. She sighed and brought herself back to the present as Debby was speaking. "Sorry. I spaced there for a minute. You said tuna's okay?"

"Yeah. Tuna's great. I asked if I could help with anything."

"You could keep me company in the kitchen. Something to drink? I have bottled water, tea, coffee, and hot chocolate."

"A cup of decaffeinated green tea sounds good, if you have it." Debby followed her into the kitchen, and Alex slowed her pace, imagining she felt the heat of her body pressed against her back as she slipped her arms around her from behind. She shook her head to fend off the image and retrieved two mugs and a box of tea from an overhead cupboard.

"Nice table." Debby settled into one of the chairs at her small two-seater table.

"Thanks. I found it at the flea market, along with my couch." Abby had wandered into the kitchen with them, and Alex made her lie down on a cushioned matt in the corner while she rummaged in the cupboards.

"I love that flea market. Kristen and I used to go every week to look at all the stuff. I found a great pair of barely used boots there this spring." Debby picked up the cup of tea Alex had set on the table and took a sip. "Thanks."

Alex stopped herself from asking Debby to go to the flea market with her. Being with her was getting too comfortable, and she hadn't heard back from Joe yet about the Martinez family. She had no right to involve Debby in her complicated life any more than she already had.

Debby had trusted her with a personal story about her ex-lover. Should she reciprocate? And what sort of story should she make up? She decided to stay safe and practice small talk. "How long have you been drinking green tea?" Alex placed two small plates with tuna sandwiches on the table.

"I decided when I turned forty, I needed to start taking better care of myself. I was diagnosed with high cholesterol, so I began making better food choices. My research indicated that green tea was good for the immune system as well as helping lower cholesterol. I've grown to like it." Debby wrapped her hands around her cup and rested her arms on the table.

Alex cringed at the memory of her fortieth birthday spent in a safe house a thousand miles away from home. She forced the memory to the back of her mind and picked up her sandwich. *Focus on her. Questions about her, and her life.* She asked things about favorite colors and foods. Things she could answer in response without having to lie. It left out so, so much, but at least it was something. *Who knew so much of who we are is tied to who we've been?*

CHAPTER NINE

The lobby was filled to capacity when Alex arrived at work. The Michigan Pharmacist Association conference appeared to be in full swing at eight in the morning. She had been off the day before, so she had missed seeing Debby check in. The buffet breakfast was being served in one of the ballrooms off the main hall, so she grabbed her clipboard and used the excuse of checking on the meal preparation to go in search of her.

"Hey. I was hoping I'd see you this weekend. I asked about you at the desk last night when I arrived, but they said you had the day off," Debby said.

Debby's tender smile urged her to relax her guard. She had to be careful. "Yeah. I switch off some Fridays if we don't have a large group or event. Yours isn't one of the bigger conventions. Is everything going well so far?" Alex needed to focus on her job, instead of the beautiful woman in front of her. Debby looked hot in a beige linen jacket and matching trousers. She wore polished brown leather boots and a chocolate colored shirt that matched the dark of her eyes. Alex felt the fluttering in her belly that was becoming the usual effect of her smile. She took a step back.

"It's going great. Do you have time to join me for lunch later?" Debby leaned against the wall next to the buffet line looking relaxed.

"I'm scheduled to cover the lunch setup, so I'll find you. Enjoy your day." She shook off the spontaneous flare of desire and returned to the front desk to make her walk through the area to pick up any clutter in the room. She then restocked the forms located on the front desk area and wiped down the countertop. She spent the rest of the morning checking in guests and avoiding thoughts of Debby. She was about to let her boss know she was heading to the luncheon hall when the computer chimed an incoming email. She opened the email prepared for a guest check-in, but the name Miguel Martinez caught her attention, and she scrolled down to read the note.

I wanted to thank the staff of the Hyatt for the wonderful job they did hosting my nuptial celebration. My darling wife and I appreciate the beautiful floral arrangements and decorations you provided to make our special day forever memorable.

I especially want to express my gratitude to one of your outstanding desk clerks. I believe her name is Alex. Her exceptional attention to detail and friendly demeanor sets her apart from any I've ever encountered.

Sincerely,
Mr. and Mrs. Miguel Martinez

Alex forwarded the email to her boss, as dictated by company policy, and logged out of the computer. *Of course he'd know my name. I was here all day.* She was responsible for checking in many of the guests that day, but what she agonized about was why he had singled her out. Was she being paranoid, or did he recognize her somehow? They were probably only newlyweds expressing their appreciation. She needed to talk to Joe.

She hurried to her boss's office, avoiding the dining area. She kept her hands in her pockets to hide their trembling. She quickly explained she needed to leave early, and her sweet, kindly boss said it wasn't an issue.

"Thanks, Betty. I need to get home and check on Jennifer. She's incredibly sick with the flu." Alex felt bad lying to Betty, but it was the first excuse that came to her in her anxious state. She needed to talk to Joe. "And I was supposed to meet a friend here for lunch. She's one of the pharmacists with the MPA group. Her name's Debra Johnson. Would you please let her know I can't make it?"

Alex raced out of the building to her car before pulling out her phone to call Joe and tell him about the email.

"But he knows my name." Alex had moved her car to the back of the parking lot, close to the exit. She sat with the windows closed and the doors locked. She twisted in her seat and switched her phone to her other ear as she scanned the parking lot for anyone lurking.

"Just try to settle down. We have Miguel Martinez under surveillance, Alex. The FBI has someone undercover in the cartel, but we don't have any evidence that Miguel is a part of it. I promise I'll call you as soon as I know something, and remember, he only knows you as Alex. I don't think you have anything to worry about. There's no way he knows your real name."

"But what if he is a bad guy and somehow recognizes me? What if…" Alex realized her fear was probably unwarranted, and she had to trust Joe to keep them safe. She worried about Jennifer, who had finally achieved some peace. She sighed and leaned back against her headrest.

"It'll be all right. You're safe, Alex."

Joe's voice calmed her enough that she was able to relax. "Thanks, Joe. I'm okay now, but I don't guarantee I won't be calling you every day."

"That's fine, kiddo. Do what you have to. I'll be here."

Alex disconnected the call and took one more look around the parking area before changing her mind. *I'm tired of living in fear.* She was supposed to be living a new life, not hiding from her old one. Determined and fighting down the fear that never seemed to release her, she locked her car and headed inside to find Debby.

"Of course. I understand. Thank you for letting me know." Debby smiled at Betty despite her disappointment at the news. She sat across from the empty chair in the luncheon hall and wondered when she had allowed spending time with Alex to become so important to her. She stood to head to the buffet line when she saw Alex standing at the door and waved when she caught her eye.

"Hey. I just heard from your boss that you'd left early and wouldn't be here."

"Sorry. I decided I don't need to leave. Where're you sitting?"

"The table over by the back door. Shall we get our food now?" Debby indicated the direction of the table and reflexively rested her hand on Alex's lower back to lead her toward the food line. Her muscles felt tight under her fingertips, and Debby suppressed the urge to massage her shoulders. She moved her hands and concentrated on filling a plate with food.

"Are you enjoying the conference so far?" Alex surveyed the room as if searching for someone.

"Yeah. It's been great this year. I'm not sure if it's because of our new association president or what, but I'm enjoying the workshops. This afternoon we cover the paradoxical effects of anti-anxiety drugs."

"I'd say how fascinating it sounded if I knew what that was." Alex grinned and took a bite of her chicken salad.

"You probably don't want to hear about the labeling regulations for unit-of-use packaging, then." Debby chuckled and smiled over her fork full of salad.

"What I'd like to hear about is your friend's wedding. Is it dressy? I'm trying to decide what to wear."

Debby recalled the invitation she had received in the mail. There hadn't been any mention of a dress code. "I don't think so, but I'm not sure what one wears to a lesbian wedding. I'll ask Kristen at the race this weekend."

"Another barrel race?" Alex beamed and grasped her hand, taking her by surprise.

"Might be the last of the season. They're talking about having an event on Labor Day, but it would conflict with the state fair." She squeezed Alex's hand and released it to grasp her water bottle.

"I'll plan to come watch the race this weekend, then. I'm working on Labor Day, but I've got the whole weekend off." Alex hesitated before continuing. "Maybe we could spend some time at the fair on Sunday? It's expanded this year, and I want to see the new equestrian show rings." Alex bit her lip and looked down at the napkin she was playing with.

"That'd be great. I'd love to go to the state fair. I haven't been since they moved it to the Suburban Showcase. We'll plan on it."

Alex grinned and relief flooded her expression. She was beautiful.

"But right now I have to get to my next workshop. I'll be in the same area Saturday as last time."

Debby stood to leave, and Alex startled her when she stood and wrapped her in a hug. "Thank you for being my friend," Alex whispered, then released her and hurried from the room.

Debby plunked back into her chair, and heat rose throughout her body at the memory of Alex's breasts pressed against hers. She'd never reacted so intensely from an innocent hug before, and she was certain it *was* an innocent embrace. After all, they had agreed upon a safe, friendly affiliation without any emotional tethers. Fleeting thoughts of her list grounded her until she was able to turn her thoughts to compounded/alternative forms of drug compositions.

Alex went through the knocking routine twice before presuming Jennifer wasn't home. She left a message on her voice mail and went home. "Hey, Abby. How's my girl?" Abby sat facing Alex, cocking her head. "Let's go for a walk."

The park was nearly empty when Alex arrived with Abby. The warm August day had turned cloudy, and a light drizzle had begun before they had gotten halfway through their walk. Alex watched the shadows begin to form as they followed their favorite path. Each silhouette of a tree became a pursuer and each sound became their footfalls. She picked up their pace until they were nearly running by the time they reached her door. She pulled Abby into the living room and quickly locked the door. Her heart felt like it was going to beat out of her chest, and her pulse raced with fear. Cold sweat trickled down her back, and she blinked back tears of frustration. She checked that the windows were all locked and turned off all the lights. She sat on her couch, her knees pulled to her chest, contemplating calling Joe again. Just as she picked up her phone, it chimed a text.

It was good to see you at lunch today. I just wanted to let you know that I talked to Kristen about the wedding. A nice pair of slacks and shirt is what she suggested. I'll probably wear what I had on today for the conference. We can talk more on Saturday. D

Alex turned to recline and put her feet up on the couch before replying. Suddenly, with this small connection to the world outside her door, she could breathe again.

It was good seeing you, too. Thanks for the info about the wedding. You looked very nice today, so I'll work on finding something appropriate. See you Saturday. A

Alex set her phone down, feeling more settled than she had all day. She put her yoga nidra DVD in her DVD player, slid down on the couch to rest her head on the armrest, and lost herself in meditation. Her past haunted her, but maybe, just maybe, there was a way to have some kind of future.

CHAPTER TEN

The stands were nearly full by the time Alex arrived at the fairgrounds. She squeezed into an empty seat next to a young blonde with a bag dog carrier hanging from her neck. A tiny, hairy white head stuck out of the opening and two big dark eyes regarded her warily. She smiled and whispered hello, eliciting a whimper and a curled tongue reaching for her. The girl shifted the bag when the little dog began wiggling and turned to face her.

"Sorry. I didn't mean to disturb you. Your small dog is a cutie." Alex resisted reaching to pet the pintsized canine.

"Thanks. His name's MacIntosh, and he loves watching the barrel racers." The girl scratched the dog's head, and he reached for her hand with his tongue.

Alex bent to eye level with MacIntosh. "Hello there, you. Do you like those big animals?"

"Oh, he loves horses, especially my sister's pinto. She's riding third today." The girl pointed toward the ring where the contestants were readying to ride.

Alex scrambled to remember the riders' names. "Kelly?"

"Yeah! Do you know her?"

"I saw her ride a couple of weeks ago. I'm here with my friend Debra Johnson."

"I know Debby. She and Kelly have been friends for years. My name's Tory." Tory shifted the dog pack and offered her hand in greeting.

"Nice to meet you, Tory. I'm Alex Reed." Tory didn't look older than fourteen, and Alex was thrown back to a time she'd taken Jennifer to the rodeo for her fourteenth birthday. Another memory she couldn't talk about. She smiled and gently squeezed Tory's hand.

They watched the competition with Alex shouting for Debby and Tory for Kelly until they both laughed and clapped for the winners, Kristen and Zigzag.

"That was fun. I hope I see you again." Tory's blue eyes twinkled in the afternoon sun.

"Me, too. I'm going to meet Debby for lemonade. See you, MacIntosh." Alex scratched under his chin and watched his eyes close in contentment.

Alex made her way down to the stand where she'd met Debby the first time and, as always, was struck by how beautiful she was. They ordered their drinks and sat down. "I met Kelly's sister in the stands today. She seems like a nice kid. What is she, fourteen?"

"Actually, she'll be sixteen this month. She's almost got her driver's license. I haven't seen Tory in months. I'm glad she was here today." Debby sat straight in the white plastic chair and bent forward to touch her toes.

"Back bothering you?" Alex laid her hands flat on the table to keep from offering to rub Debby's back.

"It's not too bad, but maybe I need some more yoga at Jennifer's." Debby grinned, and Alex squirmed in her seat at the fluttering Debby's smile always caused in her stomach.

Debby's mention of Jennifer reminded her that she still hadn't seen her since her dinner party, and Joe hadn't gotten back to her yet about the Martinez family. She stood, awash with anxiety. "I've got to go. Let me know what time you'll pick me up for the wedding." She hurried to her car without looking back. *Please be okay. Please be okay.*

Debby watched Alex's hasty departure with astonishment. *What did I say?*

"Hi, Deb. Was that Alex?" Kristen sat across from her with a cup of iced tea.

"Yeah. She had something to do today and had to leave." Debby struggled to figure out what had caused Alex to rush off, and her gut twisted at her lie to Kristen. She hated lying, nearly as much as she hated liars. But she didn't want to make Alex look bad, either.

"Ah. Good riding today. You and Shadow seem to have settled in. You looked great out there."

"Good job, yourself. I think Zigzag gets faster every week." Debby looked toward the parking lot, wondering if Alex would return. And why it bothered her so much that she had left.

"You okay? You seem distracted."

Debby blew out a breath and leaned on the table with her chin on her palm. "I don't know. Alex and I were supposed to talk about the wedding today, but she left in such a hurry that we barely spoke at all."

"Huh. But you said she had something to do. Maybe it was important, and she forgot about it?"

Kristen was a good friend, and she trusted her. She'd never had to resort to her list with her, and she questioned what was different about Alex. Why couldn't she relax and let Alex be who she was, without turning to her list for protection? What was she trying to protect herself against? "I can't figure her out sometimes. We get along great, and for the most part, I'm comfortable with her. There's just something that bothers me, and I can't put my finger on it." She leaned back in her chair and shook her head, trying to figure out an answer to her dilemma.

"You like her, don't you?"

"Yes. I like her, but I've known her since July, and I know virtually nothing about her. She avoids questions and offers little personal information."

"Maybe she's a private person. A month and a half isn't a long time to know someone, my friend."

"I told her about Evelyn. I would have thought she'd reciprocate." Debby took a drink of her lemonade to try to wash away the taste of disappointment.

"So that's what this is about. Just because you disclosed the painful end to your relationship you think she should, too? Maybe she has nothing to tell."

"Yeah. Maybe I'm expecting too much. I'll wait till the wedding and see if I get any more information out of her."

"That sounds like a good plan. The wedding's going to be fun, and you don't need to know all her deep, dark secrets just to have a good time with her. Let me know if you want to ride with me and Jaylin. We're going to leave about three thirty." Kristen finished her iced tea and stood.

"I will." Debby walked back to her car with Kristen and began planning her questions for Alex. She didn't know why it mattered so much, but something about Alex captivated her and awoke long-suppressed emotions. Emotions that scared her to death.

Alex tried Jennifer's door before leaving another voice mail message. If she didn't hear back from her later, she'd contact Joe to see if he knew where she was. She didn't believe they were in immediate danger, but she'd feel better if she could locate Jen. It could be this was her Saturday to work. She tried her work number but got the office voice mail. She tossed her phone on her nightstand, fed Abby, and plopped on the couch to watch TV.

She flipped through several of the hundreds of cable channels before turning it off. She ought to call Debby and apologize, but she had to figure out an excuse for her rudeness first. They were supposed to talk about the wedding, and she hadn't given her a chance to say anything. *Reason enough.*

Her phone was flashing a missed call so she flopped on her bed and checked the readout. She listened to Jennifer's voice mail message and sighed in relief. She was out with Phil and wouldn't be home until late. She called up Debby's number and got her voice mail.

"Hi, Debby. It's Alex. I just wanted to apologize for leaving so abruptly today. I had some personal issues to resolve. I'm looking forward to the wedding next weekend. I'll talk to you one day this week to plan, okay?"

She knew her excuse sounded lame, but she couldn't tell Debby the truth. *About anything, apparently.* She paced the room, riffling through her memory for a clue as to how to explain her behavior. She understood the deputy marshals did their best to prepare them for the transition, but they didn't have to live through it. They were living the lives they chose, while she felt like a social recluse. How could she make and keep friends when she had to worry about everything she disclosed? How could she build trust with someone when she had to hide the truth of her identity? She slumped back on her bed and covered her eyes with her arm. *People do this. Other people manage to live this way. I just have to be comfortable with lying about who I've been and trade in the truth for who I am now. Easy.*

Alex blinked the sleep from her eyes and shook off the disorientation. She glanced at her clock radio, surprised that she'd been asleep for an hour. No answers to her dilemma had appeared in her dreams, so she rolled over and grabbed her phone.

"Hey, Dad. How're you doing?"

"I'm fine. Going to meetings and…well…you know. It's good to hear your voice, honey."

"It's good to hear yours, too. Jennifer's dinner party went well, but we missed you. Do you think maybe you'd like to come to my place one day for a quiet dinner?"

"I'd like that. I'm working nights now, so you plan a day and time and let me know."

"Sounds good. I wanted to ask you something."

"Go ahead. You know you can ask me anything."

"Has it gotten easier? I mean…more comfortable, maybe?"

"Oh, honey. I'm so sorry. If I'd have known how this would've turned out, I never would have agreed to testify. I never intended to ruin your lives."

Her gut clenched at the sound of her father's sobs.

That answers that. "Dad. It's all right. You did the right thing by turning in those drug dealers. You probably saved many young lives from being destroyed. Neither Jennifer nor I blame you for anything." Her tension eased when she heard him sigh. She saw no reason to express her anger and resentment. His remorse was genuine.

"Thank you, dear. You two take care of each other. And make sure you stay in touch with Joe."

Alex heaved a sigh when her father disconnected the call. She believed he had done the right thing by testifying, and although she worried about his potential return to drug use, she had to trust he was going to NA meetings and taking care of himself. She needed to figure out what she was going to do about Debby and how to maintain a friendship based on untruths. As long as she stayed with uncomplicated details like favorite foods and opinions on current events, she should be okay. Friends shared those things without getting into details about their past all the time. She lay down on the couch and closed her eyes, hoping to dream of dancing with Debby.

CHAPTER ELEVEN

K risten and Jaylin offered to drive. Would that be okay with you?" Debby shifted her phone to her other ear as she pulled on her slacks. She'd ended up having to go in to work for the morning to oversee the distribution of IV antibiotics for a new resident. She had gotten home just in time to feed Buddy and Shadow and get ready for the wedding.

"Absolutely. It'll be nice to get to know them better."

"I'll pick you up at three o'clock, then, and we'll head over to their place."

"Sounds good. I'll see you later."

Debby disconnected the call and pulled out her ironing board. She and Alex had texted several times throughout the week, and Alex had apologized profusely for her abrupt retreat from the fairgrounds. She had said something vague about her father being in town and that she had forgotten her promise to take him to Jennifer's. How could she forget about her dad? And where did her father live? She had more questions than answers about Alex, but she planned to amend that soon. She finished dressing, ignoring her growing excitement at seeing Alex.

"Hi, Debby. I'm almost ready to go. I just needed to take Abby out one more time before we left. Come on in."

Debby pushed aside her irritation at the delay. She'd arrived early enough so they wouldn't be rushed, but punctuality was near the top of her list. She wondered why the lines between friendship and *more* were so blurred with Alex that she felt the need to relate to her list.

She followed Alex and Abby into her apartment, indulging herself in the view of her ass in jeans as she moved. Alex was a sexy woman, and she saw no sense ignoring it. She hadn't paid much attention when she had been there before, but now the sparseness of the apartment stood out. She scanned the living room, noticing few pictures and none that looked like family photos. She sat on the couch to wait for Alex, who had hurried to her bedroom to change clothes. Other than a stack of yoga magazines on the coffee table, she saw no indication of who Alex was. Her musings were interrupted by Alex returning. She glanced at her watch. Three o'clock exactly.

"Sorry. I couldn't decide between black or gray slacks. I'm ready now."

Debby's breath caught when she looked up at Alex, and she swallowed to make sure she wasn't drooling. She had chosen gray slacks with a soft looking, long sleeve, cream colored silk blouse. A thin gold chain suspended from her neck and rested on a spot Debby would have loved to run her tongue over. She tossed on a light gray, tailored blazer a shade lighter than her eyes, and Debby stood to distract herself. "You look great. Let's go to a wedding."

The ride to Kristen's took less than twenty minutes, and Debby was aware of Alex sitting next to her, watching the road as if memorizing the route.

"You don't have to concentrate so hard, you know. I'm not going to test you on it to get you home," she teased her, hoping to lighten the intensity of Alex's mood.

"I've never been to this side of Novi," Alex said.

"She lives on the outskirts. Her parents built the house when Kristen was a kid. It's pretty nice."

"Whoa. Nice doesn't do it justice." Alex looked enthralled as Debby pulled up next to the house. "She must keep her horse here." Alex pointed to the barn across the yard from the house.

"Yep, and she has a pony that keeps Zigzag company." Debby smiled as Alex stepped out of the car and turned in a circle, taking in the property. They reached the porch just as the door opened and a fluffy dog bounded out and sat quivering in excitement. "And this is Jaylin's dog, Railroad."

Alex laughed as Railroad wiggled into her arms.

"Sorry, you'll be full of hair in two minutes." Jaylin called Railroad back inside the house and held open the door. "Come on in."

"I've got a Lab mix, so I'm not afraid of a little dog hair."

Debby waved Alex in ahead of her.

"Can I offer you anything to drink? Kristen will be out in a minute." Jaylin pulled a bottle of water out of the refrigerator and handed it to Debby.

"I'll take one of those, too," Alex said. "This is a great house." She walked to the door wall and gasped at the view.

"Lovely, isn't it?" Debby stood next to her and rested her hand on the small of her back, though for the life of her she wouldn't have been able to say why. Alex didn't move away. "Want to check out the barn before we leave?"

"I would, but maybe we could do it on a day we're not all dressed up for a wedding."

"Good point." Debby moved her hand and turned to Jaylin. "Thanks for offering to drive today."

"No problem. It'll be nice to have company on the ride." Jaylin shot her a quizzical, amused glance and tilted her head slightly toward Alex.

Debby shook her head and put some distance between them.

"Okay. Let's get out of here." Kristen appeared, dangling her car keys in front of her.

Debby slid into the backseat next to Alex, surprised by the desire to put her arm around her. She remained silent for the trip, despite the many questions hanging between them, and let Kristen and Jaylin carry the conversation.

❖

They pulled into the church parking lot twenty minutes early. The trip had been uneventful, and Alex had felt comfortable with the light conversation with Jaylin. She had often turned to address

Alex in the backseat and pointed out interesting facts about areas as they passed them. She worried about what Debby's silence meant. They had texted throughout the week, and she seemed to accept her explanation about leaving the fairgrounds in such a hurry, but something still felt off.

"This is a nice little church," Kristen said. She and Jaylin walked hand-in-hand ahead of them.

"It is. I've only been here once with Maria, for a choir event. She has a beautiful singing voice." Jaylin stopped and pointed to the other side of the parking lot. "And the view of the river is great. It's peaceful here."

Alex followed Kristen and Jaylin into the small entryway, aware of Debby close behind her. Her back still held the feel of her warm hand when they were at Kristen's, and she fought the urge to stop so she would press up against her.

"Welcome. I'm Girard Wright, pastor of this lovely little church." Pastor Wright stood at the entryway to the sanctuary where people were filling the pews. He introduced himself and shook everyone's hand as they entered. "I'm thrilled to see such a wonderful turnout for our dear Maria's wedding."

Alex sat next to Debby on the end of a row toward the back of the room.

"Have you ever been to this side of the state, Alex?" Jaylin had to lean across Kristen and Debby to see her.

"No, I haven't, but I like it so far. I love being by the water." *It isn't the Gulf of Mexico, but it's water.*

The organist began playing softly, and Alex relaxed back into her seat. She recognized the hymn from the Sundays spent sitting in church with her mother. She and Jennifer would take their mother as often as they could, until she became too difficult to handle, and her father had to join them. Those were some of the best memories she was supposed to forget. The four of them together, acting like a normal family at worship. She sighed and concentrated on the people streaming into the room.

A tall, elegant woman with an engaging smile and deep auburn hair with gray highlights caught her eye and nodded before moving to the pastor's side and pecking a kiss on his cheek. She stepped away and sat down in the front pew.

A stately couple made their way to the front arm in arm. It looked as if the man leaned slightly on the woman despite the cane in his left hand. They slid onto the pew across the aisle from the auburn-haired woman, after exchanging smiles and a few words.

Alex presumed these were the parents of the brides. She shifted on the hard wooden seat, enjoying the music and the feel of Debby sitting next to her.

The room hushed as Pastor Wright proceeded to the podium. He stood quietly with bowed head for a moment before looking up to speak. "Before we begin the ceremony this afternoon, I'd like to thank all of you for being here today. Maria came to me over a year ago, searching." He paused and looked over the crowd. "She wasn't searching for faith; she brought that with her. She was searching for a church that understood that love was love. That God's love is inclusive, not exclusive, and not judgmental. She was looking for a church home for her music ministry, and I feel blessed that she chose our little house of worship. It's my privilege to now introduce to you our soon-to-be-wed couple, Maria Spencer and Dana Langdon."

The couple walked toward the altar hand in hand, beaming. The older couple stood and the elderly man shuffled to stand beside Maria, the older woman moved to her other side. Maria's parents, Alex assumed.

Pastor Wright began the ceremony.

"Maria Spencer, do you take Dana Langdon to be your lawfully wedded spouse forever?"

"I do." Maria glowed in her cream colored satin gown. Her dark hair was pinned away from her face, and she wore a string of pearls around her neck, with matching earrings. Her smile lit up the room as she placed a gold band on Dana's left ring finger.

"And do you, Dana Langdon, take Maria Spencer to be your lawfully wedded spouse forever?"

"I do." Dana looked relaxed in her custom tailored black tuxedo, silver earrings, and a huge grin as she placed a matching band on Maria's left ring finger.

"I now pronounce you legally married. May God's love live forever in your hearts and reflect your love for each other."

Dana and Maria kissed and whispered something to each other before turning to the crowd, smiling and holding hands as they walked to the back of the church to the enormous applause and cheers of their friends and family. As they'd wished, it was standing room only.

Alex followed Debby out of the building to where Dana and Maria stood with their parents, greeting people as they passed. She'd thought Kristen and Jaylin made a striking couple, but Maria's dark eyes and hair were in direct contrast to Dana's strawberry blond hair and blue eyes. They complemented each other beautifully, and Alex pushed aside her twinge of envy.

She felt the warmth of Debby's hand throughout her body when she rested it on the small of her back as they followed the line of well-wishers toward the newlyweds.

"Congratulations, you two. Dana, I think you've already met my friend Debby, and this is her friend Alex." Debby moved a step away as Kristen spoke, and a chill settled where her hand had been.

"We're so glad you could be here to share our day." Dana smiled and pulled Maria close to her side.

"It's great to meet you both. Congratulations," Alex said.

"We look forward to talking to you later at the reception." Maria kissed Debby's cheek, then Alex's.

"We'll see you there." Debby took her hand, and they followed Kristen and Jaylin to the car.

Alex lost herself for a moment in the natural feel of their fingers intertwined. *Friends can hold hands.*

Chapter Twelve

"Wow. This is nice." Debby took in the gigantic swan ice sculpture set on a round table in the middle of the room. Huge shrimp, cocktail sauce, various cheeses, crackers, and bowls of nuts nestled in beds of lettuce and kale around the ice carving. A few early arrivals stood talking and sampling the appetizers.

"It sure is. Let's grab a seat and check it all out." Kristen tugged on Jaylin's hand and led her to one of the round tables, where they set down their coats and bags.

Debby pulled out a chair for Alex and settled into the one next to her. "Can I get you a plate of hors d'oeuvres?"

"I'd like to go see what's there myself." Alex stood and reached for her hand.

Debby hesitated before taking it and strolling to the giant ice swan. She couldn't deny it felt right holding Alex's hand, but she would need to make sure their boundaries were clear. They were there to keep each other company. Nothing more. *But friends hold hands sometimes, right?* She couldn't remember ever doing so with Kristen or Kelly, but maybe different friendships meant doing different things. She tried to concentrate.

The tables in the dining area of the hall were covered with white tablecloths and pale blue cloth napkins, a fresh flower centerpiece, and two bottles of sparkling grape juice. The chairs had white cloth coverings over the backs, embroidered with matching intertwined wedding bands in the same blue as the napkins. There was an uncarpeted space Debby figured was large enough for a band and dance floor taking up half of the room. She hoped that whatever music they'd chosen would be good. She looked forward to moving across the dance floor with Alex. They returned to the table to wait for Kristen and Jaylin.

"This is great. Thanks for inviting me." Alex popped a piece of cheese into her mouth.

"I'm glad you could join me. I'd have felt awkward being here alone. I don't know anyone but you, Kristen, and Jaylin. I met Dana in July, so I don't really know her." Debby filled two glasses with grape juice and set one in front of Alex.

"Thanks. Where'd Kristen and Jaylin go?" Alex tasted her juice and looked past her, across the room. "Oh, here they come."

Debby wondered if Alex was uncomfortable being alone with her, and felt the faintest hint of disappointment. *Friend. Meeting other friends. Get over yourself.*

Kristen plunked into her chair and set a plate heaped with shrimp and cheese in front of her.

"You know there'll probably be a dinner, don't you?" Debby grinned as Kristen ignored her and picked up a shrimp.

Debby turned to Alex, determined to learn more about her. "Do you like to dance?" she asked.

"I love to dance. I hope we get to later."

"Good. Me, too." *She likes to dance. Number four on my list.*

Debby's interrogation was interrupted by the entrance of the wedding party. Dana and Maria made their way through the room, stopping to greet each table and introduce their parents.

"We're glad you and Alex could make it to our celebration, Debby." Dana glowed as she embraced her new spouse.

"Congratulations again, both of you," Alex said.

"Thank you. You two have a good time. We've got a great DJ for tonight." Maria chuckled as Dana pulled her away toward the next table to continue their greeting chain.

"Would you pass the water pitcher, please?" Alex asked.

Debby began filling her glass until Alex rested her hand gently on her arm. "No ice."

"Yeah. Me, too." *We both like water with no ice.*

"So, Kelly wasn't invited, huh?" Alex swallowed a drink of water.

"No. Kelly's a long-time friend of Kristen's, but I don't think Dana and Maria have ever met her."

"But she's your friend, too, right?" Alex furrowed her brow when she asked.

"Right." Debby wondered if Alex thought there was more to their relationship than friendship, and why it bothered her if she did.

They finished their meal and waited for the DJ.

"Whew. Is it warm in here, or is it the dancing?" Alex removed her blazer and hung it over the back of her chair. She watched Debby do the same, stirred again by the sparkle in her eyes as she turned toward her.

"I think it's the dancing, but it's pretty warm for September. Let's sit for a while," Debby said.

They both took a long drink of water, and she watched Debby's tongue catch a drop off her lip. She lost herself for a moment in the fantasy of kissing her and feeling the caress of that tongue. "I'm glad the summer's sticking around this year. I don't look forward to the snow coming." She fought to concentrate on their conversation.

"Well, I'm glad it hasn't been too hot this summer. You like hot weather, don't you?" Debby turned in her chair and rested her arm on the back while holding her glass on the table. She looked laid-back and sexy.

"I do." Alex rested her elbow on the table and her chin on her hand as she watched Dana and Jaylin dance. She was enjoying herself more than she had since she had been relocated, and she liked it. She savored her contentment at being out with friends and being the focus of Debby's attention. She shoved away fears of Martinez and drug lords and concentrated on Debby. As long as Debby stopped asking questions, she could stay relaxed. "The only way I'd ever enjoy a ski trip would be if I could stay inside by the fireplace with a book."

Debby laughed. "I agree with you. I'm not a skier, but I love a good book and a fireplace." She turned in her chair and arched her back.

"Shall we walk around a little? Will that help your back?" Just as Alex asked, the DJ started a slow song.

"I have a better idea. Let's dance." Debby stood and held out her hand.

Alex smiled up at her. "I like that idea."

When Alex stepped into Debby's arms, her uncertainties fled, but her heart beat like a frightened bird. How could something dangerous feel so safe? Her head knew that it wasn't fair to either of them to let their relationship evolve into anything besides friendship, even if her heart resisted it.

Debby must have felt her hesitancy because she pushed away, holding her at arm's length. "You okay? We can sit out the slow songs if you're more comfortable."

"No." *I can do this.* "Let's dance."

Alex eased into Debby's embrace and concentrated on the dance steps to distract herself from the feel of her warm hand on the small of her back. She eased closer as they moved in perfect time to the music, smoothly rotating around the dance floor between the other couples. She barely noticed when the melody changed and Debby drew her tightly to her body. She floated in pleasure at the feel of her breasts pressed against Debby's. The music ended, and Alex wrenched herself back to reality.

"Thank you," she whispered. She knew it meant more than Debby could possibly understand. Her uncertainties and reservations had fled while she was wrapped in the security of Debby's arms, and for a moment, she had felt free.

Debby shivered as a chill settled where Alex's body had been nestled against hers. She followed her back to their table where Kristen sat with her arm around Jaylin. Happiness for her friend warred with frustration. Why, so many years ago, had she chosen a woman who couldn't be honest with her? She could have been sitting with a lover's arm around her, enjoying that connection, instead of demanding that anyone she got close to satisfy conditions of a list she'd written to determine whether or not someone was worthy of being in her life.

And how was it that Alex had met so many requirements on her list, but she knew so little about who she was or where she came from? That had to change. "Anyone want anything from the bar?" she asked.

"I'll take a club soda with lime," Kristen said.

"That sounds good," Jaylin and Alex said at the same time.

"Okay. Four club sodas for the heavy drinking table."

Debby returned with the drinks and settled next to Alex. "Are you having a good time?"

"I am. Thanks for inviting me."

"I'm glad you could make it." Debby poked her lime wedge with her straw, pushing it to the bottom of her glass.

She likes to read and isn't a heavy drinker. Numbers nine and ten. What else can I find out? "Have you been to many lesbian events?"

"Not too many." Alex took her lime wedge out and squeezed it into her glass.

The DJ played a popular song and Kristen and Jaylin got up to dance.

"How's your dad doing?" Debby hoped Alex would explain further about her father and family situation.

"He's good. I'm hoping he'll come over for dinner one night this week. I'd love for you to meet him, if you're available."

Maybe I'm getting somewhere. "I'd like that. Let me know when. Does he live close by?"

"Not far. He's in Plymouth."

"I like Plymouth. They have a great ice sculpture festival every year. Is that where you grew up?"

"No. I didn't live there long, but he likes it. How about more dancing?" Alex stood and held out her hand.

Debby took it and put the rest of her questions on hold, wondering if that was Alex's intention. Another two songs, and they went back to their table, breathing heavily and laughing.

"I don't know about you guys, but I'm pooped. I haven't danced that much in years." Jaylin pushed her chair next to Kristen's to lean on her.

"I'm with you, Jaylin. My daily walks with my dog aren't quite enough to condition me for a night of dancing." Alex took a swallow of water and leaned her elbows on the table.

"Everybody ready to leave then?" Kristen asked. She rubbed Jaylin's back with one hand as she spoke.

Debby stood abruptly. She'd had enough of this lovey-dovey stuff, and she needed to put a stop to the desire to pull Alex to her, run her hands over her body, and see just how soft her lips were. "Yeah. Let's get out of here."

❖

"Thanks for a wonderful day." Alex took Debby's hand and squeezed it as they walked to her door.

"I enjoyed it, too. I was a little worried that I was crashing their wedding, but everyone was great. I doubt they even noticed, with the amount of people there. Are we still on for the state fair tomorrow?" Debby turned to face her but didn't release her hand.

"Sure. Shall I meet you there?"

"Unless you'd like to stop by my place first. I believe I owe you a meal. I make a pretty good omelet."

Alex considered the wisdom of spending more private time with Debby. They got along great, and she liked her. A little too much, she feared. She let go of her hand and unlocked her door. "I think I'll pass on the omelet. How 'bout if I meet you there at eleven?" She winced at the fleeting look of disappointment on Debby's face.

"Sure. Eleven it is. Good night, Alex." Debby turned and left without another word.

Abby's usual exuberant greeting did little to lift her threatening pall. She walked her before returning to her apartment and dropping onto her bed. Abby jumped to lie next to her so she rested her hand on her back, taking comfort in the warmth. Debby had asked questions she couldn't answer truthfully, and she was tired of avoiding questions. She was tired of feeling like an imposter, but no solution materialized in her whirling thoughts. The one thing she knew for sure was that she was going to have to keep her attraction and growing feelings for Debby to herself. *Yet another pretense.*

She'd met several potential new friends to whom she'd never be able to be close. How long could friendships survive based on superficiality? And a lover would certainly need to know more about her than her favorite foods or that she liked to dance. She flopped to her side in frustration and let the tears fall.

CHAPTER THIRTEEN

I'm sorry about this, Alex, but I have to go in to work this morning. How 'bout if I call you later? Maybe we can still make it to the fair this afternoon." Debby held her phone tight against her ear and ran her free hand through her hair. She hated last-minute cancelations, especially if she had to make them.

"It's okay. I understand. A resident with seizures sounds serious."

"Yeah, and the wife of the Sunday pharmacist went into labor last night, so he's at the hospital with her. Thanks for understanding. I'll call you later."

"Sure, whenever. No biggie. Bye."

Debby disconnected the call and hurried to get showered and dressed, trying not to let Alex's blasé response bother her. It was the response of a friend, and that's how she needed to look at it. And Alex was right. Seizures were serious, especially in an eighty-nine-year-old.

Seizures in the elderly weren't uncommon, but certainly weren't normal either, and there were many drugs or conditions that could cause them. Mrs. Martinez was one of the newer residents, and she didn't know much about her. The nursing facility certainly would have called her doctor and the consultant pharmacist already. She mentally reviewed the prescribed drugs she'd delivered over the past few days. She couldn't remember the name Martinez being on her list, but there were forty residents in the home, and she had been the only pharmacist working all week. She hurried into the building, sliding into her lab coat as she walked.

"Morning, Deb. Sorry we had to call you in." Kelly stepped out from behind the nurses' station, holding a chart as Debby passed by.

"Hey, Kelly. What's up? Janis called me early this morning."

"Yeah. Fernanda Martinez starting seizing about four o'clock this morning. Her doctor's with her now, and she's resting comfortably. I'm sure Jan will fill you in, but I think she just wants to go over all her prescribed medicine with you."

Debby rushed to the pharmacy where she found Janis waiting for her.

"Thanks for coming in today, Debby. Mrs. Martinez is one of our new patients. Her grandson moved her in a month ago, and she hasn't had any problems until this morning. I have her chart here, and I'd like to review her pharmacy records."

Debby and Janis spent the next hour reviewing computer files and notes for Fernanda Martinez.

"I don't see anything here that seems off." Debby spoke as she continued her analysis. "She was treated for a urinary tract infection two weeks ago, but that's about all I see as a potential possibility."

Jan wrote the dose prescribed and closed her notebook. "I'll go talk to her doctor about it. Thank you again for coming in today. I don't think it's necessary for you to stay if you're willing to be on call."

"I'm here now. I'll go check on Mrs. Martinez and leave after lunch."

Debby stopped at the nurses' desk to find out which unit Mrs. Martinez occupied and followed one of the nurse assistants to her room.

A stocky man with shiny black hair stood speaking softly next to the elderly woman's bed. He turned and she knew what the term "hard eyes" meant as his, black as coal, narrowed slightly, assessed, and then dismissed her.

"I'm Debra Johnson, one of the pharmacists at this facility." She offered her hand, which he stared at for a moment before speaking.

"Good." He nodded and turned back to Mrs. Martinez.

"That's her grandson, Miguel," the nurse assistant whispered.

"Ah. Well. Call me if you need anything. I'll be in the pharmacy." Debby spoke into the room for anyone who was listening. It was rare she had to deal with rude people anymore, and she found she had zero patience for it now. If they didn't want her input, that was fine with her.

She rushed to the pharmacy to give Alex a call and wait for any new developments.

❖

"It's good to hear from you. How're things going?" Alex sat on her couch and propped her feet up on the coffee table.

"It's going. I'm still not sure what the issue was, but the resident seems okay now. Her grandson is here watching everyone like a hawk."

"Do you think you'll make it home this afternoon?"

"I'm planning to leave at noon, as long as everything stays quiet. I'll have to be on call in case they need me, though. What're you doing?"

"Right now, I'm sitting on my couch with my feet up, and quite honestly, I wouldn't mind staying this way for the rest of the day. I have a new book from the library I'd like to read." Alex shifted so Abby could fit on the sofa snuggled against her.

"We don't have to go to the fair today if you don't want to. Relaxing with a good book sounds like a wonderful idea to me."

"Do you like pizza?"

"I love pizza. Why?"

"I'm going to order whatever kind you'd like, if you come over and sit and read with me." Alex swung her feet to the floor and held her breath.

"I'll have to stop home first, feed Shadow and Buddy, and get my book and change. How does three o'clock sound?"

Alex exhaled. "Perfect. I'll see you then." *It's just pizza. And reading. That's not exactly romance on fire.*

She disconnected and phoned Jennifer.

"Hey, Alex. How're you doing?"

"I'm good. I stopped by your place a couple of times this week, but you weren't home."

"I worked every day this week, and Phil and I went to the show a couple of times. Something up?"

Alex shifted the phone to her other ear. She had deliberated telling Jen about Martinez, but she was an adult as vulnerable as Alex was and deserved to be aware of any threatening issues.

"Well, I'm not sure it's anything to worry about, but I worked a wedding a couple of weeks ago for a couple named Martinez."

"Oh, crap. Like the drug cartel, Martinez?"

"I'm not sure, Jen. You know how common the name is, but there was a hell of a lot of money being thrown around, and it did feel…off, I guess. I'm still waiting for confirmation from Joe, but the last time I talked to him, he assured me that the marshals were on top of it. They have someone undercover gathering intelligence, and he told me not to worry."

"Huh. Easy for him to say. I suppose we need to trust him, though."

Alex understood the frustration in Jen's voice. Their peace of mind was at the mercy of the U.S. Marshal Service. She considered calling Joe after hanging up with Jennifer, but decided to wait until her weekly check-in, the following day. Joe had kept them safe so far, so she had to trust he was still there for them.

She sat back and allowed herself to feel the anticipation of Debby's visit while questioning the wisdom of letting herself get too close. The ease of being with her was both comforting and scary. It was natural for new friends to talk and get to know each other, but she feared how long she could avoid so many of her questions. She rested her feet on the table, picked up her book with one hand, and placed her other on Abby's warm belly. She'd take it a day at a time.

Startled awake by Abby's bark, Alex sprang from the couch and pulled a baseball bat from beneath it. The knocking at the door slowly crept into her consciousness, and she realized Debby must have arrived. Abby stood between her and the door growling. "It's okay, Abby. Good girl." She stuffed the bat back under the couch, recognizing how unnerved she was about Martinez. She hadn't been this jumpy since she had first moved in. She took a settling breath and opened the door. *Normal life. A friend to read with. Normal.*

❖

The first thing Debby noticed when Alex opened the door was her slightly disheveled look and wide eyes. Like she'd just woken up, but something wary lingered in her gaze, and gentle Abby stood as if on guard until her tail began to wave in recognition. "Everything okay?" She waited for Alex to answer before entering the room.

"Of course. Come on in. I fell asleep reading, so I'm a little groggy. Sorry."

"No problem. I brought tea and a couple of light beers." She held up the plastic grocery bag as she pushed past Abby.

"Cool. Have a seat and I'll order the pizzas. Olives and extra cheese okay?"

"Sounds good." She picked up the book lying on the floor next to the couch and recognized her favorite author. *She reads romance. Number eleven.*

She looked up when Alex came back into the room and was glad to see she looked considerably more relaxed.

"The pizzas will be here in twenty minutes. I think I'll have one of those beers you brought. Can I get you one?"

"Sure. Thanks."

Debby sat on the end of the couch with Abby curled next to her when Alex returned with the beers.

"I see you've made a friend."

"It seems so." She scratched Abby's belly as she rolled to her back. "Kelly's sister has a Maltese that she brings to the nursing home every week. He makes the rounds of the place visiting the residents. Do you think Abby would like to do that occasionally? It seems to be good for morale."

"Is that Tory? I met her and MacIntosh at the last riding event." Alex sat on the opposite end of the couch and took a drink of her beer.

"Yes. Tory's her sister."

"I think Abby would love to go visiting. Let me know when."

"I'll talk to Janis Tuesday and let you know."

"What book did you bring?"

"It's my favorite author's latest. I see you like her, too." Debby held up her book for Alex.

"Oh yeah. I haven't gotten that one yet." Alex grabbed it out of her hand.

"You can read it when I'm done, if you'd like."

"Cool. Maybe we can get together for another reading event." Alex handed the book back to her and smiled.

"Sounds like a plan."

They discussed a few of the other authors they liked and found they had a number of them in common. *It just keeps getting better.* Debby shook off the thought.

Their conversation was interrupted by the arrival of the pizzas, and Debby and Alex settled at the kitchen table to eat. "So, was something up just before I got here today?" Debby asked.

"No. Why do you ask?" Alex took a bite of pizza and didn't meet her eyes.

"I don't know. You seemed…scared, maybe. And Abby definitely looked like she was shielding you."

Alex shifted in her seat and finally looked directly at her. "There are things in my life that I can't talk about. It's not that I don't want to. I just can't."

"You can't? Meaning you don't trust me?" Debby hoped she was getting close to the reason Alex seemed so reluctant to open up to her.

"It's not a matter of trust, Debby. Honestly. I'm just not at liberty to talk about some stuff. Please don't pry."

Debby stopped her questions, moved by Alex's imploring stare. She stood and stretched before taking her plate to the sink and following Alex into the living room.

"I have to tell you something, Alex. Honesty is very important to me." *Number one on the list.* "In fact, I consider it essential in any type of relationship. We agreed to no dating, but we're friends, and I respect your privacy. I just wanted you to know that I like you a lot, and I'd hoped you felt you could openly share who you are with me."

Alex shook her head and opened her mouth as if to speak and then closed it. She looked stricken, and Debby reached out and gently pulled her into a hug.

"I'm sorry," Alex mumbled against her chest.

Debby felt her tears soak through to her heart. Whatever Alex couldn't talk about clearly hurt, and Debby felt bad for her part in making Alex cry. *Like Kristen said, I don't need to know everything about her to be her friend. So be it.*

She brushed away the tears on Alex's cheeks. "What do you say to us getting down to some serious reading?"

Alex stepped out of her embrace and smiled. "You're pretty good at making me feel better. I'm not sure I deserve your compassion. You said you have a brother and sister. I'm presuming you'd avoid doing anything that would endanger them. Please try to understand. That's what's going on for me right now. I'll open up to you the best I can because I like you a lot, too, and I want us to be friends. It's not that I don't trust you. I don't trust me."

"Okay. It means everything that you want to be open and honest with me. Let's agree to do the best we can. We'll be as truthful as possible, and I'll work on respecting your boundaries."

"Thank you. I think we can make that work. It's early, and I have some ice cream in the freezer." Alex looked at her expectantly.

"I think ice cream goes great with lesbian romance novels." Debby shook off her vision of licking ice cream off Alex's nipples and followed her into the kitchen.

Chapter Fourteen

Alex rushed Abby through her morning walk, anxious to get to work. The state fair was a fun event, even though she would be busy most of the day checking in and out guests who were there for the whole weekend. But she planned to spend half an hour of her lunch break checking out the equestrian show rings. Thoughts of the horses reminded her of Debby, and she winced, remembering her behavior the night before. She had fallen apart in Debby's arms, and unexpectedly, Debby had held her and allowed her to have her feelings without censure. She had left with a warm hug and a gentle good-bye. Alex wondered now if it was a final good-bye.

She focused on her driving as she considered various explan-ations to defend her evasion, although she wasn't sure she needed to, now that she'd simply said there were things she couldn't talk about. Maybe that was enough. She arrived at the center early enough to spend a few minutes meditating before going inside. She hoped she hadn't ruined her chances of friendship with Debby. She recognized what she didn't want to admit, that she was beginning to desire more than just the companionship they'd agreed to. She craved the connection she had felt when they had held each other dancing, and the closeness and familiarity when they had sat together quietly reading. What she craved and what she desired wasn't to be. Debby had made it clear how important honesty was to her, and it was the one thing Alex couldn't give her. She hoped Debby would follow up and let her know about taking Abby to the nursing facility. If not, she planned to call the Serenity Care nursing home herself to find out. It would be good to work on her skills of interacting with people to try to make it feel more natural, if not easier. She stepped out of her car and slammed the door shut, slightly too hard.

"Good morning, Betty." Alex greeted her boss, stepped behind the front desk, and booted up the computer. The busy morning did little to keep away thoughts of Debby's arms around her, comforting her. By lunchtime she was more than ready for a break. She logged off her computer and headed outside to lose herself in the festivities.

She wandered through the midway carrying a lemonade, another reminder of Debby, and watched the squealing kids on the Tilt-A-Whirl. She passed the Ferris wheel and envisioned herself and Debby, feet dangling, holding hands as the bucket swung and the breeze blew that piece of hair Debby always had to move off her face.

There were only two riders performing in the show ring, but they were impressive. She watched the choreographed dressage performance for a few minutes, thinking how much more she enjoyed watching Debby ride.

She checked her watch and turned to head back to work when she caught sight of Miguel Martinez walking toward her in the middle of the walkway. Her gut twisted, but she held her head up and smiled as he approached.

"Alex!"

She didn't like the way her name sounded in his heavy Mexican accent. She smiled anyway.

"I'm so happy to see you. You remember my beautiful bride, Rosita?"

"Yes. Of course. Hello, Rosita. Are you enjoying the fair?" Alex reminded herself that he only knew her as Alex, the hotel employee. She pressed her palms tightly to her thighs inside her trouser pockets to keep them from shaking.

"Oh yes." Rosita's accent was lighter than her husband's and made her words float melodiously. "I love the Ferris wheel." Her chestnut eyes sparkled as she spoke and her black hair shone in the late summer sun. She was a beautiful woman and projected an air of innocence Alex hoped was genuine.

"It's good to see you both. I have to get back to work now. Enjoy yourselves." Alex smiled and began walking back to the hotel when she spotted several men dressed in all black flanking the couple from behind. She started when she recognized Phillip, but he was walking away and didn't see her. She picked up her pace, looking back over her shoulder every few feet.

She finished her workday and rushed to her car, where she locked the doors and pulled out her phone.

"I saw Martinez again today, Joe, at the state fair. Do you have any more information about him?" Alex checked the area surrounding her car as she spoke.

"We don't have any intelligence linking him to your father's case, Alex." She heard Joe sigh and waited for more. "It's not much, but I'll tell you what I know right now."

"Thank you. I may be paranoid, but I'm worried." She wondered about Phil, but decided to wait to hear what Joe had to say.

"We're watching a warehouse full of drugs we discovered in the area, and the FBI suspects the cartel is involved. So far, they've only seen sporadic activity, so they'll continue to monitor the situation."

"What the hell does that mean? Sporadic activity! It seems to me there's activity or there isn't. Is it Martinez of the cartel family or not, Joe?" Alex didn't try to disguise her agitation at Joe's rhetoric.

"I don't know for sure yet, Alex, but we're on top of it. You have to trust us. We…I…promised to keep you safe, and I will."

Alex tipped her head back against her headrest. "There's something else, Joe. Remember the guy, Phil, you met at my place who's dating Jennifer? I saw him with Martinez today. I'm really concerned that if this Martinez is part of the drug deal, that Phil could be a dirty cop. I need to keep Jennifer from being hurt."

Joe was silent for a moment. "I'll check into it. You and Jennifer just keep doing what you've been doing. If there's a problem, I'll let you know. And, Alex? Thank you for expressing your concerns. Call me anytime."

"Okay, Joe. Keep us informed, please." She disconnected the call. She was tired of being "handled" by the deputy marshal. He was as close to them as an uncle, but he wasn't real family. She'd been responsible for taking care of Jennifer her whole life, and if she was involved with someone working for a drug dealer, something had to be done about it. She wasn't sure what she was going to do, but she'd figure it out. *Somehow.*

❖

"That was a great wedding wasn't it?" Kristen and Debby sat on Kristen's porch, sharing a pitcher of iced tea.

"Yeah. I was a little nervous about not knowing anyone, but it was fine." Debby took a sip from her glass and watched the birds at the feeder battling for the best perch.

Jaylin came out of the house and pulled a chair close to Kristen. "I started the grill for you, babe." She kissed her lightly on the lips. "How's Alex, Deb?" she asked.

"She's fine. She had to work today."

"We'll have to plan another day so you can both come over."

The truth was, Debby hadn't told Alex about Kristen's invitation to dinner. Her growing feelings for her unsettled her, and Alex's apparent mistrust of her convinced her to distance herself for a while. Spending time alone with friends felt good. There was no reason to complicate things.

"Can I help with anything?" Debby asked.

"I've got it covered, but let's go sit on the back deck." Kristen stood and she and Jaylin followed her.

"I'm going to get the salad ready," Jaylin said.

Debby settled on one of the chairs at the outside table and watched Kristen place three sizeable steaks on the hot grill.

"So, how're things going with Alex?" Kristen asked.

Debby considered a short vague answer, but Kristen was her friend and she trusted her to tell her if she was off base. "Not so well. I spent the afternoon at her place yesterday."

"That doesn't sound bad. Did something happen?"

"Not really. We ordered pizza and read for a while, just hanging out, really. She seemed upset when I first got there, so I asked her about it and she told me there were things she couldn't talk about. Basically, she can't be honest about who she is, and that's important to me."

"She knows about Evelyn and you probably expressed the importance of honesty, so maybe whatever she's not telling you isn't about her." Kristen flipped the steaks over.

Debby thought back at her conversation with Alex. She had said there were things she *couldn't* talk about, not that she didn't *want* to.

"Maybe. I can't remember her exact words, but the message that she doesn't trust me came through loud and clear. I did tell her I'd work on acknowledging her boundaries, but I'm still bothered a bit by it all."

"Well, you guys'll work it out, or you won't. I kind of hope you do. I like Alex and it would be nice to have her around more often. Just remember, you don't have to know everything about someone just to be their friend. Let's eat." Kristen piled the steaks on a plate just as Jaylin came out with the salad. "Perfect timing."

Debby hoped she and Alex could work out their relationship, too. If she thought about it, Kristen was right. If she and Alex were to only be friends, pushing her to disclose everything about herself was fanatical. She just wasn't sure anymore that all she wanted with Alex was friendship.

Alex considered calling Debby, but decided to wait until she contacted her. She didn't want to seem pushy or needy, and if Debby didn't like that there were things she couldn't discuss, then it was best they didn't spend a ton of time together anyway. The thought made her sad, and she wanted to talk to someone who understood. She settled on her couch with Abby and punched in her father's number.

"Hi, honey. How're things in Northville?"

Her dad's cheerfulness surprised her. "Good. I was calling to say hello and ask you something."

"Shoot."

"Does the name Miguel Martinez mean anything to you?"

"I've heard the name, but it's a common one. Why are you asking?"

Alex wondered if her father was hesitating because he was hiding information. "I met him and his wife at their wedding at the convention center where I work. I told Joe about it and he's checking on him. Something feels strange about him."

He was silent for a moment. "Huh. I think you should trust Joe, honey. He'll keep you safe."

"You know about Martinez, don't you?"

"I told you, I've heard the name, but I don't know anything 'about' him. The drug guy that I helped put away was a Gonzalez, and yes, there was a Martinez involved somehow after that, but it's a common Hispanic name. You and Jennifer are just going to have to trust the marshal."

"All right, but I'm worried. I saw him today, and Phil, Jen's new boyfriend, was with him. I don't know how to tell Jennifer. I'm concerned he's a dirty cop."

"I think you should talk to Joe. The guy you saw might not be involved in drugs at all. Maybe he's someone Phil's protecting or something. Plenty of cops take guard type positions to make some money on the side. Talk to Joe, honey."

"I'll try to be patient and wait for him to get back to me, but I'm nervous, Dad."

"I understand, honey. I'm so, so sorry you have to go through this. I love you, you know that don't you?"

"I love you, too, Dad. I'll wait for Joe, but like I told him, I may be calling him every day."

She disconnected the call and grabbed Abby's leash to head to the park.

Her suspicions about Phil frightened her more than running into Martinez. If he was a dirty cop on the take by the drug cartel, Jennifer could be in danger. Martinez might be off doing his thing at some warehouse while Phillip was wooing Jen in her own home. She had to make a plan to protect her. *Just another reason to keep Debby from getting too close.*

Chapter Fifteen

Debby closed her laptop and stood to stretch, causing Buddy to meow his displeasure at having his naptime disturbed. She had made good progress in her studies for the geriatric pharmacist exam and hoped to complete her certification by the end of the year. She made herself a cup of tea and thought of Alex. Would she be at work today? She had left a message on Alex's voice mail with Jan's contact information as promised, in case she wanted to take Abby to the nursing home. She had spent the week in the pharmacy without even leaving for lunch, both because she was so busy and because the desire to call Alex was too tempting. Her avoidance of Alex seemed less important now that they'd had no contact for over a week, though. She missed her and questioned how essential it was to know *everything* about her. Couldn't she simply accept Alex for who she was and be friends? She was a kindhearted, gentle, and caring person. Couldn't that be enough? She picked up her phone and texted her.

Just wanted to say hello. Did you talk to Janis about Abby visiting the nursing home? D

She rolled out her new yoga mat on the floor and loaded her new yoga DVD into her player. She thought of Alex again when she reached the meditation segment. She lay quietly, attempting to empty her mind when her phone chimed. She picked it up while lying on her back and read the text.

Glad to hear from you. I hope you're well. I did talk to Jan, and Abby and I will visit Serenity Care on Friday. A

No indication that Alex wanted to see her. Debby finished the yoga DVD and returned to her lessons.

Her phone interrupted her concentration just before her planned break for dinner and setting Shadow up for the night. Alex's number showed on her readout.

"Hello."

"Hi, Debby. I wanted to know if you'd have time for lunch on Friday. I'm planning to be at the nursing home about eleven o'clock. I figured Abby could visit a few residents for an hour and then we could go to lunch."

Debby faltered for a heartbeat. "Yes. I'd like that. I'll plan to see you on Friday."

"I'll make sure we find you. See you then."

Debby disconnected and contained her eagerness at the prospect of seeing Alex. *I can let go and just let people be who they are. I can.*

Alex paced her living room while Abby sat watching her from the couch. "Debby agreed to meet us for lunch Friday, Abby. I guess I'm still her friend." She smiled at Abby's tilted head.

She tried to figure out a solution to the situation with Phil as she paced and mentally checked off details. She had seen Phil with a possible member of a drug cartel. She didn't know for sure, however, that Miguel Martinez was a member of the Knights Templar. There was a chance that Miguel was just another Martinez without connections to the offshoot of La Familia, but there was the drug filled warehouse Joe had told her about.

The speed of her pacing increased as her anxiety escalated.

If Martinez was a drug dealer, and Phillip was involved with him, he certainly wouldn't tell Jennifer. Jennifer had said she trusted him. What if she slipped one night and he found out who she really was? Her life could be in danger, but the more she thought of it, the more she doubted Jennifer would slip up. She and Alex had been through too much for her to jeopardize their safety.

Phil knew them as Alexandra and Jennifer Reed. Miguel knew her as Alex, a desk clerk at the Hyatt. Joe knew about Phil and he knew about Martinez. They'd entrusted their lives to him for two years, and she had no choice but to continue to do so.

She took a deep breath and released it slowly. There was no way Martinez could find out who they were. Whatever Phil was doing with Miguel was his business, but Jennifer needed to be warned, just in case. She snatched her phone to call but got her voice mail.

"Hi, Jen. It's Alex. I just have something I'd like to talk to you about. Give me a call when you get this message. Love you."

Alex hung up and collapsed on the couch next to Abby. Between her flip-flopping feelings about Debby and her concern for Jen, it felt like she was spinning wheels in mud. It would have been so nice to be with someone she could talk to. But if the thing with Debby was any indication, that could never happen.

❖

"My name's Alex Reed. I'm here to see Janis Smith." Alex held tightly to Abby's leash even though she sat quietly by her side. She noticed the faint scent of antiseptic as she waited for the nurse on duty.

"Hi, Alex. Debby told me you were coming in today. I'm Kelly, and this must be Abby." Kelly squatted to Abby's level and was rewarded with a whine, a wagging tail, and a paw placed on her arm.

"I'm glad to meet you, Kelly. I met your sister and MacIntosh at the last barrel racing event at the fairgrounds."

"Cool." Kelly stood and leaned back against the nurses' desk. "I'm sorry I missed meeting you before this. It would have been nice to get to know each other."

Is she flirting with me? Alex felt the blush creep up her neck. She was saved from replying by Jan's arrival.

"Hello, Alex?" Janis's sincere smile put Alex at ease.

"Yes. Janis Smith? It's good to meet you. This is Abby." Alex pulled on Abby's leash so she was standing.

"I'll see you later, Alex. Have fun." Kelly grinned and winked as she turned to head away from them.

"Please call me Jan. Thank you so much for bringing Abby today. We have several residents who had to leave pets behind when they moved here. Needless to say, they miss them terribly. Have you met Tory and MacIntosh yet?" Jan automatically reached to pet Abby when she leaned against her leg.

"Yes, I have. Are they here today?"

"No. Tory has some school event today. Come on, I'll give you a tour."

Alex followed Jan along the hallway. The building reminded Alex of a square donut. The center was an open outdoor patio space where a few residents sat in wheelchairs enjoying the fresh air. Spotless ceiling to floor windows gave the nursing staff a full view of anyone outside. The residents' rooms were off to their right, with every door wide open. Each room had a number painted above the entrance and a plastic name tag in a holder mounted on the wall next to it. A nurse's call light hung above each door like a beacon. She shivered, awash with empathy for the apparent lack of privacy as they passed a woman sleeping, mouth agape.

Janis must have noticed her discomfort because she gently rested her hand on her shoulder. "Is this your first visit to a nursing home?"

"Yes." Alex took a deep breath, surprised to feel herself trembling.

"Come on. I'll get you a cup of tea."

Alex followed Jan to a closed door labeled break room. Like the rest of the building, the tiny room was spotless. The walls were painted a seafoam green, and the cream-colored sofa and matching cushioned chairs with forest green accent pillows were positioned facing a window overlooking a landscaped area with ornamental trees and a pond.

"Sometimes we need a peaceful place to decompress. Have a seat." Jan smiled as she spoke and handed Alex a cup of delicious smelling tea. "It's my special blend I call 'relaxation.'"

"This is awesome." Alex sipped her tea and felt the tension leave her body. Abby curled up at her feet, seeming to understand she wasn't allowed on this furniture.

Jan sat opposite her in one of the chairs. "We have room for forty residents here, and we're usually at full capacity. We have people with family who visit regularly and patients who have no one. They all have health issues that prevent them from caring for themselves and require nursing care. We aren't an Alzheimer's facility. We send those patients where they can get specialized care." Jan sipped her tea and looked past her to the window.

They sat in companionable silence for a few minutes before Jan stood to collect their cups. "Let's go visit someone."

Alex had no reservations about Abby's behavior with strangers, but she was astounded by her interaction with the wheelchair bound elderly woman. Her tail never stopped its quiet waving as she gently nudged the woman's arthritic hand. She nuzzled her head underneath it and rested her muzzle in her lap. The woman's cloudy eyes sparkled when she looked up at Alex and beamed a toothless smile.

She watched in awe as Abby tipped her head so the hand could slide down to her neck and back. It was as if she realized the woman's pain and offered relief with the warmth of her body.

"Abby is very good at this." Jan had supervised their first visit, introducing them to various patients throughout the facility.

"She is. I figured she'd be good, but I'm impressed." Alex loosely held her leash.

"It looks like Abby's got everything under control. I have a staff meeting to get to. If you have any questions just ask one of the nurses or assistants. It was great meeting you and Abby, and I look forward to seeing you often."

"Thanks, Jan. I think Abby would never forgive me if I didn't bring her back."

Alex let Abby visit another ten minutes before thanking the woman for her time and going in search of Debby. A familiar figure pulled her attention away from the signs directing her to the pharmacy. Miguel Martinez walked directly toward her, concentrating on a paper in his left hand.

She pulled Abby close to her and ducked into one of the rooms. A man slept soundly in the hospital bed, and she moved farther into the room and listened for voices in the hall. She could make out Miguel's heavy accent, but he wasn't speaking English. *What is he doing here?*

Alex's paranoia threatened to overwhelm her, and she took several settling breaths. She reminded herself that he only knew her from the Hyatt. She waited until the only sound was the man's snoring and led Abby out the door. The hallway was empty, so she continued on her way to the pharmacy.

"Hey. How'd it go today?" Debby hung her lab coat over the back of a chair and turned to face Alex in the doorway. "Everything okay?"

"Yes. It went well. Janis is wonderful and Abby loves visiting."
Alex glanced behind her for the second time.

"Good. I'm sure that whomever you visited enjoyed it, too. You
look a little nervous. You sure you're okay? If it's about last week—"

"No. Thank you for that, by the way. I'm sorry I was such a
crybaby."

"No problem. Ready for lunch?"

"I am, but I didn't think about the fact that I'd have Abby with
me today."

"Come on." Debby led Alex to the back of the pharmacy where
she had a small table set with paper plates, silverware, and bottles of
water. Two small pizza boxes sat in the center.

"Wow. This is great." Alex filled a bowl with water for Abby and
settled onto a chair.

"So, how many residents did Abby visit today?"

Alex watched Debby bite into a piece of pizza. She refrained
from reaching to wipe a drop of sauce off her lip. "Only a few, and Jan
supervised. I think she wanted to make sure Abby was trustworthy."
Being with Debby helped settle her apprehension, but she couldn't
help waiting for Miguel to kick in the door and execute them both.
Alex blinked to dispel the vision.

"Are you all right? You still seem jumpy."

"I'm fine. I guess I'm a little tired. I'll probably head home
soon." She set her unfinished piece of pizza on her plate.

"I wanted to ask you something before you go. The U.S. women's
soccer team is playing this Sunday. Would you like to come over and
watch the game with me?"

Debby's question surprised her and brought her back to reality.
"I'd love to. I watched as many of the World Cup games as I could."
She grinned, and for the first time in days, felt more anticipation than
fear.

"Great. I'll order carry-out and we'll cheer for our team." Debby
wrapped the remaining pizza in foil and handed it to Alex. "For a
snack later."

Alex left, incredibly grateful for the upcoming reprieve from the
rest of her worries.

Chapter Sixteen

At twelve ten p.m., Debby left to pick up their order of Chinese food. Alex planned to arrive at one so they could eat and relax while they listened to the pre-game discussions. She felt anything but relaxed now. *Number twelve, must like women's sports.* She looked forward to spending time with Alex, and she was happy to find out how much she liked women's soccer, but her growing feelings for her were getting in the way of her intention to allow her to be who she was as a friend. She inadvertently kept resorting to her list whenever she thought of her lately. Today would be a good test to see if her resolve would hold.

Alex arrived at twelve forty-five, and they settled on the couch with their food. Buddy snuggled into Alex's lap, and Abby settled at her feet.

"Buddy likes you." Debby took a bite of her food and watched Alex stroke his back. She wondered why she hadn't noticed how attractive her hands were.

"He's a lover. Thanks for letting me bring Abby. I think she likes Buddy, too."

"I rescued him as an adult, so I'm not sure if he's ever seen a dog before. If he bothers you just push him off. He tends to think he's the center of the world."

"He's a cat." Alex grinned and shrugged.

Debby laughed. "Yeah. I guess that says it all, doesn't it."

"This is turning out to be a lopsided game." Alex had shifted to sit next to her on the couch to make room for Abby, who had curled up on the opposite side of her.

Heat flowed up her leg from where their thighs pressed together. Neither made an effort to move away. "Yeah. It sure is. Hey, would you like a glass of wine?" Debby needed a distraction.

"I'd love one, if you have red."

"My brother sent me a white and a red for his birthday in June." She reluctantly moved off the couch to retrieve two full wine glasses.

"Is that like 'it's my birthday and my present is a gift to you' philosophy?"

Debby shook her head. "I've never met anyone before who knew what that meant. My family's been doing it for years." She settled on the couch and nestled her leg against Alex's.

"It makes sense. Everyone eventually gets a present, just not on their own birthday."

Alex took a sip of wine, and Debby noticed her hands again. This time she lapsed into a fantasy of those hands on her body, so she took a swallow of wine.

The game continued to be uneventful, and within fifteen minutes, Alex slumped against Debby's side, sound asleep. She put her feet up on the coffee table, carefully snaked her arm around her shoulders, and relished the feel of Alex in her arms. She tipped her head and Alex's hair tickled her cheek. Her cradlesong of soft snores and even breathing lulled Debby into dozing. A few minutes later, she turned her head to inhale the clean scent of her shampoo and caught her sleepy gaze.

At that moment, thoughts of Alex's evasion, her list, her exam, and any other reservations fled, and she bent slowly to capture her lips.

❖

Alex was aware of three things as she tugged herself from sleep: Debby's arm possessively holding her, her warm body pressed against her, and her silky lips on hers. She savored the faint taste of red wine and the desire coursing to her core as she slid her arm behind Debby and pulled her closer. Their breasts met and her nipples tightened. She deepened the kiss, and their tongues met as she reached across with her free arm and shifted nearly on top of her. They both moaned, and Alex's resolve to keep their relationship platonic slipped away. Debby's need called to her, and her heart seemed willing to answer.

She altered her position and allowed reason to slowly take over. She stroked Debby's cheek and placed a light kiss on her lips before sinking back on the couch. "Whew. That was some kiss."

Debby wrapped her in a hug and kissed her forehead before replying. "Yes, it was. It was a remarkable kiss."

Alex permitted herself to absorb the feel of Debby's embrace before allowing thoughts of WITSEC, Martinez, and La Familia to invade the serenity. "I probably should head home. Who won the game?"

"We did." Debby pulled her closer and took a deep breath.

Alex permitted herself another heartbeat before disentangling herself and standing. Abby jumped off her position on the couch, and Buddy strode into the room to rub against her leg.

"Buddy wants to eat, and I need to set up Shadow for the night," Debby said.

"Yeah. I need to get Abby home and feed her. Thanks for a wonderful day." Alex hooked on Abby's leash and searched for parting words. She didn't want to leave, but she knew she couldn't stay. Debby seemed to understand her dilemma and wrapped her arms around her.

"I'll talk to you tomorrow. Be careful driving home." She whispered in her ear and kissed her lightly on the side of her neck before walking her to the door.

The realization of what she had done hit her as she drove home. *This isn't good.* A state of panic had her taking deep breathes by the time she reached her parking lot. She hoped this huge mistake didn't cost her the first friend she had made in her new world.

Debby concentrated on filling prescriptions and organizing the pharmacy shelves, but her mind kept wandering to Alex and their kiss. She had started the day resolved to enjoy watching the soccer game with a friend and ended up totally absorbed in Alex. She couldn't accept anything less than honesty from Alex if they were to move to beyond friendship, but they had both expressed the desire for no dating when they first met, and one kiss wasn't going to change that. Now she just had to convince her heart.

She locked the pharmacy door and went to find Kelly for lunch.

"Ready for some soup and salad?" She leaned on the counter at the nurses' desk.

"I sure am." Kelly set the chart she was holding on the desk and they walked to the cafeteria. "So, how's that attractive friend of yours?"

"Do you mean Alex?"

"Yeah. I met her last week when she brought her dog to visit. She's pretty hot." Kelly picked up a tray and headed for the buffet line.

Debby bristled, taken off guard by a sudden surge of possessiveness. "She's fine. We watched the U.S. women's soccer game together yesterday." She filled her tray with a plate of salad and proceeded to a table.

Kelly settled opposite her. "Is she single?"

"Who?" Debby knew she sounded defensive.

"Alex. She is just a friend, isn't she?" Kelly looked uneasy.

"I'm sorry, Kelly. Yes. She is just a friend." Debby sighed.

"Uh huh."

"What does that mean?"

"That maybe you'd like to be more than friends?" Kelly took a bite of salad and grinned.

Debby picked at her plate, considering her response. "You know about Evelyn and how that ended, and you know how important honesty is to me. Alex told me that there are things in her life that she can't tell me about. I don't know why, but the bottom line is that she doesn't trust me, or, at the very least, she simply can't be totally open. I can't accept that if we have anything more than a friendship."

"But you'd like more?"

"There's something that draws me to her, and we're so comfortable together. I'm pretty mixed up about her." Debby took a mouthful of salad, but hardly tasted it.

"She's not Evelyn, and maybe she's just especially private." Kelly stopped eating and took a drink of water, staring at her thoughtfully.

"You sound like Kristen. She said the same thing. I think I'm still too scared to take a chance. I was devastated when Evelyn left, and I could never go through something like that again."

"Yes. But like I said, Alex isn't Evelyn, and you deserve to move on and have someone special in your life."

"Thanks, Kelly. I'll either figure it out, or I won't." She vowed to review her list as soon as she got home. *There're plenty of items Alex can't satisfy, so I won't have to worry about it going further.*

❖

"Hi, Dad. How're you doing?" Alex decided to try her father again, for information about the warehouse.

"I'm well. It's good to hear from you. Are you and Jennifer getting on all right?"

"We're fine, but I'm a bit uneasy. Joe told me that the FBI thinks the Knights Templar cartel was using a warehouse north of Novi to store drugs. Have you heard anything about that?"

"No. What else did Joe tell you?"

"That's pretty much it. He said there was sporadic activity going on there and that they had the group under surveillance and to trust him. His usual." She took a settling breath.

"The marshals have done a good job of keeping us safe. I think we should just trust them to do their job."

"Would you mind asking your handler please? I'm nervous about this whole thing. I'm starting to have a life here, and I don't want to move again. But with Martinez here, I'm constantly jumping at shadows."

"Of course. I'll call him today and see what I can find out. I'd have thought he would've told me something if he was suspicious."

"I doubt it. Jen and I were given mere minutes to pack a bag and get out without any explanation last time." Alex heard her dad sigh, but ignored it. She was tired of stifling her anger at having her life upended.

"I'll do my best, honey."

She heard him hang up, as usual without any good-bye, and tossed her phone onto her coffee table. She lay on the couch with her feet up, and a minute later, her phone rang.

"Hi, Debby."

"Hey there. I told you I'd call today, so are you okay?"

Alex shook her head to dislodge the effects of her conversation with her dad and concentrate on Debby. She sounded hesitant. "I presume you're asking about yesterday and our kiss."

"Yeah. I was worried that you may be upset about it. I know we agreed to keep our association platonic."

"It was only a kiss, Debby. We didn't sleep together, and I have no intention of doing so."

"Good. That's good. I figured the same thing. That a little kiss wouldn't change our agreement."

Alex shook off the twinge of disappointment at Debby's words. "No change at all. We're good. It was just one of those things, spur of the moment and all that."

"All right, then. Did you get the email from Nat about the next Meetup? It's a trip to the cider mill."

"Oh yeah. Let's plan to go."

"Sounds good. We'll talk before then. Take care."

Alex ended the call and reclined back on the couch, trying to convince herself that their kiss didn't change a thing. She ignored the wave of desire when she thought of Debby's soft lips, gentle touch, and warm hands. She'd kissed several women over the years, but had never before felt the tenderness with which Debby had held her, as if she was precious. Her sense of humor and attentiveness when they were out together was something else she'd never experienced. She could easily imagine them together, reading, going out to dinner or a show, or dancing, or riding horses side by side along a wooded path. The thought that scared her was the one where they awoke together on a Sunday, made love, and spent the rest of the morning drinking coffee and reading the paper in bed. She tried to push her feelings aside and persuade herself that she was only a friend, but hard as she tried, she couldn't deny she was falling for Debby.

CHAPTER SEVENTEEN

Jennifer perfected her downward facing dog pose while Alex made them hot chocolate and waited for her to finish.

"I'm going to change." Jennifer waved and disappeared into her bedroom.

Maybe Debby would like to go to the outdoor market with us one day. The fall vegetables had arrived, and she had a great recipe for squash soup. Her thoughts seemed to wander to Debby a lot since their kiss. She considered the consequences of disclosing her situation to her. She would never put her in danger by telling her about her previous life, but would it be so bad if she knew she was in WITSEC? She knew she couldn't tell her, but she lost herself in the fantasy until Jennifer returned.

"So what's up with the Martinez guy?" Jennifer asked as they walked the few blocks to the market. The sun warmed the late summer air, and Alex took a deep breath before answering.

"I'm not sure. Joe told me they were watching a warehouse full of drugs, but he couldn't connect this Martinez with it. If it is him, he's covering his ass well."

"I suppose we have to trust Joe. Surely if they thought we were in danger, they'd move us again."

"Yeah. We do." Alex squelched her frustration at being totally at the mercy of the marshals. She clenched her hands and released them in an attempt to expel her tension. "Let's get a few squash and make some soup tonight." Alex grabbed Jen's hand and squeezed, wanting to make the worry lines around her eyes disappear.

"Sounds good to me. Isn't *Criminal Minds* on tonight?"

"Yes." Alex wondered if Debby liked the crime show, and the idea of criminals brought her back to their situation. Alex needed to find out if Jennifer knew anything about Phil and Martinez, and how to tell her if she didn't. When they were back in the kitchen and getting dinner ready, she said, "How're things going with Phillip?" Alex and Jennifer worked together peeling and cutting while they talked.

"It's going well. I feel *seen* by him, you know? Like I can relax and be myself." She chuckled. "Myself as Jennifer Reed, anyway."

"Do you ever wish you could tell him? I mean tell him that you're in Witness Protection, not who you were before." Alex considered her earlier fantasy and cringed from the desire to be known and loved.

"I do." Jennifer's voice was soft, quiet. "But I'm afraid. Not for me, but for him."

Alex knew exactly what she meant. Jennifer obviously had feelings for this guy, so she decided to wait a few more days for Joe's call. "How do you manage when he asks about your past?"

Jennifer looked pensive. "We don't really talk about it. We enjoy each other's company, whether we're going to the show or out to dinner. We go dancing and listen to music together, or just sit quietly reading or watching TV. I guess the past doesn't matter much. We are who we are today, and it seems to be enough. He doesn't ask, so I don't have to tell, and that way no one is in danger."

Could it be so simple? She thought about what was important to her about Debby. She knew about some of her family and where she grew up, but that wasn't the information that triggered her feelings for her. She was kind, gentle, honest, and sexy. Debby evoked contentment and accepted her for who she was. She quivered at the memory of Debby's strong arms and clean scent when she's held her while she'd broken down into tears. Her questions felt probing but not intrusive, and she'd accepted her evasions but still remained her friend. Jennifer's statement struck a chord. For the first time since becoming Alexandra Reed, she feared for someone besides herself and Jennifer. But what was she going to do about it?

❖

Debby settled into her swivel rocker and nearly spilled her cup of tea when she lifted her arm so Buddy could jump into her lap. She reviewed the paper in her other hand while she sipped her tea. She had written her list after Evelyn left and had never revised it for anyone. It had kept her from being hurt again, but at the cost of finding love. She'd become comfortable being single and proficient at ignoring loneliness, but Alex seemed to easily fulfill most of the requirements on her list. *Except the most important one.*

She knew there was something Alex wasn't telling her about her past, and she needed her to be forthright if there was going to be something romantic between them. No matter what questions she asked, or how much time they spent together, she remained evasive.

"I'm not sure what to do, Bud." She rubbed his ears, and some of her tension eased at the sound of his purring. "It doesn't matter anyway. Our kiss meant nothing to her. Maybe I need to try the club again. At least maybe I can find someone who'll want to sleep with me." She set her list aside and turned on the TV. These days, it felt like she was in constant need of a distraction.

She startled when the phone rang just as someone on TV jumped out from behind a door.

"Hello."

"Hi, Debby. It's Alex."

Debby sat up to orient herself. "Oh, hi, Alex."

"Were you sleeping? Sorry. I didn't think it would be too late to call."

"No. It isn't. I was just watching *Criminal Minds*."

"I love that show. It's a commercial now, so I called. I wanted to ask you something."

Debby pushed Buddy off her lap and went to get a bottle of water. "Ask what?"

"I'd like to go to dinner after the cider mill next week. Will you go with me?"

Debby wasn't sure how to interpret Alex's question. Did she mean as a date? That didn't sound right. "As a friend, correct?"

"Yes. I wanted you to know that I value your friendship, and I hope our kiss hasn't spoiled that."

"I value your friendship, too. I won't deny that kiss was quite nice, but I agree that we need to keep our relationship friendly. It seems like neither of us are in the right place for more. I think."

"Okay. Good. I'll see you next Sunday then."

Debby set her phone back on the end table and stretched before heading to bed. She tossed and turned, pushing aside thoughts of Alex. As hard as she tried, she couldn't convince herself that their kiss was inconsequential. Something had shifted in her core while she'd held Alex, and she wasn't sure she could settle it back again. Or if that's what she wanted.

❖

"What do you mean a private party? That's not my job. I don't know anything about hosting at parties." Alex stared at her boss, horrified.

"Mr. Martinez specifically asked for your help with this, Alex. He's a huge sponsor of events here, and I told him we'd help him out. He only needs you for a couple of hours, to check in his guests and keep an eye on things. He's having a fundraising dinner for one of the state senators. It isn't unusual for our more wealthy clients to ask for assistance outside the hotel occasionally. It's just part of the job."

Alex froze. Why would Miguel ask for her to come to his house? Joe would never allow it. "When is this party, Betty?"

"Saturday. You're to be there at six o'clock sharp. I'll have directions for you tomorrow." Betty stood to leave.

At the end of her shift, Alex sat in her car, debating with herself. This job would get her into Miguel's home, and maybe she could find out how Phillip knew him. If she had proof he was involved in illegal activity or working with a drug dealer, she could turn him in to Joe and save Jennifer some heartache. She would do it for her sake. She should call Joe, but he would never let her go alone. She was on her own with this plan, but she realized she needed some sort of backup. If Martinez was a bad guy and somehow knew who she was, she might not get out of his house alive and could be putting Jennifer in danger. She pulled out a pen and pad of paper from her glove box and composed a note explaining what she was doing and why. When she got home, she'd address an envelope to Joe.

She took a minute to meditate and made a last-minute decision to stop at the nursing home. She wasn't sure Debby would still be at work after five, but she had an overpowering need to see her. She rushed to the nurses' counter and was told that Kelly and Debby had left together a half hour earlier. *Together?* She pushed aside the unbidden jealousy. It was none of her business what Debby did after work.

She had just reached the exit when she heard someone call her name. She turned as Debby waved at her.

"Hi, Alex. What're you doing here so late?"

"I was looking for you, but the nurse said you'd left already."

"I forgot my lunch pack on my desk, so I came back to get it. What's up?"

"You want to get a cup of tea or something?" Alex jangled her keys in her jacket pocket.

"How about dinner at Pete's?"

Relief flooded her at the prospect of not having to go home to her little empty apartment. "That would be perfect."

The small diner was crowded when they arrived, but Alex didn't mind waiting for a table. Her uneasiness about her intended evening at the Martinez house eased as she stood close to Debby. She ached to hold her hand.

Their server led them to a table at the back of the restaurant and took their orders. Alex unwound as the scent of food cooking and coffee brewing permeated the air, and the quiet chatter of the patrons infused Alex with a sense of normalcy.

"So, what brought you out tonight?" Debby poured them each a cup of coffee from the carafe the waitress had set on the table.

Alex measured her words. "I needed a friendly face, I guess." She weighed her need to talk against the safety of disclosing too much. She studied Debby's face searching for disinterest and found only concern. "I've been given a side job."

"That doesn't sound typical for your position at the Hyatt. Is it?"

"Not exactly. That's why I'm bothered by it. I have to go to some rich guy's house Saturday night and tend to his guest list for a fundraiser he's hosting."

"It doesn't sound awful. Who is this guy?" Debby sat back as the server placed her salad with grilled chicken in front of her.

"I guess he's a big financial sponsor for the events at the showcase, so my boss wants me to cooperate." She pondered the wisdom of telling Debby his name.

"Maybe it'll be interesting. If he's rich he probably has a huge house, and maybe he'll offer you a part-time job."

Alex winced, thinking about what he might offer her if he knew why she was there. "Thanks for helping me try to put a positive spin on this." She took a bite of her turkey sandwich.

"What is it you're worried about, exactly?"

"I'm just not sure who this guy is, or why he specifically requested me."

"Wow. He requested you?" Debby looked confused.

"Yeah. I worked the desk the day of his wedding in July, and I guess I impressed him with my stellar desk clerk duties." Alex shook her head and snickered.

"Was that the Sunday wedding after Jennifer's dinner?"

"Yeah."

"That was a while ago. You must've made quite a good impression. What's his name?"

Alex sighed. Debby probably didn't know anything about the Knights Templar, and it wasn't like normal people ran into drug cartels on a daily basis, but should she take a chance? She took a sip of coffee, wishing it were wine. "Miguel Martinez."

"Huh. That name sounds familiar." Debby paused and furrowed her brows. "Mrs. Martinez and her grandson. She's one of our newest residents, and I remember because she suffered a seizure a couple of weeks ago. I think Martinez is a common name, though."

Alex stopped mid-chew as she processed the information. *That explains what he was doing at the nursing home.* She set her fork down before speaking. "You're probably right. Maybe there's no connection, or maybe Miguel and his wife were married here because of his grandmother."

"Well, I look forward to hearing all about it Sunday at the cider mill." Debby's smile calmed her further and gave her reason to hope that she would still be around on Sunday.

They finished the meal between small talk and chuckles about Leslie, who they'd nicknamed "mushroom woman." They each finished a cup of tea before leaving, and Alex allowed herself to revel in the feeling of normalcy, even though she knew it was only for a fleeting moment.

CHAPTER EIGHTEEN

G ood morning, Kelly." Debby leaned on the nurses' counter. "Hi there. How's everything going?" Kelly walked around the desk to hug Debby.

"It's going well. I'm working on my geriatric certification, and I love it here. I have a question about one of our residents, if you have a sec."

"Okay. Who?" Kelly leaned against the counter and waited.

"Fernanda Martinez. Do you know anything about her?"

"She transferred here from a home in Florida, and her grandson, Miguel, is her guardian. She doesn't have an extensive medical record that we can find, but I know she's had that severe reaction to Cipro. Remember when you were called in to review her meds?"

"Yes. We got that all straightened out. So, you don't know anything about her grandson, huh?"

"Just that he seems especially protective of her and visits daily." Kelly tilted her head and looked concerned. "Why do you ask?"

"My friend Alex knows him from work and was wondering about him, so I thought I'd ask. We on for lunch today?"

"Sounds good. I'll see you then." Kelly returned to her chair behind the desk.

Alex had said this guy was rich, but instead of looking forward to the possibility of extra income, she had seemed almost fearful about the job. She detoured to Fernanda's room on her way to the pharmacy.

"Good morning, Mrs. Martinez. I'm Debra Johnson, one of the pharmacists. We met a few weeks ago, and I wanted to see how you were feeling." Fernanda looked half asleep, and Debby regretted her decision to bother the elderly woman.

"Hello, dear. Thank you for the lovely flowers, and I loved the chocolate covered cherries."

Debby wondered who she thought she was. "I'm glad to see you doing so well. Maybe those chocolates helped."

"Is Miguel with you this morning? I know you two have a long drive to get here, and I appreciate your visits so."

She must think I'm Miguel's wife. "Miguel will be here later. I just wanted to make sure you were well."

She quietly left the room when Fernanda smiled and fell sound asleep.

Debby Googled Miguel Martinez and waited. She spent the rest of her fifteen-minute break reading about Mexican actors, a Chilean soccer player, a musician, an artist, and a professor. They were correct in presuming Martinez was a common name. She closed her laptop and put any further thoughts of Miguel Martinez out of her mind. Perhaps Alex was just nervous about doing something different.

❖

"Of course you're invited, Jen. I'm making a couple of different soups, a salad, and my yogurt pie. Dad'll be here about one. You come over whenever you feel like it..." Alex pulled on her jeans while squeezing her phone between her ear and shoulder. "No, he still hasn't gotten his license back, so he's bringing a buddy from the program...Willy...No, I don't know him either, but Dad says he's solid...Good. I'll see you then."

Alex set her phone on the kitchen counter and began cutting up carrots. Excitement at seeing her dad warred with anger as she thought of her father and the reason he'd lost his driving privileges. He had been doing well after their relocation, going to NA meetings and working for the department of public works in Plymouth. She thought he had cleaned up and settled down until the day he called from the local jail. Now he had a DUI on his record. At least he had been drunk, not high on drugs.

She had only spoken to him on the phone since then, and she missed him. She allowed forbidden memories to surface, as if they could keep them all safe. Her father had been the one who made their breakfasts and prepared their lunches before taking them to school, while her mother lay curled in a fetal position in bed. He would pick them up from school, often stopping on the way home for an ice cream cone. It wasn't until years later she found out he was using his lunch hour for that parental duty. She was already in college when her father had turned to drugs after years of dealing with her mother's mental illness. She had tried to help by balancing her study time with trips home to help her dad search the streets for her mother, who'd begun to wander off more and more. They had usually found her curled up in the corner of an abandoned shack on the beach. The final, futile search had been with the help of the local authorities, and there was probably still a missing person's report somewhere in their files. Alex shook her head to clear the worthless musing and concentrated on stirring soup.

She was in the middle of preparing the salad when Jennifer arrived. "I brought sparkling grape juice." She put the bottles in the refrigerator. "Something smells good."

Alex wiped her hands and turned for a hug. "Thanks. Everything's ready except the salad. Sit and relax. Just push Abby off the couch."

"This is fine." Jennifer sat at the small kitchen table. "So, do we know anything about this Willy?"

"Not a thing. I'm glad Dad has a friend in the program, though." Alex finished her preparations and sat across from Jennifer.

"Me, too. He seemed so lost and remorseful for so long. Maybe he's ready to be in our lives again."

"I hope so. I know I miss him. Even after everything…"

"Me, too. I think they're here."

Alex answered the door and introduced herself to Willy. He reminded her slightly of Phil, with his clean, scruffy brown hair. His wrinkled shirt and jeans hung on his thin frame, and he wore thick black-rimmed glasses that emphasized his clear dark brown eyes. The wrinkles in his clean-shaven tanned face hinted at a hard life, but his warm smile emitted serenity. He removed his shoes before entering the living room.

"Hi, Dad." Alex hugged him and reluctantly stepped away. He looked thinner than when she'd seen him, but his neatly cut hair and clear eyes implied good health and sobriety. "Have a seat. Dinner's ready whenever we are."

"It's so good to see you two," her father said. He opened his arms to hug them both.

"I hope this means we'll see more of you now." Jennifer spoke as she filled glasses.

"You might, honey. Willy has a place close to Novi, and you're on the way."

Alex was pleased to see her father making friends other than drug dealers, but she couldn't deny a twinge of resentment that he'd only stop by to visit on his way somewhere else. "Just remember that you're both welcome anytime."

The dinner conversation revolved around Willy, the NA program, and their father's public works job. Alex would have thought it odd if she didn't know how important it was for her dad to maintain a routine and stick to the program. She thought about her own struggle to make friends and strive for stability. Talking about it made it real.

Alex lay on her couch with Abby at her feet after everyone left, inhaled, and expelled her bottled-up nervous energy. She relished having her father in her life again and was delighted that he had found a friend to connect with. He had Willy and Jennifer had Phil. She missed Debby.

She slid her note explaining her reasons for going to the Martinez house into an envelope with Joe's name in bold print on it and leaned it against the salt and pepper shakers on her kitchen table. She hoped she'd return home to toss it into the garbage.

Alex double-checked her GPS and then glanced at the map she had printed from the Internet. She had expected Martinez to have a large house, but the mansion that sat atop a hill at the curve of the circular drive was beyond anything she had imagined. She stopped in front of the enormous mahogany doors and gave her keys to the valet.

She understood the request for formal attire when she was escorted into the foyer by a muscular man who made his tuxedo look a size too small. There were paintings lining the entryway, and a huge Mexican flag hung above the entrance to what looked like an enormous dining room. She read some of the artists' names as she passed the works. Diego Rivera, Carlos Merida, Rufino Tamayo. She didn't know a thing about art, but they sounded like Mexican artists, and she presumed they were famous.

She followed her escort to the corner of the lobby, where what looked like a bar was set up with a chair behind it. There was a gold trimmed guest book embossed with the Mexican flag on a raised podium. A feathered fountain pen rested in a holder to the left side. *He knows I'm left-handed.* She swallowed and took a deep breath.

"Is this where I'll be stationed?"

The giant grunted and nodded while he waited for her to settle into the surprisingly comfortable chair and then disappeared into the dining room. She reviewed the list of names printed on the linen paper in the book. She recognized a few as prominent business owners and a few politicians. She formulated a plan to go in search of the restrooms later, so she could look for Phillip.

"Alex. Welcome to our home."

She pasted on her desk clerk smile before replying. "Good evening. You both look fabulous tonight." She didn't have to lie. Miguel was dapper in his black tux, white shirt, black cummerbund, and red carnation. Rosita looked like a model in a slinky black evening gown and glittering jeweled earrings with matching necklace and bracelet. Her hair was pulled up into a French twist, showing off her slender, pale neck.

"Please help yourself to a beverage and some hors d'oeuvres. I believe all the guests will arrive by six thirty. Thank you for doing this tonight. Please let me know if there are any problems." Miguel and Rosita retreated to the dining room to await their guests. Neither his words nor his actions suggested he was anything more than professionally interested in her, and the weight on her chest eased a little.

Alex could only see one table from her corner and the more she thought about it, the more she guessed that Phil probably wouldn't be here as a guest. When she had seen him with Miguel at the state fair, he had looked like one of his bodyguards. She would investigate when all the guests were checked in.

Well over an hour later, when she checked in the last guest on the list, she closed the guest book and strolled into the dining room. She stayed close to the outside wall as she ambled past the tables. She kept the location of the restroom in her sight in case she was stopped and needed an excuse for her wanderings. She smiled and nodded at several people as she passed. She had reached the opposite side of the room and debated whether to return or continue, when she saw him. She recognized Phil when he turned and she saw him in profile, talking to Miguel. They were standing close enough she could hear Miguel's distinct accent and saw his animated gestures as he spoke in hushed tones. She ducked behind a huge plant next to a back exit to the room and eased closer to listen.

"I want you to personally take care of it." Miguel's manner indicated he was upset about something.

"I'll see to the shipment. You don't have to worry. I'm leaving now to supervise the loading and select a driver. You stay and enjoy your party." Phil turned to survey the room and Alex pushed back farther into her corner.

"See that nothing goes wrong this time." Miguel moved away from Phil to join a group at a nearby table.

Alex waited until she saw Phil leave the room before venturing away from her hiding place to the restroom. She hurried into the expansive washroom, locked the door, and tried to calm down. She leaned on the marble counter and tipped her head back. So, Phil was involved with Martinez. She wanted to confront him and tell him to leave Jen alone, but she was sure he had left the house, and she had to consider how to handle it so she didn't put her in any danger. She washed her hands, retrieved her valet ticket, and walked out the front door. As far as she was concerned, her job here was done.

Alex wrapped her arms around herself to still her trembling. Her warm coat kept away the October evening chill, but her emotional response to seeing Miguel and Phil had her shivering on the inside. She couldn't let a dirty cop take advantage of Jen, but she had to figure out how to protect her. She grabbed Abby's leash as soon as she had gotten home and now she stood on a grassy area on the edge of the parking lot waiting for her to find a spot to pee.

"Come on, Abby. It's getting cold out here, and I need to call Joe."

She reset the thermostat higher when they went inside, tossed the note in the garbage, and cuddled on the couch with Abby for a minute before making her call.

"Hi, Joe. I'm taking advantage of your offer to call anytime."

"I'm glad you did. What's up?"

"I just need to know if you have any more information on Miguel Martinez. I want to know if I should be worried about this guy."

Joe's hesitation did nothing to diminish her concern.

"I can tell you that we believe he's involved with the drugs in the warehouse we found, and that's probably why he's in Michigan, but we have no solid evidence that he's the one doing anything with them yet. The FBI doesn't want to move in prematurely and risk the kingpin getting away."

"So, you know it's this Miguel Martinez who's involved?"

Joe exhaled noisily before answering. "I've only seen pictures of this guy, but yes, it's *a* Miguel Martinez who we're watching. I told you I'd keep you safe, and I will. I've no reason to believe that you or Jennifer are in any danger. Your dad didn't testify specifically against any Martinez family, and he doesn't appear to be part of the other groups your dad made nervous."

"There's more, Joe. I had to go to his house tonight for work. He had a political fundraiser and hired me through the Hyatt to cover his guest list. While I was there, I saw Phil talking to Martinez. They were discussing some kind of shipment, and Martinez seemed upset."

"A shipment, huh? Thanks for letting me know, kiddo. I don't want you to ever go to his house again, though. I'm going to the FBI and won't leave until I get some answers. I *will* let you all know if something happens."

"Okay. Thanks, Joe."

Alex disconnected the call resigned to waiting. She calmed herself with thoughts of Debby and their plans for the cider mill.

CHAPTER NINETEEN

Debby arrived a few minutes early so Alex made them a cup of hot chocolate. "Do you think Leslie, the mushroom woman, will be there today?" Alex blew on the hot liquid in her cup and grinned.

"I don't know. She posted that other Meetup for next week, to spend the day mushroom foraging, so maybe not."

"Well, I'm looking forward to this. I haven't been to a cider mill in years."

"I went to the same one we're going to with Kristen and Jaylin last year, and it was packed. Have you been to this one before?" Debby took a drink from her cup and cradled it with both hands.

"No, not this one." Alex hoped Debby didn't press for more information.

"We should probably get going. It may take us a while to find a parking spot." Debby picked up Alex's cup and carried them both to the kitchen. *Such a normal thing for couples to share.* She shook off the fruitless pondering.

Alex pulled her down vest out of the closet and had one arm through when she felt Debby behind her, helping her snake in her other arm. She rested her hands on her shoulders, and Alex reflexively leaned back into her arms. She stood still for a heartbeat, wrapped in Debby's embrace, allowing herself a moment's respite from her fears and uncertainties before stepping away and turning to the door. "Thanks." She meant a whole lot more than just appreciation for help with her vest.

"My pleasure. Let's go drink cider and eat donuts." Debby held the door as Alex stepped through.

Nat and Joy from the Meetup group stood at the entrance to the cider mill as they pulled into the parking lot. It took several passes before they found a spot at the far end of the lot. Alex didn't have to wonder long about how many people were already there. As they turned toward the log building, she saw the crowd surrounding Nat. The scent of ripe apples permeated the air, and her mouth watered at the smell of donuts.

"Wow. I guess we have a good turnout." Alex turned to Debby and smiled. Debby took her hand and squeezed but didn't let go. It felt wrong, dangerous, but so right. Would it hurt to believe they could have something special just for today? She was tired of hiding who she was. Tired of fearing for Jen's safety. Just plain tired. She leaned against Debby, imagining she could feel the heat from her body through the wool sweater covering her arm.

"Hey, you two. Glad you could make it." Joy waved to them as they approached the group. "We don't have anything specifically planned for today, but some of us are going to walk the path along the river, and you're all welcome to join us. First, we're going to get some cider and donuts, though. Have fun." The majority of the group followed Nat into the building to stand in line, but Alex tugged Debby toward the river's edge. Suddenly, the opportunity to get advice from someone who seemed so level-headed, and who actually cared, felt incredibly important. She certainly hadn't planned on it, but now she couldn't shake the desire to talk.

"You okay?" Debby asked.

"Yeah. I just wanted you alone for a minute. And I hate standing in lines."

"I don't think you'll be able to avoid lines today." Debby sat at one of the benches alongside the path and pulled Alex down next to her. "We're about as alone as we can be among this throng of people. Something wrong?"

"No. I just wanted to ask you something." Alex took a deep breath and allowed the words to tumble out. "If you knew something bad about someone who was important to someone you cared about, would you tell them the bad thing?"

"I told you how important honesty and openness are to me, so I'd say that I probably would." Debby tipped her head and sat quietly.

"Even if it was a hurtful bad thing?"

"If it was that bad then I guess I'd figure it would be better for them to find out from me sooner, than from the one doing the bad thing later." Debby shook her head. "This conversation is pretty weird. Does this have anything to do with your side job at the rich guy's house?"

"Never mind. It is weird, and that job went fine. I was only there for a couple of hours. Let's get in line." Alex gave up struggling to make a decision about Phil. At least for today. And just being able to voice the concern out loud felt a tiny bit freeing. Hopefully, Debby wouldn't think she was deranged. She put the thoughts aside and decided to pretend, just for today, that her life was normal.

Debby removed her jacket and tied the sleeves around her waist. The tiny room in the cider mill was wall-to-wall people. The line Alex had wanted to avoid was out the door, and they were squeezed in the middle of the warm room. Alex stood close enough that over the aroma of apples and sugar she caught the scent of her coconut shampoo. A scent she was growing to like a lot.

"You sure their cider and donuts are worth this wait?" Alex flinched at anybody trying to move past them.

"If I remember correctly, they are. I hope so, anyway." Debby stepped out of the way of a kid pushing to the front of the line. He grabbed a handful of taffy pieces wrapped in wax paper off the counter, stuffed them into his pockets, and sprinted out the door.

Alex groaned next to her, and she wondered if this was worth it after all. "We can leave if you want. I have some bottled water and a box of protein bars in my car."

"Sounds like a feast. Let's go." Alex took her hand and pulled her out the exit and back into the fresh air.

"You're right. This is better." Debby held Alex's hand as they walked along the river trail, pleased that she didn't pull away. They passed young couples cuddling and laughing, elderly men and women sitting on the benches, and children pushing the limits of their caretaker's patience. She pushed away thoughts of her list and the fact that there were only a few conditions left Alex didn't fulfill, and why she was even keeping track.

They followed the asphalt pathway to the end, where several women from their groups sat at wooden tables, the seats worn smooth from years of use.

"Hello!" Leslie stood and waved as they approached. "Come sit with me. I've got a whole gallon of cider and a dozen donuts to share."

Debby looked at Alex and shrugged. "Looks like we'll get cider and donuts after all."

"How are you two? You look great together. Did you see my Meetup notice?" Leslie looked at her and then turned to Alex and back again. Her voice rose with each question, and Debby wondered if she was drinking hard cider.

"I got your notice yesterday, and I told Alex about it. I hope it goes well for you." Debby filled two tiny waxed cups with cider and handed one to Alex.

"Cool. I hope you can make it. We're going to the state park, north of Flint, to look for brick tops, bear's tooth, and velvet foots. It's going to be great fun." Leslie took a bite of a sugar-coated donut, and sprinkles of sugar fell to the table. She swallowed and continued. "You have to be careful with the bear's tooth. If they're yellow, you mustn't eat them, but they're delicious when you find them at just the right time." She took another bite of donut and washed it down with cider.

"We should probably start back." Debby finished her miniscule cup of cider and stood.

Alex emptied her cup like a shot glass and rose from her seat. "We should. We'll see you at the next Meetup, Leslie. Thanks for the cider and donut."

Debby tugged Alex's arm as she rushed away before Leslie gathered up steam to continue.

"Sorry, but I just couldn't listen to another lecture on fungus."

"That's okay with me. I need to get home and take Abby out anyway."

"It's been a fun event, though, don't you think?"

"It was. The walk along the river was my favorite part. It was good cider, though."

"Do you still want to go to dinner?" Debby wondered if Alex's weird "bad thing" question meant something was wrong.

"Would it be all right if we made it another day?"

"Sure. Is everything okay? I'm still a bit weirded out about your earlier question. Did something else happen at your side job?"

"No. I'm a little tired. It ended up being a later night than I'd planned." Alex rolled her shoulders.

Debby stopped herself from pulling her into her arms and kissing away the sadness on her lips. "The line's gone now. Let's get a bag of apples before we leave. I actually like making homemade applesauce."

The ride home was quiet as Debby wrestled with her emotions. She had resolved that she would never allow herself to be deceived again after Evelyn, and here she was falling for a woman who had "things in my life that I can't talk about." She knew enough about Alex to believe whatever she couldn't talk about wasn't illegal or immoral, but it stung to think she didn't trust her enough with it. And that odd question about someone doing bad things puzzled her. She pulled into Alex's parking lot determined to say good-bye and go home.

"Would you like to go for a walk with me and Abby?" Alex had turned to lean her back against the passenger door, and the late afternoon light highlighted her beautiful face.

"Sure." *It's only a walk.*

She followed Alex into her apartment and waited while she hooked on Abby's leash. She stood by the door, grappling with her desire to enter or leave. She knew she wanted to stay and take Alex in her arms. Then what? There was nowhere for them to go. Alex had her secrets, and she had her list to protect her heart. She should go.

"The park isn't too far. Is that okay with you?" Alex looked pensive.

"That's fine. I like that park." *It's only a walk.*

They were well along the darkening wooded path before Alex spoke. "Thanks for coming with me. I'm feeling a little unsettled."

"Anything I can do to help?" *Will you trust me?*

Alex was silent for so long Debby figured she wouldn't answer.

"I don't think you can help me, but I appreciate your friendship. Just your presence helps settle me. I just have stuff I have to work out alone."

"Well, I hope you do work it all out. I'd be happy to help if you let me, but I don't want to be where I'm not wanted. I won't push." Any expectation she had that Alex would open up to her vanished like the setting sun. "We ought to head back. It's getting dark."

Debby stood in the foyer while Alex unlocked her door. She willed Alex to say more. To show her she wanted to be known as much as she wanted to know her. When it was obvious Alex wasn't going to say anything more, she left without going back inside.

❖

Alex could feel Debby withdrawing and had no idea what to do about it. How could she make and keep a friend when she was unable to honestly share who she was? When she feared being asked about her life? How long could a one-sided friendship last? Debby was willing to be her friend, but she deserved the respect of truthfulness. When she had entered the protection program, she'd been given a new identity, and there was no reason she couldn't come up with a past life to go along with it. She'd never be able to return to her previous life anyway, so why waste energy and potential friendship by worrying so much about concealing it? Debby knew Jennifer and her father, and she didn't need to tell her anything about Florida or her previous job. She would show her who she was as a person and a friend. She would find a way to really become the person she was now, rather than the one she used to be.

If Alex was being truthful with herself, she had to admit she wanted more than friendship with Debby. She wanted to hold her hand and cuddle on the couch. She wanted to kiss her until her smoldering desire ignited and burned away all her fears. She wanted to reveal herself and see who they could be together. She wanted all of her, but couldn't offer the same.

"What am I going to do, Abby?" Alex dropped onto her couch and allowed the tears to fall. Her mind was a whirlwind of questions without answers. She couldn't tell Jennifer about Phil without hurting her. She might not believe her anyway, and what if she was wrong? What if he was an undercover agent or something? She had to wait for Joe to confirm her suspicions about Miguel Martinez, and she couldn't tell Debby about any of it. She hadn't felt so alone since her first day in Michigan as Alexandra Reed.

CHAPTER TWENTY

Debby sorted pills and thought of Alex. She hadn't been able to get her out of her mind despite throwing herself into her work and studies. She felt close to finishing her preparations for the geriatric pharmacy certification exam and set a reminder notice on her phone for the registration deadline.

She ate lunch and pictured Alex. She longed to turn the anxiety she saw in her eyes into happiness. She didn't know how to reassure her that everything would be all right when she had no idea what caused it.

"Anybody home?" Kelly stepped into the pharmacy and held up her lunch bag. "May I join you?"

"Of course." Debby set her sandwich on the counter and waited for Kelly to settle in the chair next to her.

"Did Jan let you know about the Halloween party?"

"No." Debby took a bite of her sandwich and a sip of water. She had always thought of the holiday as a silly event meant for children.

"We have it every year for the residents. The lucid ones seem to love it." Kelly opened her plastic container of macaroni and cheese and swallowed a forkful.

"Huh." Debby couldn't come up with a reason to care about the event.

"Don't get so excited. It's for the benefit of the residents. Many don't have any family or visitors, so anything like a party is a big deal to them."

Debby chuckled. "I've never cared about Halloween, but I understand what you're saying, and I hope they have fun." She finished her water in two swallows and rolled the empty bottle between her hands. She thought of the cold, and often rainy, Halloween nights she and her brother had spent traipsing from house to house in silly costumes for pieces of candy that her parents had to pick through to assure they were safe to eat. She'd had friends and classmates who loved the disguises and skipped down the sidewalks pretending to be ghosts and goblins. Maybe the party reminded these older folks of their youth, too. If it brought some joy into their lives, she could live with it.

"You okay?" Kelly asked.

"I'm fine. I was just reminded of my not so fun times with Halloween."

"Ah. Well, these people are restricted in so many ways that a little letting loose is a welcome distraction. Anything else going on behind those beautiful brown eyes?"

"I'm studying for the geriatric exam and…well…I'm not sure if I'm coming or going with Alex." She tossed the empty bottle into the wastebasket.

"Are you thinking you'd like more than friendship with her?"

More. Everything. "I'm not sure if I can. There's too much she isn't saying."

"How much do you need to know? You said you two were comfortable with each other, and did I mention how hot she is?" Kelly grinned and took a drink of water.

"Yeah. She's hot, but she's so much more. She's mature, sensitive, self-sufficient, gentle, and strong." Debby retrieved another bottle of water from her cooler and sighed.

"It sounds to me like you know the important things about her. Sometimes our hearts recognize rightness before our brains. Don't let your brain's quest for perfection get in the way of your heart's desire. You deserve to have love in your life. Remember, Alex is not Evelyn."

Debby blew out a breath. "No. She isn't. But secrets are secrets, no matter who is keeping them."

Kelly tossed her paper lunch bag into the trash and gave Debby's arm a squeeze before rushing out the door to answer a resident's alarm buzzer.

She went back to work, pushing aside any more thoughts of what she didn't know about Alex Reed. The things she knew were wonderful. The things she didn't were the ones that could break her heart.

❖

"Again? I thought his request was only for the one fundraiser." Alex ran her hand through her hair in frustration.

"I guess this is a party for his wife's birthday. You'll be paid overtime again, and you said it went all right the last time." Betty stopped scrolling through emails on her laptop and turned it so Alex could read the screen.

My wife and I would be honored to have Alex check in and greet our guests on the occasion of my new bride's birthday celebration. Please be sure she arrives promptly by six p.m., Saturday. Sincerely, Miguel and Rosita Martinez.

"Betty. That's tonight. What arrogance! He isn't requesting anything. He's expecting me to show up whether I want to or not. Why can't his guests sign the damn book themselves? Why does he even need one?"

"Alex. Relax. Like I told you before, he's a huge supporter of ours and it's only for a couple of hours. His reasons don't concern us." Betty closed her laptop and sat back in her desk chair.

Alex clenched her fists at her side but refrained from pacing. It might give her a chance to find out something more specific about Phil's involvement with Miguel, but Joe had said never again, and a little overtime wasn't worth the risk. "I'm not doing it, Betty. Maybe one of the other desk clerks needs the overtime."

"Well, I'm not going to force you to go, but he did ask for you specifically."

"Tell him I'm sick or something. I'm sorry, but I just can't."

"All right. I'll see if June will go. But I'll need you to fill in for her tonight." Betty reopened her laptop and clicked a few keys but didn't look up again.

Alex hurried out of her office and stopped in the restroom for a moment of meditation before heading to her station at the front desk.

"Hey, Alex. It's lunchtime. Take a break." Betty called to her from the opposite end of the counter.

"I'm going in a minute." Alex logged off the computer and snatched the paper off the printer. She wasn't allowed to use the hotel's computer for personal business, but she figured if she had been asked to work at the Martinez residence, she could find out as much about him as possible. She had Googled Miguel Martinez and found only one reference related to a Mexican drug gang, with a different first name. There wasn't anything on Miguel, but she had printed out the information anyway. She had another thought as she was leaving and turned back to the computer. She Googled just the last name of Martinez and found an article about a Gomez Martinez who had been part of the cartel and had died in prison. She printed out that article also.

She sat in the lunchroom at the same table she and Debby had shared during the pharmacy convention. She remembered her smile and the sparkle in her eyes that never failed to ignite her desire. She missed her. They had texted a few times over the past two weeks but made no plans to get together, and the texts were brief and stilted. As much as she wanted to, she couldn't bring herself to involve Debby in her life any more than she already had. She pushed aside her half-eaten lunch with a heavy heart and called Joe.

"Hey, kiddo. What's up?"

"I just got asked to work at the Martinez house again. He's having a birthday party for his wife, and I thought I'd let you know that I told my boss I wouldn't do it."

"Good job, Alex. I'll let the FBI know about the party, and you relax. I don't know if there's a danger, but you did the right thing by not involving yourself with him anymore."

"I suppose. I looked him up on the Internet but didn't find anything significant. I found a Gomez Martinez, but nothing on Miguel."

"Gomez was Miguel's uncle. The FBI will let my boss know as soon as they have anything to report, and I'm on their 'pain in the ass' list because I call so often."

Alex took a huge breath and expelled it loudly. "Fine. I'll wait to hear from you."

She turned her thoughts to Debby and to figuring out her plan to be a better friend.

❖

"What in the world is that?" Debby pointed to what looked like a huge cotton ball blocking most of the hallway.

"It's a cobweb. A Halloween decoration," Kelly said.

"Well, it looks stupid, and it's a hazard for anyone walking through here." Debby stomped toward the netting and intentionally knocked part of it down.

"All right. I'll make it smaller. Don't rip it apart, you Scrooge."

Debby made it to the pharmacy without running into any more holiday trimmings, grateful to begin her daily routine. She had awakened grumpy and sore. She did a few more back stretches and poured a cup of coffee. She missed Alex, and she didn't want to. It felt like everything was conspiring to irritate her.

She sorted capsules and reviewed the medication orders for possible drug interactions. Then she looked up the latest state and federal regulations for handling medications and prepared her reports for the upcoming monthly review with the consultant pharmacist.

She stretched her back again and settled at her desk to have lunch when she heard clapping and laughter filtering into the room. She went to investigate the commotion that became louder the closer she got to the community dining area. She rounded the corner and stopped.

Alex stood in the center of the room, and Abby was covered with a blue and red cloak with a large white S on her chest. She was furiously wagging her tail and prancing as Alex called her "Super Dog." The residents surrounded the duo, clapping and calling for Super Dog to fly. Abby jumped and yipped with her tongue hanging out and her cape flapping. She finally stopped her theatrics and sat panting to face Alex.

Debby felt her belly flutter when Alex turned and caught her gaze, smiled, and raised her hand in a tentative wave. She hadn't expected to see her, but she couldn't deny she was glad she was here. She returned a friendly smile and resisted adding a wink. She watched for a few more minutes as Alex led Abby to each resident for petting and nuzzling. Her attention was drawn to movement on her right as MacIntosh raced into the room wearing a miniature orange striped Tony the Tiger costume, complete with orange bandana, followed by Tory. She cheered with the crowd as he jumped and spun in circles. She guessed a nursing home was a perfect place for folks who would recognize the mascot for a breakfast cereal that had been around since 1951.

She watched the two dogs sniff each other and play for a moment before being called back to visit the wheelchair-bound and the men and women sitting at tables. MacIntosh curled up in laps while Abby rested her head on bony thighs and burrowed her snout under arthritic fingers. The dogs were impressive, but it was Alex who drew her attention. She rested her hand on each person as she bent to speak to them or adjust the throw on their lap. She kept one hand on Abby when they came to anyone especially feeble. Abby seemed to sense their frailty and quickly darted her pink tongue to barely touch their hand.

Alex followed Abby, supervising every interaction, and when she turned and looked directly at Debby, she knew she was smitten. Alex was kind, gentle, and sweet. How much more did she need to know?

CHAPTER TWENTY-ONE

Debby sat at her desk finishing up the final paperwork for the monthly review when she heard the door open.

"I'm almost done. I'll be right there, Kelly." She continued to work, presuming Kelly would wait for her by the front door.

"Sorry. It's not Kelly." Alex walked up behind her and rested her hands on her shoulders. Abby sat quietly beside her.

Debby felt her soft lips and warm breath on her neck as Alex lightly massaged her shoulders. She swiveled her desk chair to face Alex, causing her to step back. They were face-to-face, and Alex straddled her legs and leaned forward, supporting herself with an arm on either side of her. She bent close enough so their lips were a breath apart. "You looked so sexy standing there with your lab coat and sparkling eyes." Alex closed the gap between them and gently stroked her lips with hers.

Debby pulled her close, deepening the kiss and exploring with her tongue. She lost herself in the feel of Alex's need and slid her hands to her buttocks, pulling her closer. Alex sat in her lap facing her, pushed her breasts against hers, and cradled her face with her hands. Debby inched her fingers up Alex's back and under her sweatshirt. Her skin was soft and warm, and desire burned away restraint as she pulled her closer and slid her hands under her bra. Alex moaned and stretched back to allow room for Debby to slide her hands around to the front and caress her breasts. Debby groaned as her hard nipples tickled her palms. She squeezed gently and stroked the smooth skin, wanting more. Fearing it wasn't enough.

Alex covered her hands with hers and tipped her head back. She thrust her hips forward, her whimpers calling to Debby's soul.

"Oh, God." Alex bent forward, forcing Debby to move her hands to her sides. She wrapped her arms around Debby and pulled her face to her chest. "I want you, now."

Debby wrestled down her hunger and allowed sense to creep in. "I'm at work." She kissed her softly. "Anyone could walk in." She kissed her again and pulled away.

Alex stood and adjusted her clothes. "Damn."

"Yeah." Debby stood, glanced at the door, took Alex in her arms, and tenderly kissed her one more time. "Have dinner with me tonight?"

Alex picked up Abby's leash and made her sit while Debby waited. "Is this a date?"

"Yes. Alex Reed, would you go on a date with me?" Debby grinned, unexpectedly realizing how important her answer was.

"I'd like that." Alex looked over her shoulder toward the door, then leaned to kiss her. "Very much."

The restaurant was crowded when Debby and Alex arrived, and Debby questioned her choice of the popular seafood lounge. "I never thought we'd need a reservation for Halloween night. Doesn't everyone stay home and pass out candy?" She willed herself to unwind. She was doing what she vowed never to do again. Offering her vulnerability.

"Not everyone, I guess," Alex said.

The maître d' finally seated them, and Debby's nerves began again. She reviewed the familiar menu. "I've never had a bad meal here, but my favorite is the grilled salmon."

"That sounds good to me. Are you okay? You seem nervous." Alex set her menu on the table. "If it helps, I'm a little scared myself, but I want to be here with you."

"Yeah, it helps. We need to talk, I suppose, but I want to be here with you, too."

They placed their orders and Alex began to speak. "I was honored when you told me about Evelyn, but I wasn't sure how, or if, I should respond. I've never met anyone with whom I'd considered having a long-term relationship. I've dated plenty, but never found anyone worth settling down for. I'm not sure where we're going, but this feels right, and I really like it. I'm feeling something I haven't felt in years. Happiness. For now, for me, that's enough." She smiled and placed her napkin in her lap.

Debby took a drink of water that the server had placed on the table, working out how to respond. "I know I've felt comfortable with you from the first time we met, but I wondered if you were holding something back when you didn't reciprocate after I talked about Evelyn." Debby wondered when the pain of Evelyn's betrayal had begun to lessen. Being with Alex filled a void she'd been ignoring, or maybe protecting. It was a safe place to hide her heart, but at what cost? "I'd like to see where we're going." She raised her water glass for a toast, and Alex did the same. "To us."

"What do you see for us going forward?" Alex scooped a spoonful of tartar sauce onto her grilled salmon.

"Well, I'd like us to spend time together and get to know each other better."

"I'd like that, too. I still have stuff I'm not allowed to talk about, but I'll try to be as honest as I can with sharing who I am with you."

"I guess that's all I can ask for." Debby took a bite of her salmon and wondered if that would be enough.

The server approached their table with a carafe and refilled their water glasses.

"I want to let you know how much I appreciate your understanding about that." Alex spooned the ice out of her newly filled water glass before taking a sip and contemplating her next words. "I enjoy spending time with you. In fact, I feel like we've know each other much longer than a few months. That's odd for me."

Debby sat back in her chair, immobilizing her with a gentle smile. "The fact that I'm here on a date with you is odd for me. Actually, it's the scariest thing I can remember doing since the first time I kissed a girl in high school. On one level, I feel like I've known you for longer than a few months, too. But I can't shake the niggling feeling that you're holding back, and that triggers my doubts and suspicions. I told you I'd try to respect your need for secrecy, but I need you to know that it's difficult for me."

"I know. I'll do my best." Her heart ached with the fear that her best wouldn't be good enough.

They spent the rest of the evening discussing Debby's work in pharmaceuticals, and the tension eased considerably. Debby grabbed the check when the server returned, and they stood to put on their coats before heading to the exit.

The night was cold, and Debby regretted their decision to walk after dinner. Alex wrapped her arms around herself despite her warm jacket. She stopped in front of Starbucks. "How about a hot tea?"

"Oh, yes. That sounds great." Alex rushed past her through the door, into the heat of the room. The scent of coffee added to the warm ambiance. A young couple occupied a table on the far side of the room. They ordered their tea and sat at one of the tables. "It's too cold to walk anymore tonight."

"I agree. Let's finish our tea and head home." Debby wrapped her hand around her paper cup to keep from taking Alex's hands in her own.

"This has been a wonderful first date. Can I pick where we go next time?"

"Sure, but I've been invited to Kristen and Jaylin's for a pre-holiday dinner next weekend. Would you like to go with me? We can call it our first and a half date." Debby considered the implications of showing up with Alex and decided her friends would be happy for her.

"Okay with me. It's not formal, is it?" Alex looked genuinely worried.

"No. Nothing formal. We'll just have dinner and visit for a while. Ready to head out?"

The car finally warmed up by the time they arrived at Alex's apartment. Debby turned to appreciate Alex in profile as she dozed. She stroked her cheek, overtaken by a wave of protectiveness. Even asleep, she looked worried.

Alex stirred and turned sleepy eyes on her. "Sorry I conked out on you."

Debby leaned and brushed her lips across Alex's. "No problem. Good night."

Alex put on her gloves and pulled up the hood on her jacket before getting out of the car and walking to the door. She turned back and blew a kiss before unlocking the door and disappearing inside.

Debby sat for a minute before backing out of the parking lot. She struggled with the desire to follow Alex, but she feared she would ask her to stay the night, and it was too soon. She was definitely attracted to her and believed Alex felt the same, but sex changed a relationship. She'd had her share of one-night stands and hot tangles in the sheets with women, but Alex wasn't just any woman. As hard as she tried to deny it, she felt things for Alex that went beyond sexual attraction, and for the first time in years, she wanted to see where they led.

Alex went through Jennifer's knocking routine and waited for her to open the door.

"Hi. Come on in. I've got the DVD ready to go."

"Great. I need this." Alex stretched her arms over her head, rolled her shoulders, and then unrolled her yoga mat on the floor. "Yoga nidra, here I come."

Jennifer laughed and began to follow the instructor. "You have to work for the nidra part first."

They posed and stretched for the half hour, until Alex was able to finally close her eyes and let the narrator's voice carry her into deep meditation. "This will always be my favorite part."

"I'll get us some water. You relax." Jennifer rustled about in the kitchen and returned with a tray of freshly baked scones, two cups of tea, and two bottles of water.

"Wow. I'm coming over for yoga more often." Alex settled on the end of the couch and set a cup of tea on the end table while she grabbed a scone.

"Anytime. I've been trying different recipes that I got from Sue at work. The cinnamons are my favorite. Phillip loves them, too."

"So, how's it going with Phil?" Alex swallowed her bite of scone and took a sip of tea.

"Pretty good. It bothers me a little that he has to work so much, but he said he'll be done with what he's involved with pretty soon. He's asked me to go with him to his parents' for Thanksgiving." Jennifer bit into a scone and smiled. "I think these are the best I've made so far."

Alex wondered what Debby did for Thanksgiving. She had said she had a brother in Lansing and a sister in Arizona. She couldn't remember her talking about any other family. She realized she might be spending the holiday alone, and the thought caused a lump in her throat. She brought herself back to concentrate on Jennifer. "Did Phillip tell you what he's working on?"

"No. I told you he's a cop, but really he's a detective, so there're investigations he can't talk about." Jennifer drank her tea. "Have you seen Debby lately?"

Alex felt the blush creep up her neck. "We had dinner together Saturday at that fancy seafood place downtown."

Jennifer regarded her closely. "How was it?"

"The dinner? It was good. I had grilled salmon."

"And the company?" Jennifer took another bite of scone and put her feet up on the coffee table.

Alex sighed. "The company was good, too. It was a date, okay? She took me there for our first date."

Jennifer smirked. "I think that's great, sis. You deserve to have someone special in your life, too. Since we're here to stay, we might as well be happy."

Alex hoped Jennifer's words could make it so, but hoping wasn't enough. Debby had said she wanted to see where they were going, but she also wanted to get to know her better. The tightness in her ribcage indicated it could be easier said than done.

Alex settled on her couch with Abby and called Joe.

"Hello, kiddo. Everything okay?"

"Yeah. I'm just checking in." Alex sipped a cup of tea and shifted position, trying to relax and say what she needed to say.

"Okay. You're not due until tomorrow. Is something up?"

"I went on a date last night."

"With Debra Johnson?"

"Yes." She wasn't surprised he knew who she was talking about. He had met her, and Joe did background checks on anyone new in their lives.

"Did you have a good time?"

"Yes. It was perfect. I just thought you'd want to know that she's become more than just a friend. I'm hoping she'll be around a lot more."

"I'm happy for you, and I appreciate you letting me know. Anything else going on?"

"I still want to know about Miguel Martinez and why Phil was with him, but I'm trying to let it go. I believe you'll keep us safe."

"Good. Keep believing that, because it's true. If I find any more information, I'll let you know."

"Thanks, Joe."

She disconnected the call and opened her laptop. She Googled Debra Johnson simply to look at her picture.

CHAPTER TWENTY-TWO

Alex laid another pair of slacks on the bed while Abby watched. "What do you think about this one?" She spoke as she shuffled blouses. She moved the blue blouse to cover the brown pants. "No." She picked up the peach silk shirt and set it on the black pants. "Maybe." Then she moved it to the brown pair. "Yes. I think this is it for our date and making new friends, girl. I'll wear it with the brown sweater that matches these pants." She smiled, remembering Debby calling this their first date and a half. Her decision made, she retreated to the bathroom to shower.

She leaned against the shower wall and allowed previously forbidden thoughts of Debby to flow like the hot water streaming over her shoulders. She imagined Debby's fingers exploring the curves and planes of her body as she spread her body wash on her belly and breasts. Her nipples tingled at her memory of Debby's gentle caresses. She lifted the removable shower head from its holder and pointed the spray at her throbbing clit. She grabbed the safety bar with her free hand and allowed the pulsing water to carry her over the edge, free-falling into Debby's arms.

Alex stepped out of the shower and imagined the heat of Debby's arms around her as she wrapped herself in a towel. She allowed herself a moment of contentment before she returned to reality. She wasn't ready to jump into bed with Debby yet, but a little fantasy never hurt.

She put on sweats and a sweatshirt before grabbing her down jacket and Abby's leash. They walked along their usual path as snow flurries swirled around their feet. Abby stopped to sniff every few feet as Alex thought of Miguel Martinez. She trusted Joe to find out if he was the drug dealer, but deep down, she knew he was shady just from the conversations she'd overheard. She reminded herself, once again, that he only knew her as Alex from the Hyatt, so his being a drug dealer didn't matter in the larger picture, as long as she could stay clear of him for the most part. Phillip's involvement remained unknown. She only hoped Jen wouldn't be a victim of his deception. A twinge of remorse reminded her of her own deceptiveness. "Come on, Abby. I've got a date tonight."

Alex stood before her full-length mirror, evaluating her choice. As she turned left and right, she wondered how Debby would see her. She still needed to lose ten pounds, and her hair was getting shaggy, but she was healthy and looked neat overall. *Hopefully, it's enough.*

Debby's breath caught when Alex opened the door to usher her in. She looked gorgeous in a soft looking silk blouse that complemented her gray eyes and skin tone beautifully. Her hair had grown into a sexy disarray. She stepped past her and turned to push her against the closed door. She gently cradled her face in her hands and kissed her.

"Now that's what I call a greeting." Alex grabbed her and pulled her so their hips met.

"You look fabulous." She stepped back and grinned. "I couldn't help myself."

"You look pretty good yourself."

Heat flared in her belly as Alex did a slow perusal of her body. She'd chosen a pair of black jeans, a white turtleneck, and a black leather vest. "We should probably get going."

Debby held her coat as Alex threaded her arms through the sleeves and wrapped her arms around her from behind. She caught the subtle scent of perfume but refrained from nuzzling her neck.

"At this rate we'll never get out of here." Alex covered her hands with hers and leaned back on her.

"You're right. Let's go." She disentangled herself and led the way out the door.

❖

"This place is amazing." Alex admired Kristen's front porch. "I think I'd probably be spending most of my time sitting out here in the summer."

"I know Kristen does."

"Hey, you two. Come on in out of the cold." Jaylin stood at the front door, holding it open.

"Thanks. I hate winter." Alex shivered before she took off her coat and handed it to Jaylin.

"We'll be sitting by the fireplace tonight, with anything hot you'd like to drink," Jaylin said.

Jaylin took Debby's coat and hung it in the closet next to Alex's and they followed her into the house.

"Hi there. Glad you could make it." Kristen hugged Debby and hesitated before Alex stepped close and hugged her. "Dana and Maria were invited, but they called off earlier, concerned about the drive."

"I don't blame them. The roads are getting pretty slick, and they have a ways to drive." Debby rested her hand on Alex's back and led her to a seat by the gas fireplace in the family room.

"This is great." Alex stretched her hands toward the fire. "I like that you don't have to haul firewood in to keep it going." She stifled the memory of the huge fireplace in her Florida home.

Kristen set a tray full of tea, hot chocolate, and coffee on a table next to the couch. "Help yourselves. If there's anything else you need, just let me know. We'll eat shortly."

Jaylin sat across from Alex with a mug of hot chocolate after handing one to her. "I'm glad to see you again, Alex. We didn't have much of a chance to talk at the wedding."

Alex relaxed in the presence of Jaylin's calm. "I appreciate the invitation. How long have you two lived here?"

"Kristen took over the house after her mother died and her father went into a nursing home, but I've only lived here about a year." Jaylin smiled when Kristen kissed her lightly and sat next to her.

Debby settled next to Alex on the couch with a cup of tea. She put her arm around her and Alex leaned into her.

"So, do you like chili, Alex?" Kristen asked.

"I love it. There's not too much I don't like, unfortunately."

"Kristen is famous for her chili," Debby said.

"Debby says you live in Northville. How long have you been there?" Jaylin asked.

"About two and a half years." Alex hoped Jaylin wouldn't ask more.

"I like Northville. Have you been to the farmer's market downtown?"

"Oh yes. Jen and I go there weekly during the summer and fall." Alex sighed inwardly in relief. She could handle the daily questions, the normal stuff. *And when in doubt, deflect.*

Their conversation was interrupted by Kristen calling them to the table. She set a huge bowl of greens for salad in the middle of the table along with warm rolls. She ladled hot chili into each bowl and set out bowls of hot sauce and shredded cheese.

"This looks great, Kristen. Thanks for all your hard work," Debby said.

"No problem. I love doing it, and I have Jaylin to help now."

Jaylin made a choking sound and laughed. "Yeah. Like I know the first thing about cooking. I did set the table, though."

The dinner conversation was light, and Alex appreciated that there weren't many personal questions. Jaylin seemed to sense her reserve and remained friendly without prying. She liked her a lot. Debby and Kristen talked about their horses and riding while Alex and Jaylin compared notes on their dogs.

"I'd love to bring Abby to your father's nursing home." Alex spoke between mouthfuls of chili. "I've taken her to the one where Debby works, and she's great with people."

"I think they'd love it, Alex. Jaylin can tell you who to talk to there."

"Absolutely. I'll let you know the next time I take Railroad."

"Sounds good. Debby and I are going to the Novi equestrian expo on Saturday. Do you guys want to go?"

"We're planning on it," Kristen piped up from across the table. "Let's meet there."

"Glad you remembered that, Alex. Yeah, let's check the schedule and decide what time to meet," Debby said.

Alex nearly quivered with excitement. She was making friends, making plans. Almost like a real person.

When Debby kissed her good night later, a kiss filled with promise and hope, she wondered if life really could be good again.

❖

Alex stomped her feet, attempting to stay warm as she waited for Abby to finish peeing. The day had started out sunny, and she'd hoped it would stay that way, but it was almost time to leave and snow had started falling.

"Damn." She tugged Abby's leash and went inside. "It's too early for this."

It was on days like this that she was grateful for her all-wheel drive vehicle, something she'd damn well never needed in Florida. She shoved the thought aside.

The road conditions had worsened considerably by the time she arrived at Debby's. She hurried to the door, and it opened before she could knock.

"Good morning. Come on in." Debby stepped aside as Alex removed her boots but left her coat on and rushed past her into the warm kitchen. "I've got hot chocolate or hot coffee."

"Coffee's good. Thanks. It didn't snow this early last year, did it?" Alex wrapped her hands around the warm mug Debby handed her.

"I don't remember. I think we tend to forget the bad winters to make them go away." Debby grinned and sipped her coffee. "I gave Kristen a call this morning to check on the road conditions out there. They suggested waiting until the road crews have a chance to salt before we head out."

"Fine by me. I hate driving in this crap." Alex settled on the couch where they'd watched women's soccer and had their first kiss.

"Come with me." Debby held out her hand. "I think you'll like this."

Alex stood, removed her coat and tossed it on the couch, and let herself be led down the hall. She hoped they didn't end up in Debby's bedroom because she wasn't sure what she would say, or do.

They turned right at the end of the short hallway, and Alex agreed. She did like what she saw. The ambiance of the room was completely different from the rest of the house. A large bay window overlooked a grassy treed area. A pair of cardinals perched on one of several different types of bird feeders and a downy woodpecker poked at a suet cake hanging from one of the trees. The quiet chaos of the snow falling made the entire scene surreal.

Her attention was drawn away from the spectacle of nature by the sound of soft music. The room took on a soft glow as Debby switched on the largest gas fireplace she had ever seen.

"This is amazing." Alex turned in a circle to take in the rest of the room. A huge bookcase took up most of the wall opposite the window, and a small couch flanked by two comfortable looking seafoam green swivel rockers were positioned to appreciate the view. The thick carpet, a shade darker than the chairs, felt cushy under her stocking feet.

"Thanks. This is pretty much where I spend most of my free time. It's a good place to read and relax. No television in here." Debby smiled and pointed out the window. "I named her Rosy because she chews on my roses in the summer."

Alex watched a young white-tailed deer rustle for something to eat on the snow covered ground. Something stirred deep in her soul as she looked at Debby watching the doe. Was she worthy of this gentle woman? She swallowed back the fear and worry, determined to let the moment be as beautiful as it could.

"I'm going to grab our coffee. Be right back."

In the kitchen, Debby took a moment to try to slow her pulse. Alex looked so beautiful, so soft and vulnerable, looking out at the deer, it had made Debby's soul ache.

She gathered their drinks and made her way back. "Here. We left these in the living room."

Alex took her cup and sat in one of the rockers. "Thanks. These are comfortable." She rocked a little and then swiveled.

Debby sat in the other chair and spun to face her. "Glad you like them."

They sat enjoying the view quietly until Debby's cell phone rang. "Hi, Kristen."

"Hi, Deb. I don't think we're going to make it today. The news just reported that this storm is getting worse. Maybe we can go to the expo tomorrow if they get the roads plowed and salted."

"No problem. I'll talk to Alex and see if she still wants to go today, but it's probably not worth risking an accident. Take care and stay warm."

"You, too."

Debby hung up, not disappointed. The thought of spending a few hours alone with Alex in front of her fireplace made her smile. "Kristen and Jaylin aren't going to make it. Do you still want to try, or wait until tomorrow?"

"Tomorrow sounds just fine to me. I could stay and watch the snowfall from this spot all day. I see why you don't have a TV in here."

Debby moved to the couch, hoping Alex would join her. She wasn't sure why she was so hesitant with her, but she'd had the room built after Evelyn had moved out, and it had become her sanctuary, her safe haven. Alex was the first woman with whom she had ever wanted to share it.

Alex stood and lifted her empty cup. "Shall I get us refills?" She took Debby's cup and headed out of the room.

Debby sat and waited, absorbing the feeling of having someone care enough to bring her a cup of coffee. Her list called to her from her desk drawer. She feared it was complaining about becoming obsolete.

Alex returned with their cups and sat next to Debby. "I love your kitchen." She took a sip of her hot coffee and snuggled closer.

Debby set her mug on the end table and put her arm across the top of the couch behind Alex. "Here. This would be more comfortable." She pushed a button on the side of the couch, and the footrest flipped up.

"Cool." Alex did the same on her side, and they drank coffee and watched nature's show in silence for the next half hour. "The snow seems to be letting up."

"Hmm. Yep." Debby shifted closer to Alex.

"Think we should go turn on the weather channel?"

"Probably." Debby didn't move.

"I guess we're not going anywhere." Alex set her cup down, slid one arm behind Debby, and reached across her with the other.

Debby only needed to turn her head and their lips would meet. She didn't need to. Alex gently gripped her chin and turned it for her.

Their kiss began as a slow exploration and quickly turned into desperate need. Debby groaned as their tongues met and Alex whimpered.

A small voice whispered for her to slow down. There were still unknowns between them, and Alex meant more to her than a one-night stand. She moved a breath away and broke their connection. She held Alex close as their breathing returned to normal. "You feel good," she whispered.

Alex's chest rose and fell as she took a deep breath and expelled it. "So do you." She sat up and pulled away.

"I think we should talk," Debby said.

"Yeah, I guess so. You have any of your brother's birthday wine left?"

Debby nodded. "I'll be right back."

Alex used the time waiting for Debby to bring back the wine to enjoy the warmth of the fireplace and compose herself. She had thought she wasn't ready to go to bed with Debby, but she had ignored her reservations and been ready to tear her clothes off. She knew it wouldn't be fair to involve her further in her life, but she wasn't sure she could resist. She had to find out about Martinez soon. She would be devastated if she allowed herself to fall for Debby and then had to leave. And it would prove to Debby that she couldn't be trusted, and it seemed like she had enough trouble trusting people as it was. Debby wanted to talk. Maybe they could come to some sort of understanding.

"Here you go." Debby handed her a wine glass half full of red wine and sat next to her with a glass of white.

"Thanks. I'll try not to fall asleep on you this time." Alex took a sip and savored the warmth spreading through her belly.

They sat quietly for a moment, the air heavy with unspoken emotions. Finally, Debby said softly, "I want to make love with you, Alex. I have for a while." She took a sip of her wine before continuing. "I've only been involved with a few women since Evelyn, my ex, and they've all been meaningless hookups. I feel differently about you. Having sex with you could never be meaningless."

Alex took a minute to consider her words and how much she could divulge. "I don't have a great deal of experience with sex. I mean, I've dated a few women and slept with a couple of them, but I've never had a long-term relationship. Sex with you wouldn't be meaningless to me, either." She fortified herself with a gulp of wine, knowing what she needed to say, though she hated to say it. "That's why I can't do it."

Debby kissed her lightly and smiled. "I kind of sensed you weren't ready either. How about if we give it a time frame? We've known each other for four months, so what if we say we wait another two? Take the time to really get to know one another."

Alex considered the offer. Surely Joe would know something about Martinez by then, and if she knew she would be staying in the area, maybe she'd be free to pursue something more. "Okay. Let's pick a nice place to go, maybe with a hot tub, in two months."

They tapped their glasses in a toast of agreement.

The snow had stopped, and Alex delighted in the serenity of the winter scene. Rosy had left a trail of hoofprints in her quest for food, and the birds flew off in search of shelter. She stood and stretched, content with her decision. She only hoped the news about Martinez was good and she would be able to keep their date.

"The dressage starts in five minutes. Let's go get a seat," Jaylin said over her shoulder as she pulled Kristen by the hand.

Debby and Alex laughed and strolled after them. Alex relaxed in the presence of these women, who were all so genuine and...real. She inhaled, enjoying the smell of horses, leather, and sawdust. Memories of Mr. Ed and the stables where she'd leased him took her by surprise. She missed him.

"Can we go watch the trainer next?" Debby asked.

"And the barrel racing exhibition, too," Alex said.

"We'll be here all day, guys. We'll see everything." Kristen grinned and squeezed Jaylin's hand.

"I'd like to stop at the Ariat boot seller before we leave," Alex whispered to Debby.

"And I want to check out the parade saddles," Debby whispered back.

"Will you two quit whispering? We'll see it all." Jaylin smiled and turned back to the riders in the ring.

Alex watched the riders barely move atop their graceful horses as they pranced, changed gaits, and skipped to music.

"Look." Alex pointed to a majestic dapple gray trotting past them. "That's a Lusitano. He's a beauty."

"Oh, he is," Kristen said. "I've never seen one before."

"They're from Portugal and were originally bred for bullfighting. I haven't seen one in years." Alex stopped herself from saying more. Her excitement at seeing the horse breed had almost caused her to slip. Another suppressed memory surfaced of her helping train a friend's two-year-old Lusitano. She relaxed when Kristen didn't ask questions.

The event was over too soon as far as Alex was concerned, and they moved to the next ring, where a horse trainer demonstrated various methods of bonding with horses. She allowed the forbidden recollections of the hours she had spent training Mr. Ed using similar methods. She felt the melancholy stealing over her and tried to shake it off by holding Debby's hand.

"Let's go check out the draft horses," Debby said.

They spent an hour visiting the draft horse stalls and checking out the various horse rescue localities advertising alongside the feed stores and tack shops.

"Anybody ready to break for lunch?" Jaylin asked.

"Yeah," they said in unison.

Alex shifted in the tiny plastic chair at the tiny round table they had picked in the food area. She took a bite of her hot dog and a drink of iced tea while enjoying the contentment of having friends. Two and a half years ago, she never would have imagined she would be sitting at a public event with three friends. *One of whom is, maybe, more than a friend.*

"The barrel race starts at one. Are we ready?" Alex willed herself to sit still and wait.

"I'm almost finished." Kristen grinned and finished her last bite of hot dog.

"I'm ready." Jaylin picked up their empty cups and paper plates and tossed them into the waste bin.

They reached the bleachers at the barrel racing area just as the competition began.

"Do you have any plans for Thanksgiving?" Debby asked after they'd settled in their seats.

Alex turned away from the exhibition to look at Debby. "I'm not sure. I know Jennifer is going to Phil's to meet his family. I haven't talked to my dad yet, but we'll get together for sure on Sunday, if not Thursday. How about you?"

"I'm going to fly out to see my mom this year. She lives not far from my sister and her family in Arizona. I haven't been out there for a couple of years."

Alex knew her father might make an effort to get together for the holiday, though it was unlikely, and she immersed herself in the brief fantasy of both of their families sharing turkey at the dining room table.

"So, how do you know so much about horses?" Debby asked as they walked to her car.

Alex had mentally rehearsed her answer since she had made the statement about the Lusitano. "I've always loved horses, so I read all I could about them and studied the breeds." She didn't need to tell her about her horse or Florida. She was getting better at lying, or half-truths, even if it wasn't getting any easier.

"You knew a lot about all those gaits and fancy footwork, too. Have you ridden dressage?"

Alex didn't need to lie about her answer. "No. I just love watching it. The Olympic events are my favorite."

"Mine, too." Debby turned and held her gaze. "Maybe we can watch them together next August."

Alex flinched at the reference to their future, but she had to admit she didn't want to dismiss the possibility. "Maybe we can."

Chapter Twenty-three

Debby set her textbook aside and stood to stretch out the kinks in her back. Spending her lunch hour daily sitting at her desk was starting to take its toll, but she wanted to be ready for the certified geriatric pharmacist exam. She logged on to her computer and double-checked that the deadline for registration was in December. Then she went to find Kelly.

"Hey, Kelly. Did you have lunch yet?"

"Hi, Deb. No. I was thinking of swinging by and seeing if you felt like joining me in the cafeteria."

"Let's go."

They filled their trays at the buffet line and sat at one of the tables.

"Are you planning to go to the Big Drug dinner next week?" Debby asked.

"I think so. I can't believe they planned it for Thanksgiving weekend. I've got my parents and my brother coming to dinner on Thursday, and my aunt and uncle on Saturday. I was planning to relax on Friday."

"It's at that fancy place downtown, so it'll probably be a good meal. And you won't have to cook."

"Good point. You're going, aren't you?"

"Oh yeah. I think the Pharmacists Association would blackball me if I didn't show up. Big Drug is one of the largest drug manufacturers in the country. We're expected to be there to schmooze and pretend we're excited about their new medications."

"I'll decide by Wednesday and RSVP. Are you bringing anyone?"

"I'm going to ask Alex if she wants to go. We've sort of started dating." Debby kept her head down like she was concentrating on her salad.

"Well, this is news. When did this start?" Kelly stopped eating and set her fork on her plate.

"Just a couple of weeks ago. We're going to see how it goes. Take it slowly and keep the pressure off." Debby sat back and took a drink of water, liking the way it sounded. Slow, sure, steady. Plenty of time for Alex to slowly open up about things.

"I'm happy for you, although I'm surprised. The last time we talked, you were worried because you felt she didn't trust you, but now you're dating?"

"I can't explain it, but I feel like I know, and like, who she is inside, and that seems to be enough for now." Debby considered her words. Alex might have secrets, but didn't she, too? She had her list, and she had never told anyone about it. That was her secret.

"Well, that's it then. I'll be at the dinner if only to see you two together. I'll talk to you later." Kelly returned her tray to the stack and left Debby sitting alone at the table, thinking about how Alex's smile made her stomach jump, and how remarkably soft her lips were.

She went back to her desk to call Alex. Hearing her voice always settled her, and she wanted to hear it before she went back to her studying. *Slow and steady. No pressure.*

"Hi, Debby. Hang on a second." Alex took her phone to the empty valet area of the lobby. "Okay. I was at the front desk. What's up?"

"I have an event that's put on by a drug company that I thought was just a show-and-tell sort of thing for their new drugs. It turns out it's a dinner event, so I was wondering if you'd go with me? It's this Friday night."

"I'd like that. I still haven't talked to Dad about Thanksgiving, but I doubt he'd want to do anything on Friday anyway. Okay if I let you know tomorrow?"

"Sure. It's sort of last-minute, but this is the first time they've had a dinner."

"Great. I'll give you a call tomorrow, and, Debby?"

"Yeah?"

"Thanks for inviting me. Second date?"

"Second date. Looking forward to it."

Alex hung up and went back to her post at the front desk. She knew her father had his NA meetings on Friday evenings, but she couldn't tell Debby that without getting into an explanation. She had bought herself time to absorb the fact that she and Debby were dating. It probably wasn't fair, but if felt so right. She was becoming more comfortable disclosing who she was without revealing her past, and it seemed to be enough for Debby. *For now.* She didn't want to hurt Debby, and she hoped she wasn't letting herself in for a big heartache. She'd take it one day at a time.

Alex pushed her father's speed button on her phone while she sat at the lunch table she now considered hers and Debby's.

"Hi, Dad. How're you doing?"

"Hey, Alex. I'm good. You on your lunch break?"

"Yep, and I thought I'd see how you were and when you wanted to get together for Thanksgiving."

"I talked to Jen, and she's going to her boyfriend's on Thursday."

"Yeah. She told me, too. How's Sunday sound instead? I'll get us a little Butterball and all the fixings." Alex began mentally making a grocery list.

"That sounds great. Uh, would you mind if I brought Willy? He has no family, and I know he'll be alone."

"Sure, bring him along. I'll call Jennifer and invite her and Phil. It'll be nice for all of us to be together, even if it isn't exactly on Thanksgiving Day."

"Thanks, honey. Please don't tell Willy I told you this, but I know that he's struggling to stay straight. He can't seem to keep away from the bad crowd he's been involved with for years. I think it will help for him to have the invitation to focus on and to be around people who aren't using, you know?"

"I understand. I look forward to having you both here. Let's make it about four."

"I'll see you Sunday."

Alex sipped her coffee and allowed herself the memory of the few Thanksgiving meals they'd shared as a family in Florida. She'd been responsible for cooking, since she was the oldest and her mother had spent most of her days in bed. She looked forward to merging her family with the new people in their lives. She'd miss Debby, but she missed her own mother and would never begrudge Debby hers. Alex finished her lunch and called Jennifer.

The Friday after Thanksgiving, Debby took her hand as soon as they entered the expansive restaurant. The red and green lights and poinsettias gave the lobby a festive atmosphere, but the event room reflected the elegance of the building rather than the holiday season. There was a small fir tree decorated with white lights and red bows on a stand in a corner by the door, but beyond that, nothing indicated that Christmas was around the corner. Crystal chandeliers sparkled above the rose colored carpet and white linen covered round tables. Sterling silver platters laden with hors d' oeuvres sat on a long table against one wall, and coffee pots and wine occupied a space at the end. She pointed to the hardwood square dance floor, and Debby nodded and grinned.

Debby squeezed her hands and pulled out a chair for her at one of the round tables. Alex wondered about Debby's newfound comfort level, as well as her own. Was Debby compromising her values of needing honesty and openness in a relationship? She would never ask her to do that, but Debby seemed to have come to a place where she accepted her for who she was, with fewer questions. Her life still felt too complicated to involve anyone but too lonely if she didn't.

"Glass of wine before dinner?" Debby asked.

"Yes, please."

Alex's perusal of Debby striding to the bar was interrupted when Kelly pulled out the chair across from her.

"Anyone sitting here?" she asked.

"No. Have a seat. I know we've met once, but my name is Alex." She smiled and leaned forward to shake Kelly's hand.

"I'm Kelly, a friend of Debby's. Your dog is Abby, right?"

"Right. Good to see you again, Kelly. This looks like it's going to be a nice dinner."

"Yeah. Big Drug does a nice job of trying to get us to buy their products."

Debby returned and handed a full wine glass to Alex. "Hi, Kelly. Glad you could make it. Can I get you a glass of wine or something?"

"Thanks. I'll go to the bar in a minute."

"Did you come alone?" Debby asked

"Yeah. I asked Mary, but she was going out of town. I can't believe they chose a holiday weekend to have this thing."

"Who knows what corporations think? I'm going to enjoy the good meal and good company." Debby smiled and grazed Alex's hand with her fingers.

Alex turned her hand so their fingers intertwined. "I think the DJ is setting up." She pointed to the area behind the dance floor.

"I hope the DJ is good," Kelly said.

Alex didn't care as long as she could hold Debby in her arms. It wasn't long before her wish came true. The music began and several couples, gay and straight, took to the dancing area.

"You ready?" Debby grinned and held out her hand.

"You bet." Alex took her hand and glided into her arms. "It's about time," she whispered as she wrapped her arms around Debby's neck.

They sauntered back to their table hand in hand when they heard the call for dinner.

"You two looked good out there." Kelly looked relaxed as she sat with one arm resting on the back of her chair and a beer in her hand on the table. "You're just in time. They called our table for the buffet." She finished her beer and stood.

Alex couldn't suppress her grin as she walked with Debby and Kelly to the food line. She filled her plate and cautiously accepted the possibility of being able to relax her guard. At least for one evening.

Alex cursed her last-minute shopping decision as she wound her way through the aisles, stopping every few feet to wait for someone browsing the nearly empty shelves to move. She occupied her time with memories of dancing with Debby. Their bodies fit together perfectly, and her pulse jumped when she remembered her warm hand on her back, drawing her closer with each dance step. The two months they had decided to wait seemed so far away, the longer they held each other. A woman with a baby stroller maneuvered past her, bumping her cart and wrenching her back to the present.

She paid for her groceries and went home. She checked the clock for the third time. Debby had promised to call when she arrived in Arizona.

The turkey was cooked, and her father and Willy arrived as Alex pulled the pumpkin pie out of the oven.

"Hi, honey. You remember Willy?"

"Of course." Alex hugged her father and Willy. "I'm glad you could make it. Jennifer called to let me know they would be a little late. Her boyfriend, Phil, is a cop, and he often has to work late. Come on in and have a seat. Coffee?"

"I'd love a cup. Thank you," Willy said.

"Me, too."

Alex handed them their cups and sat across from them on her comfy chair. "How's work going, Dad?"

"Good. I've transferred to the day shift, so I feel like I have a life again. Will and I can make it to the Friday night meetings now. How're you doing at that fancy hotel?"

"Great. I like it a lot." Alex checked her watch. Debby's plane should have landed. "We had a large group last week for a girl's bat mitzvah. I found it interesting that Jewish children aren't required to observe their commandments until the girls are twelve and the boys thirteen."

"I have a cousin who married a Jewish man last year. My Catholic mother refused to go to their wedding. I went and had a great time." Willy shrugged and took a drink of coffee.

The buzzer sounded and she rose to let in Jennifer and Phil.

"Hi, sis. The turkey smells great."

"It's ready and waiting to be carved. Come on in. Phil hasn't met Willy yet."

Jennifer introduced Phil and Alex sensed something akin to fear in Willy's eyes. A swift look of concern crossed Phil's face when their eyes locked, and he extended his arm in front of Jennifer slightly and took a step back. She shook off the weird uneasy feeling and called everyone to the table. Conversation was light and quiet as everyone dug in.

"This turkey is wonderful, Alex. Thank you for inviting me. I'd have probably opened a can of Spam for dinner tonight." Willy reached for a second helping of turkey and potatoes while he narrowed his eyes at Phil.

"Thank you. It's hard to ruin a Butterball turkey."

"How's your job at the dentist going, Jen?" Their father leaned his chin on one hand and leaned around Phil to see her.

"It's wonderful. I'll be done with my degree this semester, and Dr. Parker will hire me full-time."

"That's great, honey. I'm proud of you."

"Thanks, Dad." Jennifer reached across Phil to squeeze her dad's hand.

"If everyone is done, we can sit in the living room and have dessert." Alex stood and began gathering empty plates.

They sat in the living room with coffee and pie, and Alex noticed Willy eyeing Phil again.

"This pie is delicious, Alex. Can I have the recipe?" Jennifer asked.

"It's on the can of pumpkin. Nothing terribly unique, I'm afraid."

"Oh. Cool. I'll make one for Christmas."

Alex pondered where she would be at Christmas and if Debby would be there.

She waited for Debby's call for half an hour after everyone left before texting her, her anxiety creating scenarios her mind didn't want to consider. She settled on the couch with Abby and looked at her phone, willing it to ring. She checked the time again and laughed. "It's two hours earlier in Arizona, Abby."

She retrieved the remaining dishes from the table and began rinsing them and loading the dishwasher. She was nearly done when her phone chimed Debby's ring tone.

"Hey. You made it."

"I did. It's a sunny seventy degrees here." Debby's voice held a smile.

"Well, it's thirty and cloudy here, but I'm eating a piece of pumpkin pie." Alex allowed the sarcasm to color her tone.

Debby laughed. "How was your dinner?"

"It turned out nice. I think my dad's friend Willy enjoyed it the most. It was like he hadn't eaten in weeks."

"You must've had some good food."

"It was good, if I say so myself. I'm not sure, but I think he might be gay."

"Yeah?"

"Yeah. He kept staring at Phil." The thought crossed her mind that he almost looked angry or scared.

"Huh. Well, I'm glad it went well for you. I'm at the Phoenix airport now waiting for Mom. Oh, here she comes. I'll call you when I get home."

"Sounds good." Alex hesitated. "I miss you."

"I miss you too, Alex. Talk to you soon."

Alex hoped it was sooner rather than later. She had enjoyed cooking for her family and was thrilled to see Jennifer so happy. Phil obviously cared about Jennifer, and she hoped that her fears about him and his involvement with Martinez turned out to be unwarranted. Willy had seemed interested in him, yet detached. Maybe the fact that Phil was a cop and Willy was a druggy made him nervous. Or maybe he was gay and interested but knew Phil was straight and with Jennifer. She hoped he managed to keep himself clean because she hadn't seen her dad so settled in years. Having a friend in the NA program seemed good for him. The only missing piece to complete the picture was Debby. She wondered with growing anticipation, how to make that happen.

Chapter Twenty-four

A lex reached for her ringing phone and checked the time on her bedside clock. Three twelve a.m. She swung her legs over the side of the bed and looked at the readout. *Joe.* Her heart raced and her stomach clenched as she answered.

"Joe?"

"I'm sorry, kiddo. You've got to go. Now."

Alex knew Joe wouldn't call if he wasn't sure of a threat, but she asked anyway. "Are you absolutely certain?" She pulled the empty duffel bag from beneath her bed and started shoving things inside.

"No question about it. Pack your bags. Jennifer is already on her way, and your father's being notified as we speak. Do you remember the drill, or do you need me to spell it out?"

"I know what to do. This is only for a few days, right?"

"I'm not sure. Better plan for a month, just to be safe."

"So it's temporary?"

"I hope so."

Alex swallowed her frustration, and for a heartbeat, seriously considered telling Joe to go to hell. "How much time do I have?"

"I'm outside your building with the engine running."

"Then keep your weapon handy because I'm taking a shower and getting dressed before I go anywhere."

She disconnected the call and stood on wobbly legs. She doubled over as dread engulfed her and panic stole her breath and her false bravado. She gulped air and held it in her lungs until her autonomic nervous system took over, and she was forced to breathe again. She rushed to the bathroom, trying to ignore the multitude of affairs she didn't have in order. She needed to contact Debby. She ran back and snatched her phone but was unsurprised that it was dead. They always cut it off immediately when they had to move. She would get another phone but not until they were in a secure location, and then all her calls would be monitored. She threw the useless phone on her bed and headed to the bathroom.

This was the way it went. No warning, little time to pack, and no information as to where they were taking them. But they would be safe. She wondered if Miguel had finally implicated himself, but she couldn't figure out why it would affect them. She packed the two bags she had designated for this purpose and grabbed her ever-ready toiletry bag. She knew from experience that Joe would get them anything they needed if something was forgotten.

She topped off Abby's food travel container, seized her doggie bag with bowls, brushes, chews, and toys, and snatched her leash on the way out the door.

"Where're we going?" Alex asked as she slid into the backseat of a black sedan.

"Someplace safe." She knew Joe's curt reply was all the information she was going to get.

She wondered if Debby was still asleep and how she was going to get in touch with her. At least the last words they had spoken to each other were positive.

Debby jumped out of bed, drawn by a pull she couldn't identify. She looked at the clock radio, two forty-two a.m. She shuffled to the bathroom and splashed water on her face. Something felt off, like when her brother had called years ago in the middle of the night to let her know that their father had died, except her phone sat silent on the charger by the bed. She shook off the unsettling feeling and went back to bed.

She awoke at five thirty as usual, to a quiet house. Her mother was probably still asleep. The earlier unsettledness remained, and she pulled on a pair of sweatpants and a T-shirt before going downstairs to brew coffee. She returned to the guest room and considered calling Alex, but decided a text would be less disturbing if she was still sleeping. Her phone pinged and the message readout showed her text had been undeliverable. *Odd.* She scrolled through her contacts and pushed Alex's number. The phone's reply bothered her. *This number has been disconnected.* She tried the number again and received the same message. She decided there was probably a problem with the carrier and would try again later. But it didn't make sense that the number would be disconnected. She must have decided to change carriers, but it was unlikely she'd do that without picking up a new one right away. *Very odd.*

She stood in the shower under the hot spray, hoping to wash away the disquieting sense. She blew her hair dry and dressed before doing her morning stretches and going downstairs to settle on her mom's couch with her coffee. Heat rose through her body as she thought of Alex and their bodies pressed together as they had danced. They had agreed to more dates, but neither had made any long-term promises. Unfortunately, her heart had. Despite her list and her uncertainties, she had fallen in love with Alex, and there was no going back.

She sipped her coffee and turned on the local newscast. Phoenix weather and traffic droned on, and she tried Alex's number getting the same troubling message, so she called Kelly.

You've reached the voice mail of Kelly Newton. Leave a message and I'll get back to you as soon as I can.

"Hey, Kelly. I'm still in Arizona with Mom, and I've been trying to get a hold of Alex, but there seems to be a problem with her phone. Would you mind trying her cell for me? Thanks. Talk to you later." She didn't know why Kelly might be able to get through when she couldn't, but she couldn't think of another option. She didn't have Jennifer's number.

"You're up early." Debby's mom settled next to her on the couch. "Thanks for making coffee."

"I'm used to being at work by seven, so this isn't early to me. Besides, it's two hours later in Michigan."

"Ah. I forgot about the time difference. How's everything going at the nursing home?"

"It's going well. I like it so much better than retail pharmacy." Debby took a sip of her coffee. It felt good being with her mother. She hadn't visited her since her sixty-seventh birthday in April, and she missed their morning chats. She had always been able to talk to her about anything. Her mother hadn't batted an eye when she had told her at sixteen that she was going to marry her best friend someday. She had only nodded and told her to be careful because not everyone was comfortable with two girls wanting to get married. She debated telling her about Alex, wondering if it was still too soon. *But then, if I can't talk to Mom, who can I talk to?*

"So, nobody special in your life?" Her mother smiled and gently placed her hand on her leg.

She shook her head at her mother's question, sometimes wondering if she could read her mind. "In fact, I'm dating someone. Her name is Alex, and she lives in Northville."

"Oh, honey, that's wonderful. You know how worried I was about you after that bitch, Evelyn, left you. I'm glad you're finally able to move on."

Debby smiled. Her mother never was one to hold back with her feelings. Unlike herself. "We still have some stuff to work out, but we're enjoying each other's company. I don't know if it will go anywhere, but it's nice to want something like that again."

"Good. She better treat you right or she'll have to deal with me. I better get busy in the kitchen. Your sister and family will be here by noon."

Debby enjoyed the feeling of knowing she could always count on her mother's support. She put her feet up on the coffee table and relaxed while she finished her coffee and thought of Alex. They'd talked honestly, and she'd expressed the same desire to see who they could be together. Alex still had subjects that were off limits to discuss, but maybe, in time, that would change. *People grow closer the longer they're together.* She only needed to be patient.

"I need a phone, Joe. I have to get in touch with Debby." Alex paced the tiny kitchen while Joe sat at the table drinking a cup of hot chocolate.

"I'll get you one, Alex, I promise. It'll be for emergencies only, however. I have to wait for my boss to let me know exactly what's going on first. I only know that the FBI is keeping an eye on that warehouse I told you about. I don't have enough details yet to break protocol. I'm to make sure your family is in a secure location and wait for instructions, but at the moment, that's all I know."

"I need to call Phil, too." Jennifer paced the opposite direction of Alex.

"I know this is hard." Joe stood and stopped their marching. "But it's my job to keep you safe. Your dad will be here soon, and maybe I'll get more information then."

Alex went to her designated bedroom and flopped onto the twin bed. She had grabbed a few books in her hasty departure, but she couldn't concentrate on reading. She turned on the small TV that sat on a rickety round table in a corner of the room and found a news channel. The picture faded in and out as the wind gusted across the outside antennae. She shut it off and paced. She had no phone, and Debby would worry if she couldn't get a hold of her. The marshals probably had their addresses expunged and all their belongings in storage by now, so once again, her existence was obliterated. Only this time it mattered. She lay down and meditated until she drifted into an uneasy sleep.

Alex awoke to the sounds of arguing voices and Abby whining. She calmed Abby and made her stay in her bed, then went to the kitchen table and sat to watch the argument in progress. Her father and Joe were in a heated discussion regarding the length of time they were to remain in the safe house.

"I've started having a life now." Her father clenched his fists and gave her a quick glance before turning back to Joe. "I want to know how long we're going to be here."

Joe looked as frustrated as she felt. "I'm not sure yet. I promise you I'm doing my best to find out. All I know is that the FBI found drugs in a warehouse near Novi, and that they've had someone undercover gathering evidence, and some of that evidence has something to do with you. I'm waiting to find out who passed on information regarding your safety and how credible a threat it is. My boss is in contact with the FBI and promises me a report soon."

"Soon? What does that mean?" Alex asked.

Joe stood and retrieved three bottles of water from the refrigerator and set them on the table. "I'll call again tonight and see what I can find out. And if someone calls me before that, I'll let you know immediately."

Jennifer joined them at the table and Joe gave her his unopened bottle of water. "What'd I miss?" she asked.

"I'll fill her in, Joe," Alex said. "You go find out what you can." She touched his arm. "But please, at least get us a phone so we can let Debby and Phil know we're okay."

He gave her a sad smile, and she knew that wasn't going to happen. Letting anyone know where they were could put that person, as well as all of them, in jeopardy. She went back to the table and wrapped her arms around Jennifer.

Just when I thought everything could be okay.

Debby tried Alex's number for the millionth time when she got home from the airport. She had enjoyed the week with her mother and sister, but each day she couldn't reach Alex increased her anxiety. There would be no reason she could imagine that would take this long for her phone to be out of order, and Kelly hadn't been able to reach her either. It was as if Alex had just dropped off the face of the earth. She headed directly to her apartment after feeding Buddy.

She knocked several times and waited ten minutes for Alex to answer the door, then went to Jennifer's and repeated the process. *Maybe they went to their father's in Plymouth.* She drove home to try to find him on the Internet, but first she sent an email to Alex, imploring her to at least let her know she was okay, even if she didn't want to talk. She spent an hour on whitepages.com looking at every single Reed over thirty in Plymouth with a male first name and checked her email five times. Nothing. Alex was gone.

She unpacked and started her laundry process, trying to imagine what reason Alex would have to disappear. It had felt like everything was going so well between them. Had she been wrong? She couldn't believe that to be true. Surely Alex had felt the way she had. Self-doubt assailed her. *But please let it be something between us, and she's not hurt or in danger somewhere.* She called Kelly while she was waiting for the dryer.

"Hi, Deb. How was Phoenix?"

"Great. I enjoyed my visit. Thanks for taking care of Shadow and Buddy for me while I was gone. How're things at work?"

"Everything's decorated for Christmas. Janis put up the tree in the lobby, and all the residents have garlands and lights on their doors. You're back on Monday, aren't you?"

"I'll be there. Thanks for helping me try to find Alex, by the way. I still haven't had any luck."

"That's weird."

"I know. I'm really worried about her, and I have no idea what to think." Debby sighed. "I'll see you Monday morning."

She disconnected the call and went to check the dryer. *Where are you, Alex?*

Chapter Twenty-five

Debby reread her notes on medication therapy management for the third time. The deadline to register for the certified geriatric pharmacist examination was fast approaching, but she found it difficult to concentrate. She missed Alex and was thoroughly perplexed as to where she could be. She didn't believe she would have left without telling her, but then, maybe she didn't know her as well as she thought. The only conclusion Debby could come up with was that something had happened to her. But what about Jennifer? How could they disappear? Too many episodes of *Criminal Minds* had her imagining a serial killer kidnapping them. She couldn't eat, and her sleep was filled with dreams of murky shadows and fear. Maybe she should call the police?

She put her study guide aside and looked up the local police station's number. The woman who answered politely explained that there was no record of anybody with the last name of Reed listed in their missing person's reports, but did she want to file one? Debby declined, unsure whether that was the right thing to do, and remembered Jennifer's boyfriend.

"Could I speak to Officer Phillip Donohue please?" She held her breath.

"We have a Detective Donohue out of this precinct, but he's out on assignment right now. Would you like to leave him a message?"

"Yes. Please tell him to call me, Debra Johnson, as soon as he can." Debby left her phone number with the woman and hung up. Maybe he would know what happened to Alex and Jennifer.

Debby stopped by Kelly's station on her way out and waited until she was done reviewing a chart with one of the other nurses.

"Hi, Deb. You heading home?"

"Yeah. I wanted to ask you something, if you have time."

"Sure. I'll buy you a cup of tea in the cafeteria. You look a little ragged."

They sat at one of the tables in the nearly empty room.

Kelly spoke first. "So, what's up?"

"I was hoping you might have more ideas as to how to find Alex."

Kelly regarded her for a minute. "She's pretty important to you, isn't she?"

"Yeah. She is. I can't believe she would go away without letting me know." Debby took a deep breath and expelled it slowly. "Her sister hasn't answered her door, either. I feel like something is really wrong."

"Okay. So what do we know for sure? The three of us were at the Big Drug dinner event. Was that the last time you saw her?"

"Yes. I took her home and we kissed good night, then I left. I talked to her Sunday and told her I'd call when I got back from Mom's. That's the last time I talked to her."

"I don't want you to take this the wrong way, but do you think there could be any chance she doesn't want to see you?" Kelly rested her hand gently on her arm.

"No...I...no! We were both looking forward to seeing each other again." Debby reviewed their last conversation and came up with nothing to indicate Alex didn't want to see her again. "Believe me, I've asked myself that question over and over again. But everything was really great. Maybe, if her sister hadn't vanished too, I might look at that more seriously, but...no. Something is wrong."

"Then we'll have to figure something out." Kelly looked thoughtful. "Let's check with Janis and see if Alex left an emergency contact on file with her."

"Good idea." Debby brightened. "She had to leave early today. I'll talk to her tomorrow."

She went home feeling a tiny ray of hope. *Please be okay.*

❖

"Come on, Buddy. You liked this food yesterday." Debby dumped the uneaten cat food in the wastebasket and opened a new can. "This is it. It's all you're getting."

Buddy sat next to his bowl, looked at the fresh food, then at her, then turned and walked away.

"Suit yourself." Despite her warning, she filled another bowl with kibble and set a kitty treat next to it. "There. You go eat whenever you feel like it."

Debby dropped onto her couch, called the number she had gotten from Janis for Alex's sister, and listened to the pleasant voice informing her that the number she had reached was no longer in service. "Now what, Buddy?"

Buddy had finished his food and sat next to her, purring and cleaning his stretched out left hind leg.

She made herself a cup of tea and returned to the couch to consider her options. Kelly had suggested that Alex had left by choice, but that made no sense. They had shared a heated kiss good night after dinner less than two weeks ago, and Alex hadn't said anything about feeling like things weren't good between them. She considered her list tucked away in a drawer. She hadn't thought of it for weeks, and she wasn't sure that was a good thing now. Maybe she should have kept closer track when she first started having feelings beyond friendship for Alex. She'd known there were things Alex wouldn't share, and that had set off alarm bells. Maybe she shouldn't have been so quick to silence them.

Somehow, Alex had managed to get past her defenses and loosen a few of the bricks in her wall. The words she had written years ago replayed in her mind.

Must be open and honest and feel about me the same way I feel about her, and willingly show it. Must feel her love, not just hear the words. Her actions must match her words.

She lifted her cup so Buddy could crawl onto her lap. "She's never told me she loves me. Maybe I've been stupid and dropped my guard. I guess I'll go back to her apartment one more time and see what I can find out. Maybe I should file a missing person's report after all." Maybe this had something to do with the things in her life she couldn't talk about.

She turned on her TV to the local news station and listened to the problems of the police, the homeless, and the city. She watched the traffic and weather before switching it off. She had to deal with her own worries. *Where are you, Alex?*

❖

"What's going on?" Alex, Jennifer, and their father all spoke at the same time as Joe walked into the kitchen. They'd been cooped up in the house for a week together, and everyone was getting crabby.

"Give me a minute, please." He hung his coat on a hook on the wall and traded his boots for loafers after he rubbed his gloveless hands together. "Let me get a cup of hot chocolate and we'll sit at the table and talk."

Alex watched the snow blowing past the drafty window. *Maybe we'll get to go back to Florida. Not without Debby.*

Joe sat at the table and took a deep breath. "Okay. Here's all I know, and it's not much more than before. The FBI knows that your guy Miguel Martinez is involved with the drugs in the warehouse, but they don't have enough evidence to convict him yet. They haven't heard anything more from their undercover agent, and right now Miguel looks squeaky clean. He's even held fundraisers at his house for a couple of state senators, so it sounds like he's got a few in his pocket. I'm afraid we'll have to keep you all here until we have proof that you're not in danger."

"So does this FBI undercover agent have information that will put Miguel Martinez away for life?" Alex wondered what Joe wasn't telling them. There had to be something besides speculation that caused the marshals to sequester them.

"I hope so, kiddo." Joe drank his hot chocolate.

Alex wished she had brought a bottle of wine. "Even if he's head of this thing, he doesn't know who we were. He only knows me as Alex from the Hyatt."

"The fact that he knows you at all is worrisome. If he wasn't part of the La Familia offshoot, I wouldn't worry, but he is, and he has so many eyes and ears in the community that I can't take a chance. You were even asked to go to his house."

"But, so what if he's part of that cartel? You've erased us from the world. He can't know who Dad was or what happened, can he? What exactly did this undercover agent tell you, so far?"

Joe shifted in his chair and sat quietly for a moment as if deliberating how much to say. "Miguel Martinez's uncle was one of the guys caught on the fringes of your dad's testimony. He was sent down and died in prison from a heart attack. Miguel blames the 'snitch' who put him away for his death and has vowed revenge. We don't know exactly what Miguel knows, or if the drugs are the only reason he's in Michigan. The agent said that he overheard one of the goons tell Martinez about a guy who told him 'there's a way out of the drug gang' and that it was via being a snitch. We're sure Martinez knows that the man who put his uncle away went into WITSEC. What we don't know yet is if the goon told Martinez who the guy is. But based on his interest in you, it seems likely."

"But you said you don't know what Miguel knows for sure, so why aren't we safe?"

"You are safe. Here. I won't take any chances until we find out who this goon is and if he's talking about your dad."

"Joe, there's no way he can know who Dad is now. Who would tell him?" Alex began pacing.

"I understand what you're saying, Alex, and you're right, but I want you all here until I know for sure. It's entirely possible he saw pictures of your dad and you girls from the trial. If he tracked you down somehow, he knew the moment he saw you."

"I almost forgot about his grandmother." Alex pulled out her chair and plopped into it. "She's in the nursing home where Debby works. Maybe that's why he's in Michigan. Maybe it has nothing to do with us." Hope flickered in her belly.

"I'll check into the grandmother, but I really believe he's here because of the drugs. Maybe it was coincidental he found you at the same time he moved his operation. But it doesn't seem likely."

"Are we supposed to just sit here and wait? It's almost Christmas, and Phil told me he had something special planned." Jennifer stood and paced while running her hand through her hair. Her eyes were puffy from all the crying she'd been doing.

Alex glanced at her father, who sat looking shell-shocked. "Hey, Dad. It'll be okay." She placed her hand over his trembling ones clenched on the table.

"I'm so sorry. This is all my fault. I think it's Willy. I think he's the goon." He lowered his head and shook as the tears fell.

"What do you mean?" Joe asked.

Her dad wiped his eyes with his sleeve. "Willy's in my NA group and my friend. At least, I thought he was my friend." He took a deep breath before continuing. "He was always talking about getting out and staying clean. I thought he was talking about getting out of NA, not some cartel. He doesn't believe it's a program for life. I tried to tell him that there was a way out, meaning a way out of the life of drugs overall, and he probably thought I meant out of the cartel. He must have said something to Martinez about me." He lowered his head and groaned. "Oh my God. I told him my last name, when I told him I'd put some drug dealers away. But I never told him my full name. I never said a word about *before*. Honest. But if he told, then Martinez might suppose I'm the snitch." He covered his ears with his hands and shook his head.

Jennifer glared at him and huffed as she escaped to her bedroom. Alex didn't follow her. She had pushed aside her own anger and resentment at their situation long enough to know how it could eat away at her, and it was important for Jennifer to have her feelings.

"Why would Willy tell Martinez anything about a friend in NA, anyway? What does this mean, Joe?" Alex's throat tightened.

"Who knows? Maybe Willy knows he's after revenge for his uncle and is trying to get on his good side. I'm only concerned that he knows your name and where you live. I'm afraid we'll have to relocate you all again." Joe finished his hot chocolate and rinsed out his cup.

"What? You think you'll have to move us again?" Alex rose and stood face-to-face with Joe.

"I don't see an alternative right now, kiddo. If he knows your last name, then we need to get you far, far away from him."

"Damn it, Joe. We have lives here now. I don't want to go anywhere." She began pacing where Jen had left off.

"Let's all just calm down. It's my job to keep you safe, and I'll continue to do that by whatever means necessary. Now, I'm going to my office to see if I can find out anything more." Joe put his coat and boots back on and slipped on a pair of gloves from his pockets. "Oh. I almost forgot." He pulled out a small, prepaid mobile burner phone from his pocket. "This is to be used only for emergencies and calling me. Understand?" He handed Alex the flip phone. "I've programmed in my number."

"Thank you." Alex pocketed the phone and contemplated how to get away with using it to call Debby, and what to say if she did. She had no way of knowing if or when they would be moved, but she figured it wouldn't be long. She couldn't leave without saying good-bye. That she knew for sure.

❖

"Thanks for coming with me, Kelly." Debby pulled into the parking lot that she still considered Alex's.

"No problem. I'm nosey enough to want to know what's going on." Kelly grinned and stepped out of the car.

Snow piles surrounded them as they traversed the plowed section of the walkway toward the manager's office.

"Good morning." A short Asian woman sat behind an old metal desk. "Can I help you with something?"

"Yes. I'm looking for a woman who lives in one of your buildings. Her name is Alex Reed." Debby watched the woman's eyes narrow as she stood and switched off her computer screen.

"Who are you and why are you asking?"

"My name is Debra Johnson, and Alex is a friend of mine. I haven't been able to get in touch with her for a few weeks, and I'm incredibly worried about her, so I thought I'd see if you could help me."

"I'm not allowed to let anyone know who lives here. If she's your friend, you should know where she is." The woman stood taller and leaned her fingertips on the desk as she looked back and forth between them. "And who is this?" She pointed to Kelly with her chin.

"Another friend of mine who's trying to help me find Alex. Listen, she lives in apartment fifty-two, in the first building on the right at the entrance. Could you please just check on her and make sure she's all right? Just make sure she's not in there, hurt or sick?"

The woman seemed to soften at the implication that she might have a sick or dead woman in one of her units. She sat and turned her computer screen back on. She clicked a few keys on her keyboard and scrolled for a minute. "Alexandra Reed's lease was terminated on the first of December. She no longer lives here. That's all I can tell you, Debra Johnson." She turned off her computer screen again and sat back in her swivel desk chair.

"She has a sister I can't find either. Apartment number eighty-nine, in the same building." Debby tried to look hopeful as she smiled at the woman.

The woman sighed and repeated the computer process. "The lease has been terminated for whoever was in that apartment, too." She turned off the monitor and the computer this time. Apparently, she wasn't getting any more information from this woman, and Alex was gone.

You just up and left me. Why would you do that?

CHAPTER TWENTY-SIX

Debby circled the Twelve Oaks Mall parking lot three times before finding a spot. She loved Christmas, but hated shopping. She repositioned her scarf and trudged toward the building, ignoring the way the lights on the trees sparkled and reflected on the snow. Light flurries danced across the tops of cars and converged on the ground to form a white blanket over the blacktop. She left a trail as she dragged her feet through the snow, her heart as heavy as her boots.

She and Alex had planned to Christmas shop together. They had discovered their shared enjoyment of people watching and were going to sit on the couches inside the center court and watch as they scurried back and forth. She had wrapped Alex's gift, a signed hard cover copy of her favorite romance novel, in red and green paper, with gold horses on the ribbon. She sighed in resignation. Alex was gone and she didn't know if she would ever be back. She had lost her heart once again to a woman who had left her, only this time she couldn't figure out why. She wondered if the not knowing was worse than having an actual reason.

Debby entered the mall and started toward the center when her phone rang. She checked the readout. *Unknown caller.* She slid her phone back in her pocket unanswered and continued to the seating area. She removed her gloves, unbuttoned her coat, and loosened her scarf before settling onto one of the couches. She could see the entrance from her vantage point and sat back to imagine Alex sitting next to her, commenting on the tall man with a ball cap holding the door for a woman wearing a Santa hat. Normal people, doing normal things, preparing for the holidays. She vowed to return to her normal life without Alex. Her phone chimed again and she ignored it. She wasn't expecting anybody to call, and she was due back at work in half an hour. She didn't want to waste time talking to someone when she could be sitting here, thinking of Alex. She turned toward the huge evergreen towering over the children playing on the carpeted area underneath. The lights and ornaments mocked her with their insinuation of joy to the world. She watched a young woman pushing an elderly woman in a wheelchair, stopping every few feet to point out the multitude of lights, ribbons, and garlands strung on the walls and ceiling.

Debby slipped back into her coat and gloves and headed to the exit. She didn't have it in her to do any shopping after all. Nothing was the same without Alex to do it with. Her phone rang again, and this time she yanked off a glove and pulled it out of her pocket. *Unknown caller.* Annoyed, she decided to answer it anyway.

"Hello."

"Debby. It's Alex. I can't talk long, but please meet me at the mall tomorrow night at seven. I'm so sorry, but I'll explain then. I hope I find you there."

"Alex…hello…Alex?" Debby held the phone to her ear waiting, but Alex was gone.

She stood stunned in the path of shoppers flowing around her. Alex had called and wanted to see her. She'd been whispering, her voice tight and anxious. *What the hell is going on?* She went back to work, the anticipation of seeing Alex again warring with the confusion of not knowing what kind of trouble Alex was in. After hearing her voice, Debby knew she'd been right. Something was seriously wrong.

❖

Alex sat on the edge of her bed for a minute to review her plan. She had given Joe a grocery list for their Christmas dinner, and he would be back soon. He planned to leave by noon to spend Christmas with his family, and then be back before the first of the year to relocate them. She had paid close attention when Joe brought her to the safe house, so she knew it was within walking distance of the mall, and that was enough for now.

She composed a note for Joe to make sure he knew that neither Jennifer nor her father had any knowledge of her plans and placed it on her pillow. Then she pulled out the gift she had planned to give Debby on Christmas Day. Jaylin had emailed her a photo of the two of them dancing at Dana and Maria's wedding, so she'd had it printed and framed. The picture reminded her of Debby's solid presence in her paranoid life and of how grounded and safe she had felt in her arms. Her hands shook as she wrapped the photo in the red foil paper she had tossed into her suitcase and positioned a white bow on it. Then she sat to meditate and build the courage to tell Debby how she felt. She couldn't imagine her life without Debby in it, but she had no idea how to make that happen. Her gut clenched at the realization she'd probably be relocated again soon and have to start a new life without her, whether she wanted to or not.

"Hey, sis. You want to play Scrabble with us till Joe gets here?" Jennifer called from the kitchen.

"Be right there." Alex tucked the package under her bed and went to join her father and sister.

Joe returned with a huge turkey, a small ham, and several bags of staples.

"Thanks, Joe." Alex began the task of putting everything away. "Would you like a cup of hot chocolate before you go?"

"No, thanks. My wife's waiting for me to bring home my kid's bicycle. He's been asking for a two-wheeler since the summer. You guys have a good day tomorrow, and call if you need anything. You know I'm always here for you, don't you?"

"Sure, Joe." Jennifer stood and hugged him.

Her father shook his hand and wished him a merry Christmas while Alex sucked in her gut to silence her angry reply before hugging him good-bye. He got to leave, go back to his normal life with his kid and his bicycle and his wife, while they were stuck in this dour little house, their lives uprooted again, their next destination unknown. *It's not his fault.*

Alex sat at the table after he'd left, measuring her words. "I have to go somewhere tonight." She looked first at Jennifer, then her father. "I'll be back before nine."

Jennifer tilted her head and glared at her but didn't ask any questions. "You better be."

Her father just shrugged, looking like the lost soul he was. "Be careful, honey."

Alex packed Debby's gift and a bottle of water in a plastic grocery bag and headed out the door.

Alex hadn't specified where to meet at the mall, so Debby stood by the entrance, against a wall. The snow flurries had turned into a heavier snow shower, so she pulled up her hood. She checked her watch for the third time. Six fifty-seven p.m. She clasped Alex's gift under her arm and peered through the snowflakes. Her heart rate increased as she watched a figure huddled in a down coat, hood, gloves, and Eskimo boots, carrying a plastic grocery bag, trek toward her. *Alex.* Debby stepped away from the wall and walked toward her, meeting her before she reached the doors.

"Hey. I'm glad you came." Alex's eyes crinkled above the scarf covering her face.

She was smiling, but Debby could see the tension and fear in her eyes. "I'm glad you called me." Debby reached to touch her. To make sure she was really there.

"Can we sit in your car for a bit?"

"Of course. Wouldn't you rather go inside the mall?"

"Yes, but your car is more private."

Alex put her arm through hers as they walked. She opened the passenger door for her and rushed to the other side. They put down their hoods and took off their gloves, and Debby started the engine and turned up the heater.

"So, tell me what's going on?" She gently stroked Alex's cheek. She needed to feel her skin. She wanted to smooth away the deep worry lines around Alex's eyes. She looked so tired.

"Before I explain, I want to give you this. You may not want it after I'm done." Alex withdrew the wrapped gift from her bag and handed it to her.

Debby looked at the gift in her hand, wondering what could possibly be so bad that she wouldn't want it. Her stomach turned in dread. She passed Alex's gift to her. "This is for you."

Alex took the gift and clenched it to her body. "Thank you." Tears pooled in her eyes and spilled down her rosy cheeks.

Debby's chest constricted and she took Alex's hands in hers and kissed them. "Please don't cry, baby. What's going on?"

Alex took a deep breath and began to speak. "I have something important to tell you, but first, I need you to understand that I would've told you this a long time ago if I'd have known this would happen."

"What happened? What is it?" Debby couldn't help from interrupting. Alex was scaring her.

"Have you ever heard of the WITSEC program?"

"WITSEC, as in witness protection?"

"Yes." Alex wiped her eyes and unzipped her coat. "About three years ago, my sister, my father, and I entered the program. I can't give you all the details, I'm not even supposed to be telling you this much, but our lives were in danger, so the U.S. Marshal Service changed our names and relocated us to Northville."

Debby stared at her, uncomprehending for a moment. "Wow. So…who are you?"

"God, Debby. I wish I could tell you, but it isn't only my life I need to worry about. My sister would be in danger, too. Please believe me when I say I've hated not being truthful with you."

"Wow." Debby let go of Alex's hands and stared at her. *It was all a lie. She's a lie.*

"All I can say is I'm sorry. I never meant to mislead you. I can't describe how difficult it is to be someone without a past. Someone I don't even know." Alex twisted her gloves and tossed them on to the dash. A soft sob escaped her and she huddled into herself.

Instantly, her own anger vanished. Those were old fears, not things she needed to put onto Alex. Debby clasped her hand and rubbed her thumb over her knuckles. Alex might not be her real name, but was that so important? "Where have you been for a month?"

"That's what I wanted to tell you. The deputy marshal assigned to protect us believes we may be in danger. He thinks we need to relocate again." Alex sat up and turned to face her. "I won't leave without you, Debby. I love you, and I don't ever want to be away from you. I don't know what to do."

Debby blinked away her own tears and leaned to kiss Alex. "I love you, too. But won't you be in danger if you stay?"

"Maybe. Probably. I don't know right now, but Joe thinks so."

"Your uncle Joe is a marshal?"

"Oh, crap. Please don't tell anybody." Alex looked frightened.

"I won't. I promise."

"At this point, I don't know anything for certain, but if I disappear, know that I'll find you again. Somehow." Alex looked at her watch. "I have to get back. Joe doesn't know I'm here, and I don't want Jen and Dad to get into trouble if he found out. I miss you." Alex placed her hand on her cheek and gently glided her lips on hers.

Debby broke their connections and searched Alex's eyes, seeing her honest plea. "I miss you, too. But how do I get in touch with you?"

Alex blew out a breath. "You can't. I'll use the same phone if I can and call you as soon as I know anything definite. Joe's talking like we may have to go by the first of the year."

"That's only a week away."

"I know." Alex covered her face with her hands.

"What if I went with you?"

Alex looked up into her eyes. "I couldn't ask that of you. You have no idea what it's like to have to pretend to be someone besides who you've been your whole life. You'd have to change your name and leave your friends and family behind and never speak to them again." Alex glanced at the clock in the car. "I have to go. I love you." Alex slid on her gloves and stepped out of the car, taking a piece of her heart with her.

Debby watched Alex tramp away through the snow and wondered if she would ever see her again. She had a huge decision to make. She drove home on autopilot, barely aware of the traffic or snow. She'd promised herself she'd never be with anyone who kept secrets again. It turned out, Alex was almost entirely a secret. What did that mean?

❖

Debby placed the framed picture from Alex on her dresser and hurried out to take care of Shadow before returning to her warm bedroom. She dressed in her nightshirt and lay on her bed, examining her feelings. She knew she loved Alex and wanted to see who they could be as a couple, but moving away with her seemed more like a detention than a romantic escape, if it was even possible. She put on a robe, brought her laptop to her bed, and propped herself up with pillows. Then she began her research on WITSEC.

An hour later, she knew more than she had, but less than she wanted. Not only would they have to move and change their names, they would never be able to talk about or return home. Her family could never know where she went, but surely the marshals would let her say good-bye to them. Then what? Her idea of a relationship was finding someone to love who was willing to meld and share their life with her. Moving with Alex meant giving up who she was, everything she had. She shut off her computer and stood to stretch her back.

The picture of them holding each other flooded her with emotions, a few of which she wanted to ignore, but couldn't. It was the moment she had begun to fall in love with Alex. An ache in her belly signaled her longing for Alex even now, and surprisingly, she didn't want it to go away. But giving up everything she knew seemed too great a price to pay for love. Should she even put a price on love, though? She kept both sides of the argument going in her head, wanting to stay safe and wanting Alex at the same time. *Compromising for the sake of the one you love is different from giving up who you are.* She shook her head. *Who does the dishes or the cooking, and who takes out the garbage, is compromise. Leaving your home and family forever…that's not just compromise. That's…sacrifice.*

Hadn't she used her list as a device to protect her heart and avoid commitment for all these years? The price of that was avoiding love as well, and remembering the feeling of holding Alex in her arms made all that seem tragic. Alex had said she'd find her, that she wanted her, and she knew in her heart that she felt the same way, but she could see no way of that happening. She rested her head on her pillow and willed sleep to calm her restless mind and hoped for dreams that would bring a solution.

CHAPTER TWENTY-SEVEN

Y ou're not going to tell me where you went Wednesday, are
you?"

"No, I'm not, Jennifer. If you don't know, you can't get in
trouble." Alex smiled and placed her new hard covered novel on her
dresser, avoiding Jen's glare.

"Okay. I think I know anyway. I was supposed to go to dinner
with Phil last night. I think he was planning to give me a ring. I'd
probably be engaged today, instead of sequestered who knows where
waiting for information about a drug bust that may not happen."
Jennifer plopped into a chair at the kitchen table and rested her chin
on her hands. "I hate this." She dropped her hands and rested her
forehead on her arms.

"Me, too, Jen." Alex sat next to her and rubbed her back with
one hand.

"Is everyone all right in here?" Her father stood in the narrow
hallway in his pajamas and robe.

"We're fine. Come on in and have some breakfast." Alex stood
and pulled a large frying pan out of the cupboard. "Bacon and eggs
with toast for everybody?"

"Sounds great. Thanks, honey. Merry Christmas, by the way."
He poured three cups of coffee as he spoke and set them on the table.

"Merry fucking Christmas," Jennifer mumbled under her breath
and took a drink of coffee.

"I'm glad you made it back safely the other night, Alex." Her
father sipped his coffee and looked at her speculatively without
asking anything further.

"Thanks, Dad. Merry Christmas to you, too." She leaned and kissed his stubbled cheek. She hadn't noticed how gray he had gotten over the past two years. This situation had taken a toll on them all, and it had the potential to get worse.

Alex turned the bacon sizzling in the pan and wished she were having Christmas morning breakfast with Debby. She had told Debby she loved her, and finding out that she felt the same way made this situation much harder. Now she had a decision to make. She could leave WITSEC, but she wasn't sure how that would affect her father and sister. She needed to talk to Joe and find out if there were any other options.

Debby pulled the ham out of the oven to cool. Her brother, Matt, and his wife, Valerie, sat in the living room waiting. They had left her an unusual message that they wanted to see her for Christmas, so she had invited them over for dinner.

"Ham's done and the potatoes will be soon." She sat next to Valerie on the couch.

"It smells great, sis. We didn't mean to invite ourselves over for dinner, but thanks." Her brother grinned.

He looked happier than he had in a long time. "Of course you'd come to dinner. I wish Mom could be here, too, but I had a nice visit with her, sis, and the kids at Thanksgiving. We missed you there. In fact, I've missed you both this year." Debby repressed tears at the thought of never seeing her brother again.

"We'll make it out there in May for Mother's Day. I've been working with a therapist who's going to hook me up with a psychiatric service dog. We have some work to do yet, but I'm looking forward to it. I'm sure I'll be more comfortable traveling."

Debby glanced at Valerie and she practically beamed. "That's great, Matt. Let me know how it works out." She thought of Alex and Abby and their bond. "I have a friend who brings her dog to the nursing home where I work, and the residents love her. I think a service dog would be great for you."

"We have other news, too." Matt looked at his wife and they both grinned. "We're planning a baby. As soon as I've finished a year of this therapy, we're going to start a family."

Debby hugged them both. "I'm so happy for you guys, and I'll be an aunt."

Debby wondered if Alex would like the idea of being an aunt, but that thought only managed to remind her of her dilemma. Could she leave and never meet her brother's baby? Could she give up her family, her friends, her career?

"Let's eat." Matt pulled out a chair for Valerie and helped Debby serve the salad and potatoes.

"So, what's new in your life?" Matt asked.

Debby took a bite of ham to stall. "I started my new job at the nursing home a few months ago, and I've registered for the Geriatric Pharmacist exam." She wondered if she could still take the exam if she left with Alex. She'd need to work somewhere, right? But then, the license wouldn't be in her name...the pitfalls were overwhelming.

"Cool. You must like working with the old folks." Matt's smirk indicated his joking.

"I don't have that much interaction with them. I just make sure all their medications are correct and available."

"No one special in your life?" Valerie asked.

"Actually, there is."

Matt looked up and stopped eating. "Really?"

"Her name is Alex, and we've been dating for a few weeks. I'm not sure where it's going, but we're trying." She took a forkful of potatoes.

"Well, good. I was hoping you'd get over that bitch, Evelyn, and move on."

Debby smiled. Her brother was like their mom in his directness. She would miss him if she left. She'd miss them all. *A niece or nephew I'd never know...*

Matt and Valerie left before dark, and Debby was still cleaning up, thoughts a whirlwind of confusion, when her phone rang. *Unknown caller.*

"Hello?"

"Hi, Debby. It's Alex. Would you be able to meet me at that hotel right next to the mall tonight?" Alex's voice was muffled, as if she were standing in a closet.

"What time?"

"Seven again?"

"I'll be there. Be careful." Debby put her phone away and fed Buddy and Shadow before heading to the shower. She might not follow Alex into her life in the shadows, but she'd damn well take any last minutes of time she could have with her.

❖

Alex was ready to leave, with her down coat, mittens, and boots on when Jennifer poked her head out of her room.

"Are you leaving again?"

"I won't be long, honest. I have to do this, Jen." Alex hoped her voice relayed the importance of her plea.

"Here." Jennifer handed her a small sealed envelope with Phillip's name printed on it. "Please see if Debby can get this to him. Please, Alex."

Jennifer looked so distraught that Alex put the envelope in her pocket, nodded, and slipped out the door. Giving Phil, who could be in Martinez's employ, a letter was probably so out of bounds as to be stupid. She'd have to think about what to do about it.

"I wasn't sure you'd come." Alex snuggled close to Debby as they sat on the couch of a fourth-story room overlooking the mall parking lot. "And this room is fantastic. Thanks for reserving it. I had to see you, and I wanted a safe place warmer than your car." She nestled closer, sliding her arm behind her and resting her head on her shoulder.

"You sounded so lost on the phone. Did something happen?" Debby kissed the top of her head.

"Not anything new. I'm still waiting for Joe to get back to us with more information. I'm not sure what to do."

"What time do you have to be back?" Debby placed a light kiss on her lips.

"Jennifer and Dad will worry if I'm gone too long." Alex turned and pulled Debby into a searing kiss.

They shifted on the couch to lie side by side facing each other, and Alex slid a leg over Debby and rolled on top of her. "God, you feel good." Debby's voice caught as she spoke and slid her hands under Alex's sweatshirt.

"So do you." She cradled her face in her hands and kissed her until all thoughts of WITSEC fled. She pulled a breath away and whispered, "Take me to bed."

Debby kissed her, then took her hand and led her to bed. They fell sideways onto it, their arms and legs entwined. Alex rolled to her back, pulling Debby on top of her. Her core clenched with need as she pushed her hips into Debby's and kissed her with insatiable hunger. Debby broke their kiss and rolled to her side. She slipped her hand under Alex's sweatshirt, drawing tiny circles on her belly toward her bra. Alex sat up and pulled her sweatshirt over her head and removed her bra. Debby pushed her down on the bed and took turns with each nipple, flicking her tongue over them, sending currents of need pulsing along her nerves to her throbbing clit.

"I could come just from this." Alex pulled Debby's head against her breast.

Debby drew away and kissed the hollow of her neck. "Not yet, baby." She pulled off her sweatshirt and bra and stepped out of her jeans and underwear.

Alex held her breath, watching her expose herself. *So beautiful.* She shimmied out of her jeans and panties and held her arms open, beckoning. Debby answered her call and pulled her into her arms. Their naked bodies fit together seamlessly. Two sculptures molded as one. Alex pushed Debby to her back and stroked the soft skin on her belly before inching her hand lower to skim her fingers over her silky pubic hair. "I love you, you know." She spoke quietly as she continued her exploration.

"I love you, too."

Debby's words and her erratic breathing further ignited her burning desire. She slid her fingers through slippery folds to squeeze her rigid clit. Debby thrust her hips against her hand and reached for her.

"Come with me." Her words squeaked out between broken moans. She skimmed the inside of Alex's thigh with her fingers and cupped her sex as she teased her opening with her middle finger.

"Oh, God, yes." Alex threw her head back and pushed her pussy against Debby's hand, forcing her finger inside at the same time as she slid hers into Debby. They remained joined, writhing in pleasure, their orgasms overtaking them simultaneously.

Alex shifted to snuggle further into Debby's embrace, ignoring the twinge of fear. She laid her head on her chest, reveling in the sound of her solid heartbeat. She never wanted to leave, but she couldn't stay.

"I hear the wheels turning." Debby turned on her side to face her. She kissed her and stroked her cheek. "Regrets?"

"No, babe. No regrets. I just wish I were free to stay here in your arms forever." She caressed her ass and back as she spoke. "I'm glad we didn't wait."

"Me, too. You have to go back now, don't you?" Debby pulled her against her and nuzzled her neck.

"Yeah, pretty soon." She rose to lean on one elbow and look down at Debby. "You know I didn't plan this, don't you? I would never want you to think I'm trying to convince you to leave with me by sleeping with you."

Debby grinned. "No, baby. I know you didn't plan this, but I did. Whatever the future brings, I want you to know that I love you, and I needed to show you how much." Debby pulled her on top of her and kissed her.

They dressed in silence, each moment allowing trickles of foreboding to creep into Alex's heart.

"Before I leave I have to ask you for a favor." Alex handed Jennifer's envelope to Debby. "Please try to get this to Phillip. I guess he and Jen were planning to get married, and…well, you know." If Phil was working for Martinez, he was still a cop, and hopefully not a killer. If Martinez already knew their names, Joe was going to relocate them again regardless of what was in the letter. If Phil was working undercover, maybe this would give him a chance to know Jennifer was safe. She sighed and slid her feet into her boots. Either way, she would probably be gone very soon.

"I'll do my best. I've left a message at the precinct for him to call me, but I'll go over there and leave this with them."

"You called him?" Alex sat on the edge of the bed waiting for an answer.

"I called the police looking for you and asked about him. They told me he was out on assignment, and he never called me back."

"I don't suppose they gave you any more information?"

"No. Sorry, love."

"Well, thanks. I'll at least have that much to tell Jen."

"Are there any other options for this protection thing? What if you moved in with me? It would change your address and Jennifer and your dad could move, too. Would that be enough?" Debby's hopeful look tugged at her heart.

"God, I wish it were that simple, but it doesn't work that way. We have a choice to stay, or to leave the program and lose their protection, and I might be willing to, but I couldn't ask Jen and Dad to put their lives in danger. I hope to know more as soon as Joe gets back. I'll make a decision then. Remember that I love you." She rested her fingers lightly on Debby's cheek as they locked gazes, and she prayed it wasn't the last time she'd see her. "I've got to go." She put on her coat, and Debby pulled her firmly against her body and kissed her.

Alex knew it was a kiss of love, but she also knew that there could be no guarantees. She hoped it wasn't a kiss good-bye.

CHAPTER TWENTY-EIGHT

D id you give her the note?" Jennifer was sitting at the kitchen table when Alex returned close to midnight.

"Yes, Jen. She'll get it to him if she can. She talked to the people at his station and they told her he was on assignment. She left a message for him to call her, but she hasn't heard anything back so far."

"This is awful, Alex. Joe can't keep us here like this, can he?" Jennifer stood to pace. "We're not the bad guys. We shouldn't be... imprisoned, for fuck's sake."

"I know. Sit and I'll make us a cup of tea." Alex got cups and tea bags out of the cupboard and set them on the counter. "Joe said we *might* be in danger. We only need to stick it out until he gets back, then we'll know more."

"What's going on out here?" Their father came out of his room and sat at the table.

"I'm making tea. Want a cup?" Alex swung a tea bag in the air.

"Sure. Thanks, honey. So what's all the commotion about?"

"I need to get in touch with Phil. This is just stupid, that we have to sit here and wait for Joe to decide if we're going to have a life. I've probably lost the best job I've ever had, and maybe the best guy I've ever dated. I want out of this whole thing. I'd rather take my chances with some drug lord than live like this." Jennifer marched to her bedroom and slammed the door.

Alex had to do something. Her heart ached for Jennifer, and she certainly could relate to her frustration. "I'll be right back, Dad." She went to her room and knocked softly. "Hey, Jen? I have something I want to tell you."

Jennifer opened her door her eyes puffy and bloodshot. "What?"

Alex closed the door behind her. "I have something I need to tell you about Phil." Alex sat next to Jennifer on her bed. "I think he might be a dirty cop." She took Jennifer's hands in hers. "I saw him with Martinez at the state fair this year, and then again at a party at the Martinez house."

"When were you at his house?"

"He went to my boss and requested that I help with checking in his guests for a fundraiser, except it was more like a demand than a request. I went to see if I could find out more about Phil's involvement with him. I was worried about you. I overheard him and Martinez talking about some kind of shipment that Phil was in charge of. I'm so sorry, Jen, but I think he's on the take with Martinez."

Jennifer stared at Alex, pale and wide-eyed. "Now I'm scared."

"Joe will protect us, Jen, and I don't think Phil would intentionally hurt you. Even if he's a bad cop, he's still a cop, not a killer."

"You don't understand. I'm not scared for me. I'm scared for him. I think he might be the one who's been undercover with Martinez."

"What makes you think that?"

"When we first met, he told me that he'd just made detective and was being assigned to an undercover operation. He wanted to prepare me for the possibility of having to break dates at the last minute. The last time I talked to him, he said something about a warehouse full of drugs. It was only in passing when we were talking about the increased crime in the area." Jennifer sat on her bed gripping the edge.

"Okay. Let's wait to hear from Joe. You know he vets everyone we get involved with, so he probably already knows about Phil's involvement." Alex considered that Joe probably knew about Phil all along, but couldn't say anything.

Jennifer sighed and followed her out of the room. "I'll have a cup of that tea, too." They joined their father at the table.

"Everything okay?" her father asked.

"I hope so." Alex drank her tea as if it were four in the afternoon instead of the middle of the night.

"I'm sorry about all of this. If I could change it, I would." He rubbed his day-old growth of beard.

"I know you would. I'm hoping Joe is just being overly cautious." She didn't say anything else. She couldn't tell him it was okay, that it wasn't a big deal. It wasn't okay, and they all knew it.

"We can hope. God grant me the serenity." He took a drink of tea, looking sad and aged.

"We don't have a choice." Jennifer dunked her tea bag several times before tasting it.

"Here's to caution." Alex raised her teacup in a toast and they clinked cups. She hoped Phil was cautious if he was undercover with Martinez. Jennifer deserved happiness.

Debby sorted pills and reviewed her list of new prescriptions for possible drug interactions. She checked the daily resident list, hopeful it was the same as last week. She was told it was common for residents to pass away during the holidays. She supposed it was due to factors other than the cold weather. Many of their bed-ridden had no family and lived alone, with only memories of loved ones to sustain them. Depression was common among those folks, and she kept a close watch on their medication orders for serious interactions with any heart medications they might be taking. *Alone. If I follow Alex and anything happens to her, that's exactly where I'll be. Alone.* But then, what did that mean for Alex, who had to live this strange, volatile existence?

She poked at her salad while she waited for Kelly to join her for lunch. She had stopped at the police station on her way in to work to drop off Jennifer's note. The sergeant had assured her that Phil would get the note as soon as he was back from assignment, and she had unsuccessfully pressed him for more information. She wished she had a way to let Alex know. Memories of Alex and their few hours together warmed her heart as well as other parts of her body. She knew she couldn't let Alex go, but she wasn't sure she could ask her to risk staying. She didn't know what the threat was, but it was real to Alex. If she went with her, she knew Kristen would take good care of Shadow, but what about her family and her house? Could she just walk away? Her head spun with unanswerable questions.

"Hi, Deb." Kelly sat across from her at the cafeteria table. "Did you have a good Christmas?"

"Yes. Matt came over for dinner and we had a nice visit. How 'bout you?"

"It was great. My aunt and uncle invited me to their new place in Toledo. It's a gorgeous Tudor, facing the Maumee River. They told me to come down anytime and bring a friend. I think you'd like it. We can sit on their deck, have a few beers, and relax." Kelly took a drink of water. "Have you had any luck finding Alex?"

Debby considered how much to disclose. "No. I suppose I'll just have to wait to see if she contacts me." She poked at her salad again and took a small bite. Alex trusted her with a secret she literally couldn't tell anyone else in the world. She wouldn't betray that, even if she really could use someone else to talk to.

"I hope she does, Deb. Hey, let's go to the club next Saturday. Celebrate the new year. I know it'll do me good to get out, and it'll take your mind off Alex."

"We'll see how the week goes." Debby was certain nothing would take her mind off Alex. *What on God's earth am I going to do?*

Debby, Janis, and Kelly sat in Janis's office, reviewing patients' charts on her laptop.

"It looks like Mr. Kline was the first patient to show signs of the infection and be diagnosed. He was seen by his doctor and prescribed antibiotics last Monday." Janis typed and scrolled to review the next chart without looking up. She turned to Debby and continued. "I spoke to the doctor and confirmed that Mr. Kline has done well with this type in the past." Janis continued through the logs checking notes on every resident diagnosed with the acute respiratory tract infection that started spreading through the nursing home a week ago.

"I'll work with the other pharmacists to keep an eye on drug interactions, but the doctors and nurses need to be vigilant in watching for adverse reactions. We don't need *C. diff* circulating through here." Debby made notes on a pad of paper.

"I agree with that. We dealt with that a few years ago and lost two residents." Kelly typed on a laptop as she spoke. "All our nurses know what to look out for, and I've scheduled them overtime. I plan to review our hygiene protocol this morning, and every resident will be evaluated by three different nurses daily."

"Good job, Kelly." Janis input the information from their meeting into her computer and looked up. "I'm concerned about Mrs. Martinez. She came in without a doctor, so her grandson agreed to have us assign her our staff physician. We don't have much of a medical history on her, but she's on heart medication. Please make sure you monitor her meds, Debby."

"No problem. We'll keep an eye on her."

Debby reviewed her notes from their meeting and updated her laptop with relevant information before making herself a cup of tea. Talking about Mrs. Martinez had reminded her of Alex, although she was never far from her thoughts. She knew Miguel's grandmother, and Alex knew Miguel. It was a small world. She wondered what Alex was doing in the safe house. They must have television, but probably no Internet, and a phone only for emergencies. She smiled sadly at the thought of being an emergency. She missed her.

She transferred all the nursing home's information she had on her laptop to the secure work computer and saved it on the backup drive, just in case she decided to disappear.

Four days later, Debby was finishing her patient drug review when commotion in the hall caught her attention. She looked out the door and saw Kelly rush past with two other nurses, the staff doctor, and the code team close behind. She finished her review and went to investigate.

"What's up, Kelly?" As soon as she spoke she realized she already knew. Someone had called a code blue on Mrs. Martinez. She watched the team work on the elderly woman for a few minutes before returning to the pharmacy.

She pulled up all the information she had on Fernanda Martinez, anticipating the inevitable inquiry. Whether she lived or not, there would be questions about her medications. She looked at all the data she had on her and closed her computer. The only issue she could find was the antibiotic prescribed for a respiratory tract infection. It looked like the correct broad-spectrum type, but there would have been no way to tell how it would interact with her heart medication. Nobody was at fault. She went back to work and awaited the outcome.

The call came before the end of the day and Debby was ready. She gathered her notes and laptop and went to Jan's office. Kelly looked drained, sitting at the table with a glass of water. She squeezed her shoulder as she slipped past her to take the seat next to her, among several of the other staff members.

"Thank you for coming." Janis stood at the head of the table, the sadness obvious on her face. "As you already know, we lost one of our residents today." She dropped into a chair. "Our crash team did an excellent job with their efforts to save her, but it wasn't to be. She died at 3:05 p.m. of sudden cardiac death. She'd been on a couple of different heart medications, as well as antibiotics lately." She sighed and poured herself a glass of water. After taking a drink she continued. "I don't believe there is any fault or blame to be assigned. Everyone did their best to try to save her. I'll call her grandson immediately to inform him of his grandmother's passing. Kelly will take care of contacting the funeral home. Thank you all again."

"Can I buy you dinner tonight?" Debby asked Kelly as she passed her.

"Thanks, Deb, but I think I'll just go home. See you tomorrow."

Debby went back to the pharmacy to close up and wondered if Alex was planning anything on New Year's Eve, and if she was even still in the state. The thought occurred to her she might never know.

CHAPTER TWENTY-NINE

"Come on, Abby. I'm not standing here all night waiting for you to find the right spot. Joe is due here any minute." Alex shivered as she followed Abby back and forth. It wouldn't be so bad being relocated somewhere warm. Abby finished, and she dragged her inside. She hated being out in the cold and dark these days, just waiting for someone to jump out of the shadows.

Alex, Jennifer, and their dad convened at the kitchen table with water and a pot of coffee to wait for Joe to arrive. Alex answered the door when he knocked.

"Hey, Joe. Come on in."

"Hi, all. I have a little new information, but I'm not sure it will save you from having to relocate again. Here's what I found out." Joe began speaking after filling his cup and taking a sip of hot coffee. "Miguel Martinez is definitely our bad guy. As you know, his uncle was one of the La Familia leftovers who were convicted, thanks to your father's testimony. He died in prison, and I'm not sure he wasn't assassinated. Anyway, he's dead, and apparently, they were very close. Miguel would love to avenge his death by finding the snitch that put him away. Your father. Because he probably knows your name, I want you to stay here for a while longer, before we actually relocate you. It could be we take him down and you don't have to leave."

Jennifer groaned and her father looked spooked.

"Only for a while?" Alex asked. She pushed aside the emerging hope.

"We'll see," Joe continued. "The problem is that the undercover agent was identified as law enforcement, so Martinez is planning to move the drugs. The agent has been sneaking back, though, and found out when the drugs are to be moved. The FBI is planning the raid for tomorrow night."

Jennifer turned ghost white. "Martinez knows he's a cop?"

"Yes. I'm going to be at my field office waiting for word starting tomorrow morning. I'll let you know anything I find out as soon as I can." Joe stood and pulled Jennifer into a hug. "I'm sorry, Jen. I know Phil is important to you."

"So, Phil *is* undercover in the Martinez gang." Alex began pacing.

"Yes. He's been gathering information about this warehouse drug distribution for months." Joe stepped away from Jennifer and sat at the table.

"What about Willy?" her dad asked.

"His name is Willard Simpson, and he's only been with this group since they set up in Michigan. It looks like he's small time and not part of the cartel. I'm sorry he got mixed up with this, because the FBI will shoot first and ask questions later after the raid."

"This is just great. Willy's a bad guy, and Phil is in danger because of him. They must have recognized each other on Thanksgiving. Just great. Thanks, Dad." Jennifer stomped to her room and closed the door.

"So, what happens after the raid, Joe?" Alex asked. She moved to rest her hand on her father's back.

"Well, since he's the last in the line of his family, if he's killed or they catch him with enough evidence to lock him up, then you can go back to your life here. If he gets away…" He shrugged slightly and looked at them apologetically. "But we'll deal with that if it happens."

He left, and the room was silent as she and her father considered his news.

Alex picked up the empty cups and put them in the sink, then sat across from her father. She couldn't imagine how devastated he was feeling.

"I'm sorry, honey," he said.

"It's okay, Dad. You couldn't have known who Willy was."

Joe had answered many of their questions, but Alex wanted to know the answer to the most important one. Could they really go home?

❖

Debby and Kelly dropped into the chairs in the cafeteria. "Whew. I think the worst is over." Kelly took a long drink of water.

"Yeah. You and your nurses did an excellent job of containing that infection so quickly."

"I'm sorry that we lost Mrs. Martinez, but she was the only one. Mr. Kline is doing well, and the couple who developed pneumonia, are doing much better. We can't let down our guard, yet, but this could've been much worse." Kelly bit into her sandwich, looking thoughtful. "Did you know Janis still hasn't gotten hold of the Martinez grandson?"

"Fernanda only died yesterday. He could be out of town for the holidays or something." Debby speared a piece of chicken off the top of her salad with her fork.

"Yeah. I guess he left the name of a funeral home and instructions for her body, but he hasn't shown up or returned messages. I would have thought he'd care that she died. His wife hasn't been around either. It's weird because they used to visit every day."

"They're newlyweds. Maybe they went on a honeymoon cruise or something." Debby sat back and took a sip of coffee.

"Maybe, but it's still weird. Anyway, I've got to get back to my reports. We have a ton of information to input into the computers. Have a good New Year's Eve. I'll see you Saturday. I'm off tomorrow."

Debby sat drinking her coffee and thinking about Alex. It had been a long week of keeping up with antibiotic medications. She was tired and still had half a day to go. She wondered if Alex was allowed to do anything tonight. She looked forward to a quiet night on the couch, watching the crystal ball drop in Times Square with Buddy, and a bowl of popcorn, though it would have been so much better to do it with Alex at her side. She went back to her desk to finish her workday and lost herself in the fantasy of what it would be like to start over in a new state, with a new name, and Alex. Indecision still roiled in her stomach, and she didn't have much time.

❖

Alex and Jennifer set the tiny TV on top of a box they had positioned on a table by the window. Alex fiddled with the rabbit ears until the picture cleared. Their plan was to watch the crowds in Times Square and toast in the New Year with a bottle of wine. Alex wished it were with Debby instead, and wondered what she was doing tonight. Was she going out to the bars with Kelly? Was she going over to Kristen's? The thought of the wonderfully normal, loving life Debby led made Alex's heart ache. She couldn't take her away from all that, not to live the life of chaos and uncertainty. They sat on the lumpy couch and put their feet up on milk crates. Abby curled up in her bed on the floor. The domestic scene would have felt normal, if they had been at home. One more day. Joe had come by to confirm the raid was the next day. Surely he'd be back to tell them they could go home.

Alex filled a plate with cheese and crackers and poured them each a glass of white wine.

"Here we are. The finest wine and hors d'oeuvres the government can buy." She set the plate on a flat area of the couch and handed Jennifer her wine.

"Do we have to wait till midnight to drink this?" Jennifer asked.

"Heck no." Alex took a swallow of hers and offered a toast. "To spending New Year's Eve in a safe house."

Jennifer groaned and finished her glass in two gulps. "It's a good thing we bought four bottles." She stood to refill her glass.

"Here." Alex finished hers and handed her empty glass to Jennifer for a refill. "It is a good thing."

They were making fun of people's outfits in Times Square, when Alex heard the chirping of their burn phone coming from the drawer in her bedroom. She stood unsteadily to retrieve it. Joe might have news.

Unknown caller.

She answered anyway. "Hello."

"Alex, it's me, Debby. I'm sorry to call you on this number, but I had to hear your voice."

Alex took the phone into the closet but still whispered. "I'm glad you did, love, but we can't talk long. I miss you."

"I miss you, too. Are you okay?"

"Yes. Fine. How did you get this number?" She realized it would be in Debby's phone from when she had called her. *And this is why I'd be a terrible spy.* "Never mind. It's in your phone, isn't it?"

"Yeah. I just thought of it today when Buddy and I were sitting on the couch missing you. I was worried Joe might have moved you already and I'd never see you again. So, what's your status? Are they moving you tomorrow?"

"God, I don't know for sure. Joe will let us know in the morning. Right now, Dad is in his room probably sleeping, and Jen and I are drinking wine and watching Times Square." Alex cringed at the normalcy of their conversation knowing that the situation was anything but normal.

"Me, too. Only not with wine. I'm having popcorn. Feel me kissing you at midnight, baby. And please call if you can. I don't want to lose you."

"Oh, I will. You feel my kisses, too, love. If I have to go, I swear I'll find you, somehow. I'll figure out a way, even if I have to leave the program." Alex stifled the threatening tears. She needed to cling to a sliver of hope. Her chest tightened as if her heart was being torn from her body.

"I want you safe. You do whatever Joe tells you to do. I've spent years denying myself love because of fear. I'm not afraid anymore, because I believe we were meant to be together. We'll find each other again. Somehow. I love you."

They disconnected the call and Alex's lightheadedness had nothing to do with wine.

Alex rolled over, swallowing against the queasiness in her belly and squeezing her eyes shut to lessen the throbbing in her head. She vowed never to drink wine again when the blare of the cell phone on the milk crate serving as her nightstand, seeped into her soggy mind. She grabbed it and sat up.

"Joe?" She used a flashlight to check her watch. Four fifteen.

"Yes. I'm at my office and can't leave for a while, so I need you guys to stay inside and absolutely no calls out with this phone. I'll call you when I know what's happening. Martinez has moved up the time of the drug move, so the FBI has initiated the raid. Keep away from the windows and keep them, and the doors, locked. I'll call before I come over, understand? Don't open the door to anyone."

"Yes. We'll be waiting for your call." Alex closed the phone and lay down to still her heart rate. *Today. It could happen today. We could be free, somewhat. Maybe.* She took some aspirin for her aching head and went to wake up her dad and Jen. She took Abby out quickly, staying as close to the house as she could, before darting back inside.

As they were shifting furniture, Jennifer asked, "So why are we moving the table away from the window this early in the morning?"

"Joe called earlier and told me that Martinez has started moving the drugs out of the warehouse, so the FBI is raiding the place now. He said to lock all the doors and windows and stay inside." She poured herself a cup of coffee and sat next to Jennifer. "Thanks for making coffee."

"Did Joe tell you anything else?" her father asked.

"No, Dad. Just that he was at his office and couldn't leave yet. He'll call before he comes over and we're not to answer the door to anyone but him." She sipped her coffee and scrutinized the darkness outside the window, wondering how long they would have to wait.

Alex recoiled at the pounding on the door. She grabbed Jennifer's hand and pulled her under the table, while her father crept to the wall behind the door ready to stop anyone from entering.

"It's me, Joe. It's safe to open the door."

Alex exhaled in relief and Jennifer crawled out from under the table.

"You scared the shit out of us. You were supposed to call before you came over." Her father ran his hand through his disheveled hair and sat at the table.

"I thought it would be better if I made a lot of noise. I figured you wouldn't believe a bad guy would be so loud. I was in a hurry and tired. No excuse for not calling first. Sorry. I just wanted to get to you with the news."

"Just sit your ass down and tell us what's going on." Jennifer picked up her cup and set it back down with shaky hands.

"Wait a second." Alex stood and grabbed a package of bran muffins from the refrigerator and set them on the table.

Joe poured a cup of coffee and sat across from Jennifer. "The raid is over. The FBI surrounded the warehouse and charged in about three hours ago." He took a sip of coffee and rolled his shoulders. He looked as if he hadn't slept any more than they had. "The good news is that Miguel Martinez is dead. Shot and killed. The bad news is that Phil was shot, and is in surgery as we speak."

Jennifer gasped and wrapped her arms around herself.

"We also lost two agents in the machine gun fire." Joe tipped his head back and rubbed his neck.

"In surgery where?" Jennifer stood and began pacing.

"I'll take you all there, when you're ready." Joe smiled and sipped his coffee. "There was paperwork with your names on it, and a couple of pictures of Alex as well. We probably moved you just in time, frankly. But with Martinez dead, you're safe. Safe as you can be, for the moment. You can go back to your lives here."

"We're ready. Let's go." Jennifer grabbed her coat, slipped on her boots, and raced out the door, with Alex and their dad right behind her.

Alex ran down the steps, and when the fresh air hit her, the fear lifted. *I'm coming, baby.*

CHAPTER THIRTY

Jennifer hopped out of the SUV as soon as Joe pulled into a parking spot at the hospital.

"Hang on, we're coming with you. Joe knows where he is." Alex rushed to put on her gloves.

"Alex. Here." Joe tossed her the burn phone and grinned.

"Thanks." She rushed after Jennifer, the phone a beacon of hope in her hand.

They hurried to the surgical floor and waited for Joe and their dad before following the nurse to the waiting room filled with Phil's fellow officers and detectives.

"Which one of you is Jennifer?" A burly dark haired policeman with sparkling blue eyes stood looking between her and Jennifer.

"I am." Jennifer moved closer to him and shook his hand. "And this is my sister, Alex."

"It's good to meet you both. I'm Sergeants Mills. Phil's told me all about you. A woman named Debra Johnson gave me an envelope for Phil, which I managed to get to him a couple of weeks ago. He asked me to give you this, in case he couldn't." The sergeant handed Jennifer a small box wrapped in paper covered in hearts.

"Thank you, Sergeant." Jennifer looked at the tiny box in her hand and tears welled.

Alex thanked him as well and sat in one of the chairs against the back of the waiting room. Her hand trembled as she dialed Debby's number.

You have reached the voice mail of Debra Johnson. Please leave a message.

"Debby, it's Alex. It's…it's over. I'm at the hospital downtown, waiting for Phil to get out of surgery. Call me on this number whenever you get a chance. I love you."

She closed the phone and went to wait with Jennifer.

"Is there a Jennifer Reed here?" The nurse called from the entry to the waiting room.

"Yes. I'm Jennifer Reed." Jennifer pushed through the mass of blue uniforms.

"Phillip Donohue is out of surgery, and he asked for you." The mass of police pushed closer to hear the nurse. "He's in recovery and it'll be a little while before I can take you, or anyone, back to see him though." She spoke to the group and smiled. "He's resting comfortably and the doctor will be out shortly to fill everyone in on his condition." She disappeared back through the door, and Sergeant Mills slipped his arm around Jennifer and hugged her.

Alex watched the exchange with gratitude. It seemed Jennifer had found a warm and loving extended family. She worried about the risks of Phil's job but understood what it meant to love someone enough to accept them. She wished Debby would call.

Joe stood and checked his watch but didn't make a move to leave.

"Do we have time?" Alex asked.

Joe smiled and hugged her. "All the time in the world. I'll have to get back to my office and finish up my report later, but you take all the time you need. Oh, before I forget, I wanted to tell you that the FBI went to the Martinez house. It's vacant. Completely cleaned out and no sign of his wife. They must have planned on moving on as soon as they'd moved the shipment." She paled slightly. "And dealt with us."

"Huh. I wonder if his wife left him when she saw he was about to get caught."

"I'm going to get a cup of coffee. Can I bring you one?" Her dad had been sitting quietly, reading a month old *Sports Illustrated*.

"I'm good, thanks." Joe concentrated on his cell phone.

"Thanks, Dad." She glanced at Jennifer, who sat with a few of Phil's fellow officers. She was smiling as they shared stories with her. "I'll go with you."

Alex and her father stood in the line at the hospital cafeteria. "Jennifer looks happy," he said.

"Yes, and I'm happy for her. How are you holding up?" She filled a Styrofoam cup with acidic smelling coffee and added cream.

"I'm glad Martinez is dead. I wish I knew how Willy was doing. He might be dead or in prison. But then, I guess he was one of the bad guys." He sighed and shook his head. "Those drugs are insidious. I think he was recruited from NA by the cartel. I remember seeing him with some shady guys after a meeting one night. They probably promised him the moon and delivered only grief."

"You're probably right. We'll ask Joe if he knows what happened to him. I'm proud of you, you know." Alex grimaced as she took a sip of the black swill.

"Proud of me? How so?" He took a drink of his coffee and coughed. "This stuff is awful."

"Yes, it is. I'm proud of you for sticking to your program and trying to help Willy. If he'd been in a place to hear you, he might have been able to stay away from Martinez. We'll never know if he knew about you before Willy told him or not."

"I've learned a lot about myself from NA, but I can only pass that on and hope it helps someone." He filled a cup with coffee and they went back to join Jennifer.

"I brought you a cup of coffee, hon, but you better take a small taste before you drink much. I got spoiled with your coffee." Her father held out the Styrofoam cup to Jennifer.

"Thanks, Dad." She wrapped her arms around his neck and kissed his cheek before stepping back and taking her coffee. "I'm sorry for lashing out at you before. I was just so frustrated and angry."

"I know. We've been through a trying time, but I think it's made us stronger and more connected. I love you, and I want you to be happy. Both of you." He set his cup on a table and opened his arms. Alex and Jennifer both stepped in for a hug.

"Look." Jennifer took a step back and held up her left hand wiggling her ring finger. A medium sized round diamond sparkled under the fluorescent lights.

"Beautiful. I'm so happy for you," Alex said. She wished Debby would call.

❖

Debby stopped at the desk on the first floor of the hospital. "I'm looking for a patient named Philip Donohue." She waited, hoping the clerk wouldn't ask questions she couldn't answer.

"Ah. The police detective. He's still on the surgical floor in recovery. Fourth floor, the elevators are to your right. You'll know where to wait." She smiled and pointed down the hallway.

"Thank you." Debby rushed to the elevator and pushed the up arrow several times. "Come on," she muttered.

She faltered slightly when she approached the waiting room and saw the mass of blue uniforms. Alex sat dozing on the end of a row of seats next to her father. Debby took a second to appreciate the sight of her, looking beautiful, if exhausted, before winding her way through the police officers to sit next to her. Her dad smiled and nodded to her. She gently slid her arm around Alex's shoulders and kissed her head when she leaned and rested it on her shoulder.

"Mm. If I'm dreaming, I don't want to wake up." Alex put her arm across her waist and snuggled into her.

"You're not dreaming. I'm here, and I'm not leaving."

A lean man in scrubs and a surgical hat poked his head into the room. "Jennifer Reed?"

"Here." Jennifer rushed to the door.

"I'm Dr. Flint. Phil is awake and asking for you." He looked up and addressed the room since it was filled with cops who wanted answers. "He was lucky he was wearing his bulletproof vest. We removed two bullets from his arm and one in his leg. One bullet grazed his neck and just missed his carotid artery. He'll need to rest and heal, but I believe he'll recover."

"Can my sister and dad come in with me?" Jennifer asked.

Dr. Flint scanned the room. Debby wondered how he was going to keep that many police officers from following Jennifer.

"Okay. We'll go three at a time." He moved aside so Jennifer, Alex, and their dad could pass him. "When they're done, you can go three at a time, but remember to let him rest."

"I'll be here waiting." Debby squeezed Alex's hand. She didn't want to let go, but she knew Alex needed to support Jen. She couldn't wait to talk about everything, to see where things stood. As Alex looked back at her over her shoulder, her heart swelled with thanks that she was safe. As long as she was safe, they could work anything else out.

❖

"Hey, baby. How are you feeling?" Jennifer grasped Phil's hand and leaned to kiss him.

"Like I've been shot." He grinned and coughed.

Jennifer poured some water from a small pitcher by the bed into a plastic cup with a straw sticking out the top. "Here, take a sip." He sat up and she held the cup until he finished and lay back.

"Thanks, honey." He reached to stroke her cheek, but the IV in his hand stopped the motion.

Alex and her dad stood at the end of the bed, giving Jennifer and Phil some space. "I'm glad you're doing well, Phil. We were worried about you." Alex smiled and squeezed his foot through the covers. She loved seeing Jen so happy, and knowing Phil was one of the good guys after all meant the world to her.

"I'm kinda tough. It takes more than a few bullets to keep me down." Phil looked serious as he spoke to their dad. "I'm sorry about your friend, Mr. Reed. Willy wasn't a bad guy. He just got caught up in a ruthless gang."

"Is he dead?" Her father looked so sad Alex rested her hand on his shoulder in support.

"Yes. I'm sorry. He was in the line of fire along with a dozen or so others of Martinez's crew."

Phil looked like his pain medication was kicking in, so they said good-bye to give some of his friends time to visit. Before they left, Jennifer leaned down to kiss him again. He held her face in his good hand and said, "Forever. I meant it."

Alex put her arm around Jen as they walked down the hall, helping her wipe away her tears of joy and laughter.

The waiting room looked as full as it was when they left, but Alex was only looking for one person, and she was sitting in the same chair as when they had left.

"How is he?" Debby asked as she put the magazine she was holding on the seat next to her and stood.

"He's going to be fine." Alex took her hand, intending to never let go.

Joe joined them in the seating area, and Alex cringed. Would his presence ever mean anything good?

"Don't look so scared, kiddo. I think the threat is over. I'm afraid you have no apartment to go back to, though." He looked at their joined hands. "Somehow I don't think that will be a problem."

"So we don't have to go back to the safe house? We're okay now?" Alex reined in her excitement in case she had misunderstood.

Joe called her father and Jennifer over to speak to them all. "Martinez is dead, and his gang is, too, mainly, or in custody. There's no reason I know of to keep you in the safe house. All of your belongings are in storage, but we had to give up your apartments."

"What about my place in Plymouth?" Their dad looked lost.

"We kept that for you, sir. I know the deputy marshal you've been working with is there now ensuring it's safe. I'll give you all a ride back to the house to collect your things and take you wherever you want to go. Just remember to check in with me and always let me know where you're living."

"I'll take Alex," Debby said. "If you want?" She looked at Alex, her gaze both adoring and hopeful.

"I'd like that," Alex said.

"I'm sorry, Alex. I can't allow her to take you to the safe house, because of its importance as a secret. I'll take you all to the safe house to get Abby and your things, and then drop you off wherever you want to go."

Debby nodded and squeezed Alex's hand. "In that case, I'll go home and get the house ready." She gave her a lingering kiss, eliciting a few whistles from the crowd of officers. "I'll be waiting."

Alex could think of nothing she liked the sound of more.

"Come on, Abby. We're out of here." Alex walked through the house to double check that nothing was left behind. She stopped at the couch where she and Jen had sat and drank wine on New Year's Eve, hardly able to believe it was only hours ago. She ran her hand over the worn Formica table where they'd played Scrabble, discussed their predicament, and ate breakfast, lunch, and dinner since November. She wouldn't miss a thing about the place except the time spent there with her father and sister. There was one last task they needed to finish there. Ready it for whoever needed shelter from the threats of the world.

Joe gave them each their own cell phone and collected the burn phone from Alex. He programmed each of their new numbers into his phone. They would probably be in the program for the rest of their lives, but she had control of her own life now, even if it was as Alexandra Reed, and that control could slip one day, if the cartels came looking. But being Alex Reed was her truth now, and she looked forward to sharing it with Debby. She pulled the door closed and waited for Joe to do the last walk through and lock up. It was a safe house she hoped she'd never need to see again, but she was glad it would be there for anyone else who needed it.

Joe dropped Jennifer off at Phil's condominium, Alex at Debby's, and then left to drop her dad in Plymouth. Each stop involved hugs and promises to get together that Alex knew would be kept.

Debby opened the door and Alex fell into her arms. "Welcome home." Debby waited until Alex hugged Joe and her dad before taking her hand and leading her into the house.

"Let's sit by the fireplace." Alex settled on the couch and reached for Debby. "I'm pooped."

"I bet you are. You've had a stressful few weeks." Debby pulled her close and held her while she dozed off.

She woke with her pulse racing.

"Hey, babe. It's okay. You're safe now." Debby cradled her head on her chest.

"I was moaning in my sleep, wasn't I?" Alex rubbed the sleep from her eyes.

"Yeah. You okay?"

"I couldn't be better. I'm sure the dreams will go away, eventually." She smiled up at Debby knowing her words couldn't be truer. "I love you." She pulled Debby's head down for a kiss.

"You rest a while. I'm going to run out and feed Shadow then I'll be back to start dinner. Then you can fill me in on everything that happened." She moved out from under Alex and gently set her head on a pillow and kissed her.

"I want to help," Alex said when Debby returned. She stood and stretched and laughed at Abby sound asleep on the floor. "I think she's exhausted, too."

"You can come into the kitchen and have a cup of tea while you tell me the whole story while I cook."

Alex thought about all that had happened in the last few days and couldn't remember what she'd told Debby already, so she decided to start from the beginning. She took the cup of tea from Debby and sat at the table. "You know about WITSEC and Joe already. Miguel Martinez was a big drug dealer, and he had a warehouse full of drugs north of Novi." Alex had to stop and think about how much to disclose to Debby. The less she knew, the less likely she would ever be in danger. "The FBI raided the place and killed Martinez and his main guys, and Phil was shot in the raid."

"Huh. So, Fernanda's grandson was a drug dealer. She died from a bad heart, by the way, and now I see why Janis wasn't able to get in touch with him. He may not even have known that she died."

"Joe didn't know about her until I told him. I guess Miguel's wife disappeared, and their house has been cleaned out." Alex stirred some honey in her tea and took a sip. She loved watching Debby fiddle around the kitchen. It felt like…home.

"I suppose I don't blame her for getting away. We'll never know if she knew anything about her husband's drug dealing, but I find it hard to believe she wouldn't." Debby checked the chicken roasting in the oven.

"My bet is that she got away while she could. That's pretty much all I can tell you, except that the threat is over, and I'm free." She walked up behind Debby, wrapped her arms around her waist, and rested her soul.

CHAPTER THIRTY-ONE

Alex rolled over and nestled close to Debby, comforted by her soft snores and her warm butt pressed against her belly. She was hers. She thought of the journey she had traveled to get here, not only to her bed, but to her heart. She still had the issue of the WITSEC program but that only involved talking to Joe once a week. There didn't seem to be anyone else from the trial who would want a crack at them, so the restrictions weren't as stringent anymore.

She glanced at the clock radio. Seven. They had time. They would always have time now. No more fear of being taken away at a moment's notice or having to close pieces of paper in the door to lookout for intruders. Debby was now her safe house. She pulled her close and slid her hand under her nightshirt to cup her breast. She was rewarded with a moan as Debby covered her hand with her own, pulled her closer, and turned on her back. Alex decided she liked her in that position. She circled her firm nipple with her fingers and then stroked the inside of her thigh. Debby raised her hips and Alex answered the plea. She stroked her soft, slippery folds and fondled her clit until it grew hard and pulsed. She squeezed and released and moved to her opening. Debby writhed beneath her touch, fueling her own desire.

She slid one leg over her and slipped a finger inside while kneading her clit with her thumb. She rubbed her throbbing center on Debby's firm thigh and whimpered as she came close to the edge.

"Come with me, baby." Debby's words were muffled by her attempt to hold back.

"Oh yes." Alex ground her clit against Debby's leg and stroked the spot inside of her to make her come. They held each other tightly as they spilled over into oblivion.

Debby stirred and Alex pulled her closer. "We need to get up, love." She didn't move.

"I know, but this feels so nice." Alex snuggled closer.

"I love you." Debby kissed her forehead and traced her ear gently with one finger. "It doesn't matter to me that your name wasn't Alexandra Reed before. I don't even care where you came from. I'm grateful that you're here with me now."

"I've been so lost, looking for a way to be a new person with a new truth. My new name isn't an issue. It's the constant vigilance to disguise who I was and where I grew up. WITSEC has probably saved my life, but it stole my identity. That's a difficult reality to live with." She turned her head, grabbed Debby's hand, and kissed her palm. "I feared I'd never find someone who would see me for who I am and accept my camouflaged past."

"My greatest fear was that I'd allow someone to deceive me again." Debby turned on her side, propped herself on her elbow, and captured her gaze. "I made a list after Evelyn left me. It had all the things I'd require for someone to get close to me. I've been using it to protect my heart, but I now know that it's been my tool to avoid commitment, thereby keeping love away. I don't want to do that anymore. I want us to be together forever, baby. I want you to be mine."

Alex's throat tightened as she forced back tears of joy. She'd hoped to hear words of love from Debby, but the overwhelming wave of emotions at her possessive expression left her momentarily speechless. She sighed heavily and found her voice. "Then I'm all yours. Now and forever."

About the Author

C.A. Popovich lives in a northern suburb of Detroit, Michigan, with her partner and their two rescue dogs. She writes full-time, loves to read, and enjoys walking in a local park. Her stories can be counted on to be sweet with happy endings.

capopovichfiction@aol.com

Books Available from Bold Strokes Books

Camp Rewind by Meghan O'Brien. A summer camp for grown-ups becomes the site of an unlikely romance between a shy, introverted divorcee and one of the Internet's most infamous cultural critics—who attends undercover. (978-1-62639-793-4)

Cross Purposes by Gina L. Dartt. In pursuit of a lost Acadian treasure, three women must not only work out the clues, but also the complicated tangle of emotion and attraction developing between them. (978-1-62639-713-2)

Imperfect Truth by C.A. Popovich. Can an imperfect truth stand in the way of love? (978-1-62639-787-3)

Life in Death by M. Ullrich. Sometimes the devastating end is your only chance for a new beginning. (978-1-62639-773-6)

Love on Liberty by MJ Williamz. Hearts collide when politics clash. (978-1-62639-639-5)

Serious Potential by Maggie Cummings. Pro golfer Tracy Allen plans to forget her ex during a visit to Bay West, a lesbian condo community in NYC, but when she meets Dr. Jennifer Betsy, she gets more than she bargained for. (978-1-62639-633-3)

Taste by Kris Bryant. Accomplished chef Taryn has walked away from her promising career in the city's top restaurant to devote her life to her five-year-old daughter and is content until Ki Blake comes along. (978-1-62639-718-7)

The Second Wave by Jean Copeland. Can star-crossed lovers have a second chance after decades apart, or does the love of a lifetime only happen once? (978-1-62639-830-6)

Valley of Fire by Missouri Vaun. Taken captive in a desert outpost after their small aircraft is hijacked, Ava and her captivating passenger discover things about each other and themselves that will change them both forever. (978-1-62639-496-4)

Basic Training of the Heart by Jaycie Morrison. In 1944, socialite Elizabeth Carlton joins the Women's Army Corps to escape family expectations and love's disappointments. Can Sergeant Gale Rains get her through Basic Training with their hearts intact? (978-1-62639-818-4)

Before by KE Payne. When Tally falls in love with her band's new recruit, she has a tough decision to make. What does she want more—Alex or the band? (978-1-62639-677-7)

Believing in Blue by Maggie Morton. Growing up gay in a small town has been hard, but it can't compare to the next challenge Wren—with her new, sky-blue wings—faces: saving two entire worlds. (978-1-62639-691-3)

Coils by Barbara Ann Wright. A modern young woman follows her aunt into the Greek Underworld and makes a pact with Medusa to win her freedom by killing a hero of legend. (978-1-62639-598-5)

Courting the Countess by Jenny Frame. When relationship-phobic Lady Henrietta Knight starts to care about housekeeper Annie Brannigan and her daughter, can she overcome her fears and promise Annie the forever that she demands? (978-1-62639-785-9)

Dapper by Jenny Frame. Amelia Honey meets the mysterious Byron De Brek and is faced with her darkest fantasies, but will her strict moral upbringing stop her from exploring what she truly wants? (978-1-62639-898-6E)

Delayed Gratification: The Honeymoon by Meghan O'Brien. A dream European honeymoon turns into a winter storm nightmare involving a delayed flight, a ditched rental car, and eventually, a surprisingly happy ending. (978-1-62639-766-8E)

For Money or Love by Heather Blackmore. Jessica Spaulding must choose between ignoring the truth to keep everything she has, and doing the right thing only to lose it all—including the woman she loves. (978-1-62639-756-9)

Hooked by Jaime Maddox. With the help of sexy Detective Mac Calabrese, Dr. Jessica Benson is working hard to overcome her past, but it may not be enough to stop a murderer. (978-1-62639-689-0)

Lands End by Jackie D. Public relations superstar Amy Kline is dealing with a media nightmare, and the last thing she expects is for restaurateur Lena Michaels to change everything, but she will. (978-1-62639-739-2)

Lysistrata Cove by Dena Hankins. Jack and Eve navigate the maelstrom of their darkest desires and find love by transgressing gender, dominance, submission, and the law on the crystal blue Caribbean Sea. (978-1-62639-821-4)

Twisted Screams by Sheri Lewis Wohl. Reluctant psychic Lorna Dutton doesn't want to forgive, but if she doesn't do just that an innocent woman will die. (978-1-62639-647-0)

A Class Act by Tammy Hayes. Buttoned-up college professor Dr. Margaret Parks doesn't know what she's getting herself into when she agrees to one date with her student, Rory Morgan, who is 15 years her junior. (978-1-62639-701-9)

Bitter Root by Laydin Michaels. Small town chef Adi Bergeron is hiding something, and Griffith McNaulty is going to find out what it is even if it gets her killed. (978-1-62639-656-2)

Capturing Forever by Erin Dutton. When family pulls Jacqueline and Casey back together, will the lessons learned in eight years apart be enough to mend the mistakes of the past? (978-1-62639-631-9)

Deception by VK Powell. DEA Agent Colby Vincent and Attorney Adena Weber are embroiled in a drug investigation involving homeless veterans and an attraction that could destroy them both. (978-1-62639-596-1)

Dyre: A Knight of Spirit and Shadows by Rachel E. Bailey. With the abduction of her queen, werewolf-bodyguard Des must follow the kidnappers' trail to Europe, where her queen—and a battle unlike any Des has ever waged—awaits her. (978-1-62639-664-7)

First Position by Melissa Brayden. Love and rivalry take center stage for Anastasia Mikhelson and Natalie Frederico in one of the most prestigious ballet companies in the nation. (978-1-62639-602-9)

Best Laid Plans by Jan Gayle. Nicky and Lauren are meant for each other, but Nicky's haunting past and Lauren's societal fears threaten to derail all possibilities of a relationship. (987-1-62639-658-6)

Exchange by CF Frizzell. When Shay Maguire rode into rural Montana, she never expected to meet the woman of her dreams—or to learn Mel Baker was held hostage by legal agreement to her right-wing father. (987-1-62639-679-1)

Just Enough Light by AJ Quinn. Will a serial killer's return to Colorado destroy Kellen Ryan and Dana Kingston's chance at love, or can the search-and-rescue team save themselves? (987-1-62639-685-2)

Rise of the Rain Queen by Fiona Zedde. Nyandoro is nobody's princess. She fights, curses, fornicates, and gets into as much trouble as her brothers. But the path to a throne is not always the one we expect. (987-1-62639-592-3)

Tales from Sea Glass Inn by Karis Walsh. Over the course of a year at Cannon Beach, tourists and locals alike find solace and passion at the Sea Glass Inn. (987-1-62639-643-2)